Coming Home to Sturcombe Bay

Coming Home to Sturcombe Bay

SUSANNE McCARTHY

Choc Lit
A JOFFE BOOKS COMPANY

Choc Lit, London
A Joffe Books company
www.choc-lit.com

First published in Great Britain in 2025

Cover art by Jarmila Takač

ISBN: 978-1781898710

*For my lovely friend Eva
who appears in these pages — in character.
And Spice, the little white mountain pony she rescued,
who crossed the Rainbow Bridge too soon.*

CHAPTER ONE

"Well, here we are. Home sweet home."

Cassie leaned over and kissed her brother on the ear. "Thanks for picking me up. You're a sweetheart."

Paul laughed. "That's not what you used to call me."

"That was ten years ago." Her eyes danced. "But I'm not guaranteeing I won't call you a few choice alternatives again — especially if you're still as irritating as ever."

"Me — irritating? Never!"

"Huh!"

They both climbed out of the car, and Paul went round to the boot to fetch Cassie's backpack.

"You really do travel light," he remarked, hoisting it onto one shoulder.

"You get further that way."

Halfway round the world. And now she was home.

The house rose above her, big and solid. Most of the large Victorian townhouses on Cliff Road had been converted into holiday flats, but not number nineteen. Three storeys of ruddy-brown brick, trimmed with sandstone quoins, with dormer windows in the roof.

Three stone steps led up to the front door, bay windows on each side. The front garden had been gravelled over to

1

provide extra off-road parking space, but several tubs of bright geraniums lent it a defiant touch of colour.

But her first move wasn't towards the house. Instead, she walked across the road and stood for a moment by the cliff wall, her hands resting lightly on the rough stone, still warm from the sun that was setting across the bay.

Sturcombe. Her home for the first eighteen years of her life — until the need to see more of the world than this little seaside village in South Devon, however pretty, had sent her off in search of adventure. Which she had found — in spades.

She had seen the sun set over the Golden Gate bridge, over the wide planes of the Serengeti, over the huge red monolith of Uluru in the dry, dusty outback of Australia. But though they had all been spectacular, there had never been a sunset to compare with the sunsets of home.

The sky was deepening to a soft cobalt blue, streaked with idle paint strokes of magenta and gold. Far out across the bay the sun was sinking slowly below the horizon, a great golden ball casting a path of shimmering sequins across the sea.

Some thirty feet below her the waves were breaking in frills of white lace that whispered softly across the sand. A couple of black-headed terns were swooping down to look for a late dinner, their mournful wheep-wheep cries echoing across the water . . .

A man was riding a horse along the edge of the beach, the last long rays of the sun gleaming on the horse's russet flanks. The man had risen in the stirrups, perfectly balanced, moving as one with the powerful animal as it galloped through the shallows, all smooth, elemental power.

"Who's that?" She really didn't need to ask.

Paul strolled across and glanced down at the beach. "That's Liam. You remember him? Liam Ellis."

Liam Ellis. Oh yes, she remembered him very well. At seventeen, eighteen, she had thought he was the love of her life, but the tug of the great wide world had been equally strong.

Liam had had a different dream. He loved horses — he'd had no interest in travelling the world. He'd started helping out at the local horse rescue society from when he was about ten years old, and his commitment to them had grown over the years.

It had led him to train as a vet, like his parents and his brother, with the intention of taking over from the society's elderly vet who was past due for retirement. She'd known she couldn't ask him to give that up.

Which had left her with an almost impossible choice — leave him behind and follow her dream of adventure, or give up on it and stay here with him. She had known that she couldn't have both. And though it had almost torn her heart in two, she had known that at eighteen she was too young to settle down.

So, in the week when she would have been starting at Exeter University, she had taken off in a big white bird from Heathrow for the long flight to Orlando. Gazing out of the window at England's green fields rolling past beneath the wing, she had wished that she could go up to the cockpit and beg the captain to turn the plane around and fly it right back home again.

But by the time they had landed at Orlando's stunning airport she had forced herself to look to the future, not the past. And within a week she had been so absorbed in completing her advanced PADI Divemaster certification that she had been able to tuck her memories into a small corner of her heart, only to be revisited rarely.

She turned at the sound of the front door behind her opening. Her mum and dad, and her sister Lisa, piled out of the house to welcome her. She found herself instantly swamped in hugs, her mother's warm arms around her, her father standing close by trying to pretend that wasn't a tear in his eye.

Her mother had no such reticence — tears streamed down her face. "Ah, my baby's home safe at last."

"Mum!" Cassie was protesting, though her own eyes were blurring with tears too. "I only went round the world — I didn't leave the planet."

3

"Ten years. Let me look at you." She held her daughter at arm's length, then cupped her face in her hands. "You haven't changed a bit. Except you're so brown! Did you get that tan in New Zealand?"

"It's winter there at the moment, though in the summer it was glorious. Hello, Dad."

She turned to hug her father — big, calm Richard Channing, kindly and much-respected headmaster of the local Community College. "You're looking well."

His grey eyes crinkled into a smile as he wrapped his arms around her. "So are you, my lovely. Welcome home."

"And my big sister!" She laughed. "Though I'm still taller than you." She caught Lisa round the waist and lifted her off the ground, swinging her around as she had been able to do since she was eleven years old.

"Hey, put me down," Lisa protested. "I'm a respectable married woman."

"Huh! You — respectable? I don't believe it." Cassie's eyes danced. "Where are the babies? Have you brought them down to meet their Auntie Cassie?"

"They're at home with Ollie — it's a bit late for them to be out." Lisa beamed with maternal pride. "You can see them tomorrow."

"Right." Cassie hesitated, steeling herself for the big question. "And . . . how's Nanna?"

Sombre looks replaced the smiles. "Not good," her mother admitted. "I think she's holding on for you to come home."

Cassie felt the guilt twist in her gut. She should have come home sooner.

"We can go up to the hospital to see her tomorrow. Anyway, come on indoors," her mother urged, dropping an arm around her shoulders. "You must be tired after that long flight."

"Well, yes I am," Cassie admitted. "I don't know why, but sitting in an aeroplane seat for twenty-four hours is more tiring than rafting down the Shotover rapids!"

Her sister laughed. "I'll take your word for that!"

4

They climbed the steps to the front door. And there in the hall, waiting to welcome her, so eager that his whole back end was wagging along with his tail, was Barney, the small brown Border Terrier who had been little more than a pup when she had gone away.

"Barney!" Cassie dropped to her knees to hug him. "You remember me?"

An enthusiastic pink tongue lapped away the tears that had sprung to her eyes. She hadn't quite dared to hope for this, to find him still here, the mischievous bundle of fun who had raced with her on the beach, chasing waves and seagulls, or snuck into her bed at night when he was supposed to stay in his basket down in the kitchen.

"Of course he remembers you. He missed you."

"Oh, Barney. I missed you too." She fussed the little dog, tickling his ears and reducing him to a bundle of ecstasy. That warm, wriggling body, that coarse brown fur, those eyes still bright with intelligence gazing adoringly into hers.

She held onto the moment until she was sure she wasn't going to cry, then rose to her feet and glanced around the hall, taking in the changes. "You've decorated in here."

Her mother laughed. "Of course."

The hall was long and bright, with a gleaming wooden floor and high ceiling. The old wallpaper she remembered had gone — now one wall was painted a rich dark blue, the other ivory cream.

"Very smart," she approved.

"We've done most of the house since you've been away. Come and look at the sitting room."

The walls had been painted a warm terracotta. It could have been overpowering, but in such a large room, running from the front to the back of the house, it had an air of opulence enhanced by the high ceiling and decorative cornices painted the same ivory as the hall.

The light fittings were new — brass and pearlescent globes. Two dark-red leather Chesterfield sofas and two

5

comfortable armchairs were arranged before the fireplace, and the mantlepiece and sideboard were lined with family photographs.

The marble fireplace itself was original to the house, and had been well cared for by the generations — the house had been owned by her mother's family since it was built, just as Nanna's family had owned her house three doors up the hill.

"It's lovely," Cassie approved, gazing round.

"Glad you like it." Her mum hesitated. "We haven't done your room, because . . ."

Ah, there it was. The unspoken question she'd been expecting. How long was she going to stay? Would she stay for good? To be honest, she didn't know the answer to that herself.

"Anyway, you can see the rest of the house later. You must be hungry. Come on through and get something to eat. We've got your favourite — lasagne."

"You waited dinner for me? Oh, Mum, you didn't need to do that. I could just have had cheese on toast or something."

Her mother looked horrified. "You think I'd let you make do with cheese on toast?"

"Don't be daft!" Lisa laughed. "The prodigal has returned — Mum's killed the fatted calf."

"Well, yes — I am pretty hungry," Cassie admitted. "They fed us well enough on the long-haul from Wellington, but it was only coffee and biscuits on the hop to Exeter."

"We're eating in the kitchen." Her mum laughed dryly. "Nanna has taken over the dining room."

* * *

Liam coaxed The Bandit up the concrete ramp from the beach. Sometimes the high-bred racehorse would take exception to the slope, but this evening he behaved perfectly.

Trotting easily, they picked up the South West Coast Path, skirting the Memorial Gardens with its neatly-clipped lawns and colourful flowerbeds, and past the white front of the Carleton Hotel.

A short distance further on he came to a low stone wall and an open gate. He rode through and across the front yard to the side gate leading to the stable yard behind the house, slipping down from the saddle and latching the gate shut behind him.

Most of the horses were out in the back paddock, but a couple were in their stalls, and at the sound of The Bandit's hoofs on the cobbles, they stuck their inquisitive heads over their half-doors like nosy neighbours eager for gossip.

As Liam led The Bandit across the yard his dad strolled out of the tack room, pausing to study the elegant horse with an expert eye. "How did he go, son?"

"Pretty good. Another few days and he'll be ready to go back to his training yard, I reckon."

Graham Ellis nodded. "You've done a good job with him. He's a fine horse. Leave him — I'll see to him now."

"Thanks, Dad."

Liam strode over to the house, entering by the back door — they rarely used the front. In the kitchen the rich aroma of coffee drifted to his nostrils from the coffee maker in the corner. His parents had no aversion to modern appliances for convenience, though his mother drew the line at an air fryer.

He poured himself a strong mug, not bothering with milk or sugar, and strolled into the sitting room. His mother was knitting, her feet up on a footstool, a springer spaniel on one side of her on the sofa, and a young grey lurcher on the other.

She glanced up as he came in. "Hello, love."

"Hi, Mum." He leaned over the back of the sofa to drop a kiss on her cheek and ruffle the dogs' heads, then he settled into the sofa on the opposite side of the fireplace with a contented sigh, sipping his coffee.

The sitting room was cosy, with rough white-painted walls and dark oak beams across the low ceiling. The big stone fireplace held a coal fire in winter, but now it was filled with ragged sprays of lilacs and irises from the garden, their scent almost overlaying the faint aroma of damp dog that always seemed to pervade the house.

The furniture was comfortable rather than stylish, with piles of mismatched cushions and an ancient wooden cabin-trunk that served as a coffee table.

He shifted his nephew Ben's toy car and leaned over to switch on the lamp on the table beside him. The room had changed little since he was Ben's age — the cushion covers had been replaced from time to time, and the television set was at least twice the size, but he was sure that some of the clutter was still in the same place as it had been twenty-five years ago.

His mother was watching a quiz show, impatiently calling out the answers while the contestants were still furrowing their brows. He smiled to himself. That hadn't changed either.

They were a good team, the Ellises. His father and older brother Luke mostly worked with farm animals, his mother ran a small animal clinic, while Luke's wife Julia managed the business side. For himself, his main love was horses, but there was no clear demarcation between them — they could all back each other up when necessary.

His mother sighed as one of the contestants fluffed a simple question. "Honestly, I think they must have to fail an intelligence test to get on this show." She slid her hand under Hobo, the lurcher, and pulled out the remote to change the channel. The dog huffed and settled down again, his tail banging against the cushions. "How's The Bandit?"

"He's doing well. I gave him a good gallop, and he was moving perfectly. Dad's dealing with him."

She nodded, her knitting needles clicking rapidly as she watched the wildlife programme she had switched to. "I heard Cassie Channing's coming home."

"Oh?" Yes, he'd heard. But he didn't want to get into a discussion about it.

"She'll have come to see her grandmother. They were always close."

"Not close enough that she couldn't make it home for ten years."

If she caught the acid note in his voice, she didn't make an issue of it. "No . . . Well . . ." She got to the end of the row and stopped to count the number of stitches to decrease. "The old lady's pretty much coming to the end now. Ninety-three — not a bad innings. Still, it's sad to see her go. First Molly Marston, now Edie Channing. Not many left of that generation."

"Except old Arthur Crocombe." Liam laughed. "He'll go on for ever. He's planning to reach his century." He finished his coffee and rose to his feet. "I'm just going to look in on Robyn, then I think I'll have a bath."

"OK, love. There's plenty of hot water."

The house was big and old, with thick granite walls and a slate roof — it had been thatched in his grandfather's time. It was effectively three houses linked together, with two staircases and several rambling corridors. His brother Luke lived with his family in one wing, but Liam and Robyn lived in the main house. He had been more than grateful for that these past few years.

He climbed the stairs and turned down the passage to his right. His small daughter's room was at the end, next to his own, the door slightly ajar the way she liked it, the soft glow of a pink night-light keeping all the shadows away. A room fit for a princess. Robyn was all girl — everything had to be pink, preferably with sparkles.

On silent feet he crossed to her small pink-covered bed. He had read her a bedtime story earlier, and watched her fall asleep. That was always the best part of his day. She was sleeping now, her breathing soft and steady, her pale blonde hair drifting on the pillow, long dark lashes brushing her round cheeks.

On the bedside table — painted pink, of course — was a photograph in a silver frame. He picked it up, smiling sadly at the image. Robyn, on her mother's lap. One of the last photos of them together.

The were sitting on a sun lounger beside the pool of their hotel in Greece. Robyn, two years old, in a yellow swimsuit — that was before the pink obsession had kicked in. Smiling into the camera as her daddy had taken the picture — a smile so like her mother's.

Natalie was squinting slightly in the sun — she had taken her sunglasses off for the picture. Holding back her blonde hair with one slim hand, the other was wrapped around her small daughter's middle, trying to stop her wriggling.

So happy — no idea that she only had a few hours to live. That was probably a good thing, he mused — there had been no darkness. He was the one who had been left with the darkness, from the moment the paramedic in her blue uniform had knelt beside the broken, bloodied body in the dusty street, shaking her head. He had already known that there was nothing that was going to bring her back.

He put the photo down, touched a light kiss to his sleeping daughter's forehead, and crept from the room.

In his own room he peeled off his clothes and strolled into the bathroom to fill the bath. As his mother had promised, there was plenty of hot water and the room was soon filled with steam.

The mirror was misted up. He rubbed his hand over it to clear it and stared at his reflection. It was three years now that Natalie had been gone, and the darkness had mostly faded. He had even tried a few dates — there were plenty of opportunities online to meet attractive women — but none of them had clicked.

And now Cassie Channing was coming home. There had been darkness there too, but that was ten years ago. And it had faded quickly. He had been young, resilient, and if she had bruised his heart when she had chosen adventure over a life with him, he had soon come to realise that she had probably been right. They had both been too young, they had had different dreams.

And now? No, there would be no going back there. If he only had himself to consider, maybe . . . A brief fling before she jetted off again to some exotic location. Casual, fun, no strings. But now he had a little girl to consider, a little girl who had lost her mother. There would be no going back.

* * *

Cassie sat on the cushioned bench seat in the dormer window of her bedroom, her feet tucked beneath her, Barney curled up beside her. His small brown head was resting against her thigh, and he was snoring quietly.

From up here she could see the whole wide expanse of the bay. The moon was waxing towards the full, tracing a silver path across the inky water, and the stars twinkled in the velvet sky like diamonds scattered by a careless hand. Far out on the invisible horizon, the lights of a large ship glowed as it made its way slowly out towards the wide Atlantic.

It was the view she had known for the first eighteen years of her life. The rather grandly named Esplanade curved in a wide crescent above the beach, strings of coloured lights swinging from lamppost to lamppost.

She could make out the windows of the Smugglers — the most popular pub in town — lit up with a warm amber glow. A little further on was the flashing red, blue and green of the amusement arcade on the corner. And at the far end, perched on top of a low cliff of reddish sandstone, was the elegant white facade of the Carleton Hotel, bathed in uplights from its lush gardens.

With one finger she traced the edge of the window frame. When she was fifteen she'd painted the walls and the sloping ceiling a dramatic shade of purple, the door and the window frame black. She'd been immensely proud of herself, though there were quite a few wobbles where she hadn't been quite accurate when cutting in with the paint brush.

This room, with so many memories. All the familiar items: the narrow single bed with its purple-and-black duvet cover, the pale oak dressing table where she had conducted her first experiments with makeup, the big wardrobe where some of her old jeans and tops still hung.

On the table beside the bed was the illuminated globe of the Earth — a Christmas present from her mum and dad when she was ten. She had loved to turn it slowly, tapping with her fingertip all the places she longed to visit, imagining that she could fly to them in a magic bubble whenever she wanted.

And the bookshelves jammed with the books she had loved reading far into the night, with a torch under the covers — ready to swiftly switch it off and lie still at the warning sound of a parental footfall outside her door.

Lord of the Rings and *The Hobbit*. A whole stack of Terry Pratchett's Discworld series with their colourful phantasmagorical covers.

Maybe it was those books which had first ignited the spark of wanderlust in her. It had been a secret she had hugged to herself, afraid that people would think it was a stupid dream. You didn't live your life like a fantasy tale.

The only person she'd ever told had been Nanna — she would understand. And Nanna had encouraged her to believe in her dream. She'd even bought her a scuba-diving course for her seventeenth birthday.

Dancing her fingers along the spines, she came to the anthology of poetry which she had reluctantly bought for her English A level and had fallen in love with.

And tucked inside, marking her favourite Shakespeare sonnet — 'When, in disgrace with fortune and men's eyes' — was a strip of small photographs, passport size, from a photo booth in Exeter. Three photos. The fourth, her favourite, was still in the back pocket of her wallet. She hadn't taken it out for years.

She and Liam. How young they looked. She had worn her dark hair long then, halfway down her back — now the tips just brushed her shoulders. His hair, also dark and curling over his ears, was just long enough to brush his collar. His dark eyes were laughing, that firm, sensitive mouth smiling. Four years older than her, already studying at Bristol for the career he had been aiming for his whole life.

She had never told him about her dream of travelling the world. When she was with him, she had put it to the back of her mind — she hadn't wanted to think about leaving him. She had just wanted to be with him, to live in the fantasy that it could be forever. Although she had known that it couldn't.

Had she made the right choice? If she had stayed, she would have had Liam, and love. But if she had stayed, would it have grown, that niggling frustration with the limited horizons of this little South Devon town? Would time have turned it to resentment? Would a couple of weeks holiday a year have been enough to satisfy her thirst for adventure?

With a small sigh she shook her head. There was no point in revisiting that decision now. It was ten years past.

Slipping her hand into the side pocket of her backpack she pulled out a small plastic folder. Inside was her return ticket to New Zealand, dated 25th September. Six weeks. She drew it out of the folder and placed it carefully in the poetry book, next to the photographs.

CHAPTER TWO

"Come on then, lad. Let's see how you're doing." Liam rose in the stirrups and urged the powerful racehorse into a full gallop, listening intently to the rhythm of his hoofs and feeling for any hitch in his movement.

It was peaceful out here on the beach at this time of the morning, long before any tourists had even thought of rolling out of bed. The pale-lemon sun was just above the horizon in a sky of silvery blue, the sea shimmering like mother-of-pearl. The air was cool, the only sounds were the quarrelling of the gulls and the soft hush of the waves sliding up over the sand.

They reached the far end of the beach beneath the rocky cliff and the caravan site, then turned and galloped back. As they turned again beneath the cliff on their third run, he realised that they weren't quite alone after all.

An early morning swimmer was rising like Venus from the waves. And he didn't need a second look to know who it was.

She was wearing a vibrant orange-and-purple swimsuit which, soaking wet, left nothing to the imagination. As a teenager she had been almost skinny, but now there were curves in all the right places.

Her skin gleamed golden brown, her legs were long and elegant, and on her shoulder was a tattoo about six inches long, in shades of blue and green and purple. It looked like a flower and a feather, delicate, but with a hint of classic Maori styling.

She was watching her footing, but as she waded into the shallows, she tipped back her head and slicked her dark hair from her face. Then she saw him.

The Bandit was prancing, impatient, but it would be impolite to just ride off without at least saying hello. "Hi."

"Oh . . ." She hesitated, a little uncertain. "Hello."

Yes, he'd remembered right — her eyes were green. Not hazel, but pure green, the colour of forest moss, and fringed by long, dark, silky lashes. She wasn't quite beautiful — her bone-structure was strong, her chin betraying a determined streak in her nature. Though her lips were soft and . . . tempting.

He pushed that thought aside. "You're out early," he remarked lightly.

"I like a morning swim."

"Isn't the water cold?"

"Not too bad." She glanced out at the distant horizon and back again. Deliberately avoiding his eyes? "You're out early too."

"I can only gallop him when the beach is empty."

"Of course." She took a couple of steps up the beach and picked up her towel, wrapping it around her body, sarong-style. "Is he friendly?" she asked, approaching the horse with the calm respect of someone familiar with large animals.

"Very friendly. He'd sign autographs if he could hold a pen."

She put up her hand and stroked down The Bandit's sleek neck. "He's a nice-looking boy."

"He's a beauty." Maybe it was just as well that she'd wrapped herself up in that towel. "So . . . you've come home?"

"Yes. To see my grandmother." She was still avoiding his eyes.

"Oh, yes. How is she?"

A crooked smile curved that soft mouth. "Not good. I'm going to see her this afternoon."

"Wish her well for me."

"I will."

Such a stilted conversation between two people who had once meant so much to each other. But that had been a long time ago. "Well . . . I'll see you around then."

"Yes." Another quirky little smile. "See you."

He watched her go, across the beach and up the cliff steps. His first love. Why the hell had she had to come back? He didn't need to have all those old memories dragged up from the furthest corners of his mind. He was doing okay — he had his daughter, his family, his friends, his work.

He was doing okay.

The Bandit seemed to pick up his tension, stomping impatiently on the sand. He nudged him forward, and the horse surged into a gallop, his movement smooth as silk. Another few days and he could go back to his training yard, and he'd be racing again in a couple of months.

Meanwhile, he had a full day's work ahead of him. Vaccinations, dental checks and visits to a couple of mares who were due to foal in a few weeks. And a pre-purchase vetting for a young show-jumping hopeful who was aiming to progress from her pony to a full-size horse.

Enough to put Cassie Channing and her orange swimsuit out of his mind. Completely.

* * *

Cassie strolled up the beach. Her heart was beating faster than usual, but that was understandable — she'd just been for a vigorous twenty-minute swim in water that was not much above fifteen degrees.

She wasn't going to watch Liam Ellis galloping along the beach . . . But as she climbed the steps up to Cliff Road she found herself glancing back, as if her gaze was drawn by a force stronger than gravity.

After all, there was nothing wrong with looking. He was just a man, riding a beautiful horse.

The motion was like poetry, as if they were one. He had been tall as a teenager, and now those wide shoulders and lean stomach were a man's physique, not a boy's. He still let his hair grow over the nape of his neck, and he hadn't shaved yet, a morning shadow darkening his hard jaw.

And his eyes . . . Impatiently she shook her head. At seventeen, eighteen she had let herself drown in those eyes. But she was a grown woman now, and she wasn't going to let herself drown in eyes the colour of espresso coffee. Nor let herself be mesmerised by that tempting mouth . . .

Yes, okay, the attraction was still there, but it was unlikely to go anywhere. They were two different people now. He had a kid, and she . . . she hadn't made up her mind yet. Use that airline ticket, or leave it tucked in the poetry book?

She still had six weeks to decide.

At the top of the steps she paused again and looked down at the village, curving around the bay. Home. She had dreamed of it so often while she had been away — that was part of the reason why she had stayed away so long, why she hadn't once come back for a visit. She knew that if she stayed too long she might never want to leave.

* * *

The Bandit was enjoying his gallop. Liam could feel the smooth power in his stride as raced along the water's edge. Maybe dreaming of winning the Derby? He turned him again at the end of the beach and gave him his head — down the home straight and first past the winning post!

Another half a dozen laps and then he turned him for home, up the ramp and along the first few yards of the South West Coast Path.

Though it was early a few of the serious walkers were already out, with their backpacks and their sensible walking shoes, some of them set to hike the whole length of the path which wound over six hundred miles around the peninsula.

Later the casual strollers would be along in their shorts and tennis shoes, with babies in buggies and kids on their scooters, admiring the view and picking blackberries along the way.

He greeted several of the walkers with a wave as he turned in through the gate and rode across to the stable yard.

"Well done, lad. You're doing great."

He slipped down from the saddle, led the horse over to the row of stables that edged two sides of the yard, and removed his tack. He stroked his hand over the warm russet flanks and down the horse's legs.

The Bandit's eyes were bright as he peered inquisitively around, his breathing already steady and slow, and best of all, he was standing square on all four legs with no sign of favouring the one that had required such delicate care for the past six weeks.

Liam sponged him down with cool water and checked his hoofs, then led him over to the trough and let him drink his fill. Then he brought the jar of liniment and smoothed it thickly over the horse's leg — he always seemed to quite enjoy the treatment, standing still to allow him to do it.

"Okay, lad — turn-out time."

The horse rested his head trustingly on Liam's shoulder as he followed him over to the gate into the grassy paddock behind the house. Liam patted his nose affectionately as he opened the gate. He would miss him when he was gone.

He leaned on the gate, watching the horses grazing happily on the lush green grass, looking for any signs that one might need more attention. Most were rescues — failed racehorses, or here to recover from neglect or ill-treatment.

Hopefully some of those could be leased out to responsible new owners in due course. Others were retired and could maybe be fostered. A couple were his in-patients, needing his extra care.

Then there were the family's horses, five of them, plus the children's two ponies. And their pet, little Spice, the small white mountain pony. He was probably too nervous to ever be ridden, but with patience he had gradually been coaxed to be less shy, and even to take a slice of apple from Robyn's hand.

That nice bay mare that his sister-in-law Julia rode now — he remembered Cassie riding her. They used to hack along the bridleway beside the coast path, the whole gang of them, or sometimes they'd load the horses into the trailers and drive up to Dartmoor for a longer trek, maybe stopping for a picnic on the banks of one of the fast-flowing rivers.

Good times, carefree times. Weekends, the long summer break from school and later from university — the sun had seemed to shine every day then. Or maybe that was just in his memory.

And then there had been just him and Cassie. The memories tugged at him. The first time he had kissed her, when she was seventeen. The first time they had made love, days after her eighteenth birthday. On the beach in the moonlight — her first time . . .

Shaking his head, he pushed those thoughts aside. There was no point stirring up those old embers now — they had long since gone cold. And he had a small daughter who would soon be waking up and wanting her breakfast.

* * *

Cassie strolled down the cliff steps, a soft breeze ruffling her hair as she breathed in the cool, fresh sea air, listening to the soft, sleepy whisper of the waves. Even with her eyes closed she would know she was home.

It was the height of the summer season. The mid-morning sun was already high in the clear blue sky, sparkling like diamonds on the waters of the bay.

The grey shape of a large ship hovered far out on the horizon — a cargo ship or a cruise liner — while closer in, a couple of small yachts set their white sails to catch the wisps of breeze.

Lazy wavelets edged with frills of white foam lapped at the edge of the sand. The beach was already crowded with families — children squealing and splashing in the waves, mums and dads flopping around on towels and deckchairs, seagulls stalking arrogantly between sandcastles and ball games, ready to snatch at any unguarded hamburgers or crisps.

Sturcombe was full of tourists staying in the guest houses along Church Road and the caravan site up on the cliffs to the east of the town. The little family-run bed-and-breakfast places would have their 'No Vacancies' signs in their windows, and most of the rooms in the Carleton Hotel would be booked.

The shops along the Esplanade would be eager to grab their custom while they could. The amusement arcade on the corner would be buzzing, the ice-cream parlour would be doing a roaring trade, and every table in the CupCake Café would be full.

At the foot of the steps she let Barney off his lead. He trotted off to sniff along the bottom of the sea wall, reading all the pee-mails and lifting his leg a little stiffly to leave some of his own.

"Cassie!"

Lisa was waving to her from the small encampment she had established with a picnic blanket and a colourful canvas windbreak a little way along the beach. Cassie waved back, the coarse-grained red-gold sand crunching beneath her feet as she called Barney to follow her, slipping him one of his favourite treats for obeying promptly.

"Hi. I was afraid I wouldn't find you with the beach being so crowded."

"I saw you coming down the steps. Noah, come and say hello to your Auntie Cassie."

A small boy, five years old and dark-haired like his mother, stared up at her — still baby enough to be shy of a stranger, too grown up to let it show.

"Hello. So you're Noah." Instinctively Cassie hunkered down to his level. "I've got a little present for you, from Australia. A road train. You can have it later."

He frowned, puzzled. "Trains don't go on roads. I've been on one."

Cassie laughed. "They do in Australia. It's a very big country and the roads go on for miles and miles, and the trucks pull so many trailers they call them road trains."

"Really?"

"Really."

He nodded solemnly before another thought brought a wide smile to his face. "I've got a sister." He pointed to the baby lying in an infant carrier in the shade of the windbreak.

"So I heard." Cassie peered into the carrier. A small pink face topped with a fluff of dark hair, a pale-yellow Babygro with a teddy-bear print, two tiny hands curved into fists. "What's her name?" She knew, of course, but she could see that Noah was almost exploding with the need to tell.

"Kyra. She's asleep. But she'll wake up soon and then she sometimes cries."

"Ah . . ." She shared a smile with Lisa. "She's so cute."

Kyra's mum was glowing with pride. "Isn't she? And this is Amy — Debbie Rowley's daughter. You remember Debbie? She and her mum run the CupCake Café."

"Of course." Cassie could have guessed who the child was. Half hiding behind Noah, she was the image of her mother — the same soft dark curls, the same wide brown eyes. "Hello, Amy. I'm Cassie. I knew your mum when she was at school."

The little girl managed a shy smile, her rosebud mouth forming a small, O.

"We're going to build a sandcastle," Noah announced proudly. "A great big one."

"That'll be fun. I used to build sandcastles, but I expect yours will be much better."

"Sit down," Lisa invited, patting the picnic blanket. "Want a cola?"

"Thanks." Cassie settled herself comfortably on the blanket and accepted the can of drink Lisa produced from her colourful tote bag. "So, give me all the goss. I know you've sent me regular updates, but email's not nearly as good as a proper natter. Tom Cullen's getting married?"

"That's right. Her name's Vicky — Vicky Marston. She's old Molly Marston's niece — well, great-niece. Do you remember her? She used to come down for the summer holidays, years ago."

Cassie pursed her lips, thinking. "I remember Molly, of course — she was a one-off — but I don't think I knew her niece."

"She'd have been a couple of years younger than you. She was great friends with Debbie. She's really nice."

"Didn't you tell me she inherited Molly's place? And that funny portrait. It looked really weird in that picture you sent me."

"It was weird. She told me her ex-boyfriend said it was rubbish and to throw it in the skip, but it turned out to be worth a fortune. Which just goes to show."

"And it was by the same guy who drew that one of Nanna Marjory?"

"That's right. Mum got a tidy bit for that, and so did several other people. Kate — Debbie's mum — and Tom's mum, and Brenda who runs the shop up on Church Road."

"That was lucky. Seems like this Vicky brought a windfall to the town."

"She did."

"And now she's going to marry Tom. What happened to that actress you told me about, that he was engaged to last year? The witch?"

Lisa laughed, shaking her head. "Oh, she wasn't actually that bad. She was very beautiful, and she could be really nice — at least when things were going her way."

"And when they weren't?"

22

"Well, yes." Lisa's lips twitched. "She could be a bit of a witch."

Cassie laughed. "You think everyone is really nice. Anyway, what about this Vicky? Didn't you say she's from London? Who's to say she won't toddle off back there sooner or later, especially now she's got all that money."

"I don't think she will." The baby gurgled in her sleep, and Lisa patted her tiny hand to quiet her. "She's buying those old cottages on Slaney Road. Some developer was going to buy them and knock them down to build holiday apartments, but she outbid him and she's having them done up to rent out — locals only."

"That's good." Cassie nodded her approval, though she was still slightly doubtful.

"Anyway, you'll probably meet her soon and you'll see for yourself. She's covering my maternity leave over at the hotel."

"Why?" Cassie slanted her sister a look of surprise. "Surely she doesn't need a job after getting all that money for the picture?"

"I told you, she's really nice. She took it on before she knew the painting was worth so much, and she didn't want to let us down. You know how Mike gets — he'd have worried himself to a frazzle. And that's not the only wedding we've got coming up. Debbie's getting married too. To Bill, who works up at the Cullen farm."

"Oh, yes. I remember you telling me that." She took another sip of her cola. "Wasn't she married before?"

"That's right — to Alan Gowan."

"Alan Gowan?" Cassie frowned. "The one who was in your class at school? You used to call him the Octopus."

"That's right." They were both speaking softly so that the children wouldn't hear, but fortunately they were too intent on their sandcastle to pay any attention to the grown-ups' conversation, Noah issuing instructions and little Amy dutifully following them. "He used to lurk in the senior library, and if he caught you on your own in there, he was all over you."

"Sounds like a right toe-rag. Why on earth did Debbie marry him?"

"Ah, you know what a little innocent she was. She was flattered that he paid her attention, and he liked that she always agreed with him about everything. They went together for a few years, then Debbie got pregnant with Amy so they got married. But it didn't stop him messing around with any bit of skirt he could get his hands on." She laughed. "Then he took up with Kelly-Anne Wallis. Remember her?"

Cassie frowned, dragging through the remote corners of her memory. "Pasty-faced girl, bad haircut? Always eating sweets, but she'd never share them."

"That's the one. The bad haircut's long gone — she's really glammed up these days, gone blonde."

"Wasn't she always a bit of a bully? I remember Dad had to take her prefect badge off her for shouting at the first years after she made one of them cry."

"That's right!" Lisa nodded. "I'd forgotten that. Anyway, she wouldn't stand for just being his bit on the side. She made him divorce Debbie and marry her."

"Sounds like she did Debbie a favour," Cassie remarked dryly.

"She did. They got married a year ago, just a few months after the divorce came through, and there's already a baby on the way."

Cassie laughed. "Well, if old Octopus gets up to his tricks now, he'd better watch out. She'll have his nuts for breakfast."

"She will." Lisa's eyes danced. "Debbie should have done that years ago."

Cassie sipped her cola, watching a seagull stalk arrogantly across the sand. The person she really wanted to ask about was Liam. She had avoided asking Lisa about him while she was away, hoping her sister would assume that she wasn't interested.

Lisa had once sent her a photograph of their gang of friends here on the beach, and there had been Liam among them, his arm around the waist of a very pretty blonde girl, both looking ecstatically happy in the sunshine. And a few months later Lisa had mentioned that she was going to his wedding — she assumed to the same blonde.

"All these weddings." Cassie took a moment to ensure that her voice held only casual interest. "Didn't you tell me Liam Ellis was married too?"

"Oh, yes — to Natalie." A shadow darkened Lisa's eyes. "But she died. It was a horrible shock to everyone. It was so sudden. They were on holiday in Greece, and there was an accident. It was so sad. She was . . ."

"Really nice?"

"Yes, she was. She was Ollie's receptionist for a while till she had their little girl. She was really good with his elderly patients — they all loved her. There were lots of tears at her funeral."

Cassie felt her heart crease. Lisa had told her about it at the time, but being so far away it had felt like something from another life. But now, having seen Liam again, seen that hint of darkness in his eyes, she could feel the depth of his loss. It must have been awful.

"Robyn was only two when it happened. Liam's done a great job bringing her up on his own. And he's a great vet. Barney's got a touch of arthritis, and he can be a bit grumpy at the vet's, but Liam's really good with him. But mostly he works with horses, of course."

"I saw him this morning," Cassie remarked, carefully casual. "He was riding along the beach on a beautiful roan."

"That would have been The Bandit. He's a racehorse. He had some kind of problem with his knee, but Liam fixed it and he'll probably be able to race again in a few months. He has a real way with any animal."

"Useful skill for a vet."

Lisa slanted her a questioning glance. "I thought at one time you'd marry him."

"Me?" Cassie shook her head, laughing. "Oh, that was just an adolescent thing. I couldn't wait to be off on my travels."

"Ten years." Lisa's smile had dimmed a little, a shadow of hurt darkening her eyes. "You didn't even come home for my wedding."

"No . . . I'm sorry — really. It wasn't . . . I didn't . . ."

Lisa leaned over and squeezed her hand. "It's okay. I missed you — I wanted you to be my bridesmaid. But I understood."

Cassie managed a smile. There was really nothing she could say. Her explanation at the time had been that she was due to start a new job on a dude ranch in Montana. The guy who owned it had already applied for the change to her visa, and if she had left the country, there had been a risk that it would be refused.

But though that had been true enough, it had also been a convenient excuse. What she hadn't wanted to admit, even to herself, was that she hadn't wanted to see Liam with his new girlfriend. Hadn't wanted to look at her and think, *that could have been me*.

And now, though Natalie was gone, the memory of her lingered. It always would. In a way, that was even harder.

She put her cola down and rose to her feet, picking up her swim-goggles. "Well, I think I'll go for a swim." She hoped her voice was casual enough that Lisa wouldn't suspect that she was escaping. "Won't be long."

She shrugged off her T-shirt and shorts, and strolled down the beach to the sea. The water was a pleasant few degrees warmer than it had been first thing this morning. She waded out until it was past her knees, then rolled forward beneath the surface and swam along the sandy bottom.

When she was a child she had always wanted to see real, wild coral reefs — not just the ones in the Aquarium at Newquay Zoo. And she had — in Florida, Tanzania, Australia's Great Barrier Reef. They had been even more beautiful, more spectacular than she had dreamed, all brilliant colours and crazy shapes, and teeming with the exotic fish which made them their home.

Here there would be nothing to see — sand, pebbles, a few rocks, seaweed. A torn plastic bag, several empty drinks cans.

She surfaced slowly and rolled onto her back to float for a while, then she began a lazy backstroke. After the long flight from Wellington it was good to stretch the ache out of her muscles. The sun was warm on her face, the gentle rocking of the waves beneath her could almost have lulled her to sleep.

Liam. She had dreamed about him last night — at least she had sensed that it was him, though she hadn't actually seen him. They had been walking side by side along the beach here. The sea had been as tranquil as a millpond in the moonlight. They had been talking, but she couldn't remember what about.

But then when she had turned, he wasn't there any more, leaving her with an aching sense of loss.

It was a dream she had had before. Quite often actually, especially in the early years after she had left. And last night, as on those other nights, she had woken to find her pillow damp with tears.

But now her stomach was warning her that it was almost lunchtime, so switching to an easy breaststroke, she swam back to the shore.

* * *

The hospital had an open-visiting policy. Cassie and her mum had brought punnets of strawberries and grapes, and two bottles of Nanna's favourite milk stout, which the doctors had agreed she was allowed to drink.

Helen Channing turned into the car park and drove around slowly until she spotted someone just pulling out of a parking space. "Ah, lucky." She eased into the spot, turned off the engine, and unfastened her seat belt. "No tears now," she warned Cassie. "Your grandmother hates any of that kind of fuss."

"Of course." Cassie forced a watery smile. "I promise."

"Come here." Her mother produced a tissue from her pocket, and taking Cassie's chin between her fingers, she dabbed it over her eyes.

"Aw, Mum!" Cassie protested, laughing. "Anyone would think I was in Year Three." They both climbed out of the car and set off across the car park to the hospital entrance. "I just keep thinking I should have come home sooner. I would have had more time to spend with her."

"She understands. You needed to live your own life. You wouldn't have been happy if you'd stayed here — you needed to fly. You've always been like that, since you were a little girl. You always wanted to go that bit farther, climb that bit higher. You were always asking questions, and then more questions when you got the answer."

"Sounds like I was a nightmare!"

"Not at all," her mum insisted. "You were great fun. A challenge, but fun."

"But I was your youngest." Cassie's eyes danced. "You didn't have another one — you didn't want to risk it turning out like me!"

They laughed, which made them both feel a lot better.

The hospital was busy with staff and visitors milling around the reception area, a few patients in dressing gowns and slippers taking a little careful exercise for a change of scene.

"It's on the fourth floor — we'd better take the lift," Helen suggested.

"Sure."

They stood aside to let a wheelchair out, then rode up to Nanna's floor. As they stepped out into the long, stark corridor, Cassie tucked both her hands into her mother's arm, feeling the comfort that had always been there for her, even when she hadn't wanted to need it.

The guilt was digging at her, tightening in her guts — she should have come home sooner.

She had always been close to Nanna when she was little, loving to run up the road to her house further up the hill and sit in her kitchen watching her bake, begging to lick out the mixing bowl or nibble the cut-offs of pastry. Then breathing the wonderful aroma that came from the oven, and finally being granted a slice of mouthwatering apple and blackberry pie or coffee-and-walnut cake.

Now Nanna was ninety-three and her heart was failing. It was that which had brought Cassie home, taking extended leave from the adventure tourism company she was working for in New Zealand and booking the first available flight when Lisa's email had warned her that time was running out.

So, she was here, and she knew that she had to do her best to keep a smiling face for her grandmother, though she felt like breaking down and sobbing her heart out.

It was a four-bed ward. Nanna was in the bed in the far corner, her white hair in wispy curls around her head, her face almost the same colour as the pillows propping her up. Beside her, a heart monitor was beeping — faster than normal, and with the occasional skip. Signs that a once powerful and loving heart was finally failing.

She turned her head as they walked in, her pale eyes twinkling as brightly as ever. Cassie's mother squeezed her daughter's hand as Cassie walked to the bed, forcing down the lump in her throat so that she could speak.

"Hello, Nanna." She bent and kissed the papery cheek. "How are you?"

"Much better for seeing you, my little Pickle."

Oh, lord. Cassie almost lost it. That had always been Nanna's pet name for her. To catch a moment to compose herself she went to fetch a spare chair so that she and her mother could both sit down.

"Ah, what have you brought me?" Nanna demanded as she spied the bag her daughter-in-law was carrying.

"A few of your favourites." Helen set them out on the bedside table. "Would you like some strawberries now?"

"Never mind strawberries." Nanna dismissed the punnet with an impatient hand. "I'll have some of that milk stout. I hope you've brought the good stuff."

Helen briefly rolled her eyes. "Of course."

The rich, dark brew poured with just the right amount of creamy head. Nanna took a good swallow and smiled happily. "Now—" she squeezed Cassie's hand — "tell me about everything you've been up to."

Cassie laughed. "Everything?"

"Of course. I want to hear all the details."

"I sent you loads of letters. I wrote every couple of weeks, and sent you photographs."

"Bah! That's not the same as hearing your voice tell it."

Still as bossy as ever, though her voice sounded a little thin, a little raspy. Afraid of overtiring her, Cassie glanced across at her mother. She smiled, nodding to indicate for her to go ahead.

"Okay." She drew in a breath. "Well, I started out in Florida, in Key West. I was the dogsbody to begin with."

"That's right," Nanna approved, nodding. "You always have to start at the bottom."

"I did — just checking and handing out equipment at first. But I'd got my Divemaster qualification, so after a few weeks they let me lead tourist groups on the reefs. I stayed there for almost two years."

"Was it fun?"

"Oh, it was wonderful. As well as the diving, I learned to sail, waterski, windsurf . . ."

"So, you weren't sorry about leaving Sturcombe then?"

Cassie hesitated. "Well, maybe a bit," she admitted. "I did get homesick sometimes. But mostly it was all too exciting."

"And boyfriends?"

Cassie smiled. "A few."

"But you didn't let any of them slow you down?"

"No, I didn't."

"Good for you." Nanna nodded, smiling in satisfaction. "So what did you do next?"

"Well, I lined up another job in Montana, working with horses on a dude ranch. On the way there I hired a car and took the long way round. Up to New York, down again to New Orleans . . ."

Nanna's eyes had closed and her regular breathing suggested that she had fallen asleep. The beeping of the heart monitor had slowed a little. But as soon as Cassie stopped talking she opened her eyes again.

"Go on," she urged, an edge of impatience in her voice. "I don't have all the time in the world anymore."

Cassie laughed uncertainly but continued her story. Her mother had slipped quietly away to get a coffee, leaving Cassie to talk quietly as her grandmother continued to smile.

At last, when Cassie's mother returned, Nanna opened her eyes. "There, I've heard all about my little Pickle's adventures. I told you it was the right thing for her to go."

"You did."

"You only get one go round, you know. It's not like a library where you can finish one book and take it back to get another one to start. You have to live your life like you mean it — don't waste a moment of it. So, go and tell the nurses I'm coming home tomorrow."

"*What?*"

"You heard me. I'm sick of being stuck in this place. I want to be back home where I can be comfortable. I don't need this stupid noisy thing to tell me what my heart's doing." She indicated the heart monitor. "I might have a few weeks left, I might have only a few days, but I'm going to spend them at home. And don't you go telling me I can't."

Cassie's mother sighed and rolled her eyes. "You're a very obstinate old woman."

"Of course I am! That's how come I've lived so long. And if I can't go out in my own way, well, I wonder what's the point?"

"Very well." Helen Channing threw up her hands. She knew when she was wasting her breath. "I'll go and talk to the nurses."

CHAPTER THREE

Nanna's homecoming had all the pomp and ceremony of a royal visit, though she had only been in the hospital for ten days. Ollie had gone with Cassie's mum and dad to fetch her in her dad's comfortable car, but Cassie was there waiting for her outside the house, along with Lisa and Paul.

When the car drew up at the kerb the grand old lady gave a regal wave, her eyes twinkling with delight as she saw the reception committee. Paul opened the car door for her with a solemn bow as Cassie's dad went to the boot to fetch the wheelchair. Paul and Ollie settled her into it with all due ceremony and wheeled her to the front door, then the two of them lifted it up the stone steps to the hall.

She gazed around in smug satisfaction. "Right. I'm home."

Cassie's mum smiled wearily. "Yes, you are." Apparently, the journey from the hospital hadn't been without its trials.

Nanna had finally been persuaded nearly five years ago to give up her own house at the top of Cliff Road, and move in with her son's family three doors down. Lisa had kept Cassie entertained for months with the story of all the toing and fro-ing as the obstinate old lady had insisted that she was perfectly fine living on her own.

It had taken two falls to put an end to the arguments. But even then she had been as contrary as possible, refusing point-blank to consider a stairlift so that she could use one of the upstairs bedrooms. 'She says it looks like a toilet,' Lisa had written. 'Can't say I blame her.'

So all the furniture had had to be moved out of the dining room, and her bed brought in, along with her dressing table which she had had since she was a bride, and her favourite armchair set in the bay window so that she could see out over the whole village.

They had brought her photographs — her wedding, wearing a lovely white lace gown, Grandpa Channing at her side, handsome and smart in his naval uniform. And they had set up her television for her to watch her favourite soaps and quiz shows.

"Do you want a cup of tea?" Lisa offered.

"Of course I do. And biscuits. Chocolate digestives."

Cassie wasn't the only one trying to suppress her laughter. Nanna had always been bossy, but as she had grown older she was worse than ever. Still, as she had said, at the age of ninety-three she was entitled to be as bossy as she liked.

"Do you want to lie on the bed or sit in your chair?" Ollie asked.

"The chair, of course. Come on, what are you standing there for? Help me up."

They settled her in the armchair, making sure that she was comfortable with several cushions round her, and her feet propped up on a low footstool. Ollie had taken her wrist and was checking her pulse. She glared up at him.

"Stop mithering me," she scolded. "That's why I wanted to get out of that damned hospital, with the way all those doctors and nurses kept mithering me all the time."

He smiled. "Humour me."

"Huh!" But she let him finish. "Now, where are the little ones? Don't they want to see their poor old granny?"

33

"Noah is down at the café playing with Amy, and Kyra's upstairs sleeping. You can see them later — you need to take it easy for a while now."

"I've every intention of taking it easy," she retorted. "Where's that tea? Ah, about time." She scowled as Lisa came in with a tray. "What did you do? Go and pick the leaves yourself?"

Cassie's mum sighed and set the remote control for the television down on the table beside her. "Is there anything else you want?"

"Not for now. I'm going to drink my tea and then have a nice sleep." She glared at Ollie. "And I don't want anyone disturbing me to take my damned pulse!"

"Okay. We'll go and leave you in peace for a while then."

In the kitchen the family settled round the big scrubbed-pine table. Cassie's mum had provided home-baked scones and mugs of tea.

"Well, she's home."

"She's going to run you ragged, Mum," Cassie warned her.

"I don't mind. She helped me a lot when you were all little. Now it's her turn to be looked after."

"I'll be here to help."

Paul slanted her a questioning look. "You're staying then?"

"For a while." For a fleeting moment she had a flash-back to herself tucking that airline ticket into the poetry book, but she pushed the image aside. "There's the two weddings coming up — Debbie's and Tom's. I'll be staying for those. Besides, I thought it was time I took a bit of a break from racketing around having fun."

Her mum looked pleased but didn't say anything. Cassie knew how difficult it had been for her to watch her young-est fly off across the Atlantic ten years ago, but she hadn't said anything then either. She had been grateful for that — it wouldn't have taken much to tip the scales, take the easy path of staying at home.

She glanced around the kitchen. The family usually ate in here — they had rarely used the dining room, unless they had guests, even before Nanna had taken it over.

The room was at the back of the house, overlooking the garden. It faced north, but it was always warm and bright, with buttercup-yellow walls, white painted cupboards, and a range-style cooker with polished brass trim.

Barney's basket was next to the range. He had been curled up, comfortably dozing, but the prospect of begging for nibbles of scone lured him out, his warm brown eyes full of adoration as he levered his front paws a little stiffly onto Cassie's lap.

"You greedy little mutt," she chided him fondly, tickling behind his ears. "Here you are." He snaffled the bit of scone she gave him, and promptly turned his attention to Paul. Cassie laughed. "You traitor!"

She spread her scone with a thick layer of Devon cream and a smear of her mother's home-made strawberry jam, and bit into it, the warmth of pure bliss spreading through her. "Mmm, I'd forgotten how scrummy your scones are."

Her mother laughed. "Worth coming home for?"

"Mm-hmm," she mumbled through the mouthful. "Nobody makes scones like you. Or maybe Nanna, back in the day."

Home. Sitting around the kitchen table with her family, the little brown terrier still hopefully begging for a bit of scone. Yes, moments like this were worth coming home for. Worth staying for? She didn't have to make up her mind about that for a while. She'd be staying for Nanna, and for the two weddings.

After that . . . The ticket said 25th September. Six weeks. There was no rush.

* * *

"Daddeee, can we go down to the beeeach today? I want to play with Amy."

Liam smiled down into his daughter's upturned face. He'd give her the moon and the stars, so a trip to the beach was the least he could do. The stack of emails and paperwork on his desk could wait until tonight, when she was asleep.

"Okay, sweet plum. Are you going to go in the sea?"

The small blonde head nodded vigorously. "I 'spect so."

"We'd better put your swimsuit on under your shorts then."

"I did awready."

She gave him her most angelic smile, and he laughed, shaking his head. Five years old, and she could wind him around her little finger.

The beach was crowded, but Robyn knew where to find her best friend. She let go of Liam's hand as they reached the bottom of the ramp and raced ahead across the sand. "Amy! We're here."

Liam let Hobo off his lead and he hirpled after her, not troubled at all by the absence of one hind leg. Barney, the Channing's small Border Terrier, jumped up to meet him, and the pair of them set off, bouncing and chasing each other down to the water's edge and back.

A small group was clustered at the far end of the beach, close to the cliff steps. Debbie Rowley's little girl Amy, the image of her mum. Lisa Cullen with Noah, who was in the same class as Robyn and Amy, and the baby in her carrier in the shelter of a colourful canvas windbreak.

And Cassie Channing.

His footsteps faltered briefly. But his little blonde whirlwind had launched herself to the centre of the group and was chattering excitedly. He managed a casual smile as he greeted them all, careful not to let his gaze linger too long on that one face. "Hi. How's things?"

"We're going to build a sandcastle," Noah announced. "A great big one."

"Sounds good. Can I help?"

"My daddy builds the bestest sandcastles in the whole world," Robyn proclaimed proudly, spreading her arms wide.

Noah looked doubtful. He'd been the foreman in this enterprise, and was afraid he would have to relinquish his position.

Liam grinned at him. "I'm good at digging. But you'll have to tell me what to do."

The little boy conceded a nod. "We have to start by making the moat. You can help to dig."

"Right."

The space was chosen — nice and flat, not too many pebbles. The outline was marked out, colourful plastic buckets and spades distributed and instructions given. All the children began to dig, chattering with excitement.

"Mummy, come and help," Noah demanded.

Lisa shook her head. "I have to stay with the baby. But Auntie Cassie will help if you ask nicely."

"Yes please, Auntie Cassie."

Cassie laughed and levered herself to her feet. "Okay, I'm coming."

Liam edged discreetly round to the far side of the excavation so there would be no risk of finding himself too close to her. But then he found himself opposite her.

He couldn't quite prevent himself from watching as she hunkered down among the children, her eyes sparkling with fun as she took a yellow plastic spade and began to dig, as instructed by their small foreman.

She was wearing that bright orange swimsuit again, with a pair of shorts. She must have been in for a swim as the damp fabric clung to every curve of her body like a second skin . . .

No. He forced his gaze away. That was a path he didn't want to tread.

Robyn's curiosity had been drawn to this new person in her world. "Have you hurted your arm?" she asked, pointing at Cassie's shoulder.

"No." Cassie smiled down at her. "It's a tattoo."

"What's a tappoo?"

"It's a pattern drawn on your skin, like this. People have all sorts of them."

"Can I touch it?"

"Of course."

Robyn stroked the design tentatively with one finger. "It's pretty."

"Thank you."

"Does it wash off when you go in the sea?"

"No, it never washes off. It's there forever."

"Can I have one?"

"You'd better ask your daddy." She shot him a look that was brimful of teasing amusement. *You deal with it*, was the implication.

"Daddy, can I have a tappoo?"

"Absolutely not!" Dammit, in his anxiety he'd spoken more sharply than he'd intended. But a tattoo? What next? Piercings?

"Oh, Daddeee!"

As her little bottom lip wobbled, he recognised the start of a wail. Heavens, had he brought up a spoiled little girl who would throw a tantrum whenever she didn't get her own way?

For a moment he thought she was going to throw down her spade and stalk off, but as he struggled to find a way to retrieve the situation before it got out of hand, Cassie came to his rescue.

"Sorry, sweetie, but you can't have one until you're eighteen years old, which is a long time yet. But you can have a pretend one, if Daddy says that's okay."

"Can I, Daddy?" The child launched herself at him, hugging his neck. "Can I have a pretend tappoo?"

"I suppose so." He laughed, shaking his head in resignation. "You draw all over everything anyway, so having a drawing on yourself won't be much different."

"I want one like yours." Now she launched herself at Cassie, clambering into her lap and raising a pleading face.

"Okay." Cassie's eyes were dancing with amusement. "But we can't do it right now. We need the proper pens to do it with."

Liam half expected the child to demand to have it done instantly. But maybe just because Cassie was new to her, or maybe there was something in her tone, the child agreed happily and picked up her spade again, returning to her sand-castle duties.

He smiled at Cassie across the excavation. "Thank you," he mouthed silently.

She smiled back. "No worries."

He sat back on his heels watching his small daughter, her face intent, her little pink tongue peeping out from the corner of her lips as she helped to dig the moat deeper.

He could kick himself for speaking to her so sharply. Much as he adored her, there were times when he just couldn't seem to get it right.

Maybe he was overanxious, overthinking everything. Struggling to be both father and mother to her. Maybe he should try to relax a little more. His mother had told him more than once that there was no such thing as perfect parenting.

* * *

Cassie was doing her best not to let her gaze linger too much on Liam Ellis. It wasn't easy. She'd met a lot of fit, good-looking men on her travels — men who did a lot of water sports or other adventure activities tended to have good bodies.

Liam didn't have such a muscular build as them — but then too much muscle didn't really do it for her. It was enough that he filled out that T-shirt so nicely. And those strong forearms and wrists, covered with a smattering of dark, curling hair . . . Strong wrists had always been her thing.

He and Robyn were laughing together as they competed to shovel sand onto the mound that would become the castle, the earlier storm forgotten. Cassie watched them covertly as she wielded her own plastic spade.

It was lovely to see the way he was with his little girl. She was a pretty little thing, with that cap of golden curls. She must take after her mother. That would be a double-edged sword for him — a constant reminder of the woman he had loved and lost.

If she hadn't left . . .

Liam smiled at her across the construction works. "How's your grandmother?"

"Not good. She came home from the hospital yesterday."

"Oh?" He looked surprised. "She's well enough?"

"Not really. But she's very obstinate. Ollie spoke to her consultant and they agreed it would probably do more harm to refuse to let her have her way. Besides," she added wryly, "she might be frail but she's very definitely mentally competent, so really they have to abide by what she wants."

"Still, it'll be nice for you to have her home," he suggested.

"It will. Though she can be pretty hard to manage."

He laughed. "At her age, I suppose she's entitled to be."

"That's pretty much what she said."

With most of the construction of the sandcastle completed, Cassie retreated to the picnic blanket beside the windbreak. The children continued the task of installing turrets, arranging pebbles strategically around the fortifications, and digging a long canal up from the sea to fill the moat.

The dogs had come back from their romp. Lisa dug a collapsible bowl out of her capacious bag and filled it from a water bottle. They lapped it up before collapsing, exhausted, in the shade.

"It's busier than ever down here today," Cassie remarked, glancing along the beach. Hardly an inch of sand wasn't covered with beach towels and deckchairs and sun loungers. The shallows were full of excited children, squealing as they skipped over the waves. The beach shop up on the Esplanade must have very nearly sold out of frisbees and beach balls, lilos and colourful inflatable rings, some shaped like flamingos or dinosaurs.

"It'll be worse than this in a couple of weeks when it's the bank holiday. Half the country will be heading for the seaside."

"Oh lord, yes. I'd forgotten that. The roads'll be snarled up all the way from Bristol."

"And everyone will be fighting to squeeze into a space in the car parks, struggling to figure out how to use the parking app. I bet there'll be a few road-rage incidents before the weekend's over."

"Lucky us, eh?" Cassie nodded towards the steps down from Cliff Road. "Out of the front door and straight down onto the beach."

"Mmm. It's just . . . Oh, I know it's good for the businesses that rely on the tourists. I suppose that's the compensation for the way the town gets overrun every summer. It just makes it so hard for anyone else trying to find a place to buy or even rent when so many houses are second homes or Airbnbs. I worry what it'll be like for Noah and Kyra when they're grown up, whether they'll even be able to live here."

"That's a long time ahead," Cassie reminded her gently.

Lisa laughed, shaking her head. "Oh, ignore me, grumbling like some old bloke at the end of the bar. I'm not really complaining — I love it here. And it's perfect for the kids." She pulled her phone out of her bag. "Hey, that's a fine-looking castle," she called out to them. "I'm going to take a photograph."

The castle was indeed magnificent — three feet square and two high, ready to repel all invaders. The construction team posed proudly behind it as Lisa took several snaps. "I can show these to Nanna. She'll love seeing them."

Robyn came bouncing over. "Auntie Cassie, Auntie Cassie, we're going in swimming. Are you coming too?"

She slanted a swift glance up at Liam. Swimming. He'd be taking off his T-shirt, his jeans, stripping down to his swimming togs. She could cope with that. Of course she could . . .

"Yes, I'm coming swimming," she confirmed.

The little ones all whooped with delight, racing to scramble out of their T-shirts and shorts. They all had their swimming togs on underneath, so this was clearly planned for.

"Wait," Lisa called sternly. "No one goes till everyone goes."

"Are you coming in?" Cassie asked.

Lisa shook her head, indicating the baby sleeping in her carrier.

Cassie slipped out of her shorts, then they all lined up to race down the beach to the sea, the dogs bounding ahead, barking with excitement. They splashed into the water, squealing and jumping over the waves as they rippled in over the sand.

The children could all swim, though more with enthusiasm than style. After splashing around for a while, they decided on a race. The two grown-ups were instructed to stand twenty yards apart to serve as the start and finish posts, and Liam called, "One, two, three . . . go!"

"Come on, come on!" Cassie cheered them loudly, clapping her hands as they surged towards her with whirling arms and flapping feet. A little to her surprise it was Amy, the smallest, who won. "Well done!" she applauded. "That was brilliant. You all did really well."

Liam smiled across at her, and she smiled back, and for that fleeting moment she felt as though she had slipped back in time . . .

"Daddy, Daddy, throw me."

Liam laughed, his delight in his little daughter evident. "Come on, then." He made a stirrup with his hands and lifted her up. Giggling, she leaped off, curling up her knees to make the biggest splash she could as she landed on the water.

"Me too!" pleaded Amy.

He lifted her, and she did a star jump from his hands. Of course, Robyn wanted to do that too, then Noah joined in to do a rather ungainly back-flip.

What was it about seeing a man playing like that with small children? Somehow it made him seem sexier than ever.

And dammit, he was sexier than any man had a right to be. His skin was bronzed by the sun, every muscle defined, his wide chest smattered with dark, curling hair. She ached to reach out and touch . . .

42

To cool her heated blood she plunged under the waves, staying down for as long as she could. She came up to find Robyn hanging around her neck. "I fort you was drownding!" she protested.

Cassie laughed, hugging the child. "No, I wasn't — don't worry. I was holding my breath."

"Holding your breath?"

"That's right."

"Me too!" Clinging tightly to Cassie's hands, the child took in a huge whooping breath and ducked down below the surface, staying down for a few seconds, then bounced up again in an explosion of bubbles. "I did it, I did it!"

Of course, they all wanted to play that game, competing to stay down the longest. Finally, they began to tire, and reluctantly trudged back up the beach to Lisa.

"Phew!" Cassie laughed as she strolled up out of the water with Liam. "They've got some energy."

"They're five years old — it's in the job description."

"She's lovely, your little girl."

He smiled, pride and pleasure clearly written on his face. "She can be a little minx."

"I'm sure."

"I'm sorry about her pestering you earlier. That tattoo . . . I really shouldn't have spoken so sharply. It was really rather funny. It's just . . . I worry. I don't want her to get spoiled."

Cassie laughed, shaking her head. "I don't think there's much danger of that. She's adorable. And it's really no trouble. I'll be happy to do it. I sometimes used to do face painting for the kids at Kalagooly. I won't use face paints, though — you can't get the fine lines, and it'd probably rub off too quickly. Felt-tip pens would be better."

"Right."

Oh, that smile . . . It could still do funny things to her insides, even after all these years.

"Kalagooly? That was where you worked?"

"Uh-huh. It's in Queensland, not far from Straddie Island — Stradbroke Island. It's a fabulous place. It's got some of the best surfing in the world, and it's close to the Great Barrier Reef. I worked there for three years."

"Why did you leave?"

"My visa was running out, so I moved to New Zealand."

"Oh." He glanced down at the tattoo on her shoulder. "That's pretty. Does it represent something special?"

"Of course." She laughed, her eyes dancing. "All Maori tattoos represent something special. This is a poroporo flower, which represents staying rooted to the earth, and the feather represents flying high."

He quirked one dark eyebrow. "Sounds like a bit of a contradiction."

"Of course. I'm a Gemini — I'm full of contradictions."

Liam watched Cassie as she skipped away up the beach and flopped down on the blanket beside her sister. She'd changed. Well, that wasn't surprising, after ten years. As a teenager she'd been bright, sparkling, eager for life. Now she seemed more . . . grounded, comfortable in her own skin. Though the sparkle was still there.

Contradictions — the flower and the feather.

Lisa was putting sun cream on the children. When that task was finished, with much wriggling and giggling, they went off to review the work on their sandcastle and add a few more strategic fortifications.

Cassie had taken the sun cream and was spreading it on those long, elegant legs. Liam sat down beside her, watching her discreetly. Memories were swirling through his head, mingling with the image of her he saw now, and he didn't know what to make of it all.

Hobo had come over to check if he had any treats for him. He snaffled the proffered biscuit, then turned his attention to Cassie. She held out her hand for him to sniff. Apparently, he approved, moving in closer to sniff her neck. Then with a contented sigh he lay down, his head on her lap.

Liam laughed. "He likes you."

"He's cute." She stroked the dog's whiskery grey head and scritched the magic spot behind his ear. "How did he lose his leg?"

Liam frowned sharply. "He caught it on a piece of barbed wire. It was the sort of minor injury that could have been dealt with in moments — a couple of stitches and a course of antibiotics. Unfortunately, his owner neglected it and it became infected, to the point where the infection spread to the bone and he developed sepsis. By then the only option was to amputate."

"Oh, poor Hobo." The dog recognised her tone and lifted his head, his liquid-brown eyes playing up to the sympathy — possibly in the hope of another treat. "What a brave boy you are." She kissed his nose. "It doesn't seem to bother him, though, only having three legs."

He laughed again. "He's too dumb to count them."

Her eyes sparkled with amusement, and Liam felt an odd little tug in his gut. The lively teenager he had known ten years ago had grown into a very attractive woman.

"Hello everyone."

"Debbie! Lovely to see you."

Cassie scrambled to her feet as her old friend, Amy's mum, came down the middle steps. Debbie was small and dainty, like her daughter, with soft brown curls and soft brown eyes. She and her mother ran the CupCake Café up on the Esplanade. It was always popular with the locals as well as the holidaymakers for its wonderful home-made cakes and scones.

"It's lovely to see you too." Debbie beamed with delight. She had always tended to be rather shy and subdued, but now she positively glowed. And the neat little diamond engagement ring on her left hand, glinting in the sun, was the reason why. "I heard you were back. Gosh, you're so brown!"

Cassie laughed. "Lots of good New Zealand sunshine. And you're getting married in . . . what, three weeks?"

"That's right." Her eyes danced with happiness. "You're coming?"

45

"Oh, I'd love to!"

"Of course you must."

Amy darted over to hug her mother's legs. "Mummy, we went in the sea and we raced, and I won!"

"Well done, sweetheart." Debbie stroked a gentle hand over her daughter's dark hair. "We're quiet in the café at the moment, so I brought some cupcakes down, if anyone wants one?"

That announcement met with instant approval. The box was ice-cream pink to match the colour the café was painted, the name CupCake Café spelled out in blue, and with three cartoon cupcakes dancing along beside the words.

Inside were six iced cupcakes. Wide-eyed, the children each solemnly selected their favourite colours, remembering to say, "Thank you."

Debbie sat down on the picnic blanket and handed round the remaining cakes to the grown-ups. "How long are you staying?" she asked Cassie.

"I . . . um . . . I'm not sure yet." Always that same question, and she still wasn't sure how to answer it. Especially with Liam sitting just a few feet behind her.

"And how's your grandmother?"

"Well, she's home — she didn't want to stay in the hospital any longer. But Ollie thinks it could be any time."

"Oh, I'm so sorry. But she'll be better off at home, if that's what she wants."

"That's what Ollie said."

"Oh . . ." Debbie's phone was buzzing, and she pulled it from her pocket. Her face paled as she glanced at the screen.

"Alan?" Lisa asked quietly.

Debbie nodded, her happy smile gone as she opened the call. "No, we're down on the beach, with Lisa and Cassie Channing . . . He's up at the farm . . . Why are you doing this, Alan?" Her voice cracked. "You were never that bothered about her before."

"Causing hassle for her, as usual," Lisa explained softly to Cassie. "He doesn't like it that she's getting married again, that she's going to be happy without him. So he's trying to stop her by threatening to go for custody of Amy."

"That's ridiculous . . ."

Liam had heard, and his mouth thinned. He held out his hand to Debbie, gesturing for her to give him the phone.

"Gowan? This is Liam Ellis. Yes, Ellis. Mrs Ellis is my mum. Remember that lurcher pup you took into her surgery a couple of months ago?" Hobo lifted his head, as if some canine instinct had told him he was being talked about. "Mum remembers. Running with fleas and badly undernourished, and with a nasty injury to his leg which should have been treated weeks sooner?"

Liam's voice held a barely restrained anger.

"She remembers how you slammed out of the surgery, refusing to pay for the treatment. You were lucky the RSPCA decided not to prosecute, but only because you signed the poor thing over to her. She'd have been happy to see you in court. And she'd be happy to see you in court now if you don't leave Debbie alone."

If Debbie's ex-husband was trying to argue, Liam wasn't giving him the chance to get a word in edgeways.

"Do you seriously think any judge is going to let you have custody of a five-year-old child if you can't even look after a puppy properly?" A brief pause. "Yes, I suggest you do that. And if any of us hear that you've been hassling Debbie, you're likely to find you've bitten off more than you can chew. Goodbye."

Debbie's eyes were wide as he cut the call and handed the phone back to her with a grin.

"He's reconsidered."

"Thank you." She laughed, half in disbelief. "Wow! I didn't really think he could get custody, that he was just trying to stir up trouble. But I was afraid Bill would get drawn into it, and . . . well . . ."

Liam gave her a quick hug. "Don't you worry about it. All your friends have got your back. Just enjoy getting ready for your wedding."

"Thank you." She shook her head. "Well, I'd better be getting back." She picked up the empty cake box. "I promised Mum I'd only be a few minutes. Bye, everyone."

"That scumbag," Lisa remarked with uncharacteristic acid when Debbie had gone. "If Tom Cullen gets to hear what's been going on, he'd sort him out quick enough."

Liam laughed. "He did once, years ago. And quite by coincidence, it was because of Vicky. She was down here on holiday, staying with old Molly. Gowan and some of his stupid gang were bullying her, here on the beach, and Tom thumped him one. Gowan ran away crying like a baby! He's been wary of Tom ever since."

"Ace!" Lisa punched the air.

"Anyway, it looks like the tide's coming in, and I have a pile of paperwork waiting for me, plus a couple of foals who are due for their vaccinations. Come along, Robyn." He held out his hand to her. "Say bye-bye."

"Bye-bye." The child smiled angelically, waving as she put her small hand in her father's large one, and they walked away along the beach, Hobo hirpling along beside them on his three legs.

Cassie watched them go, all the way to the ramp up to the Memorial Gardens. That casual, athletic stride — it had been one of the things she had found so attractive about him all those years ago.

That phone call . . . She'd never heard him use that tone — ice-cold menace. She doubted that he or Tom Cullen would ever resort to violence, but when it came to cruelty to animals . . . And she'd hold their beer.

She became aware that Lisa was watching her, a small smile curving her mouth. "What?"

Lisa shook her head. "Nothing," she said, but there was a knowing glint in her eyes. "Anyway, tide's coming in. Time to go." She began to pack up the towels and discarded swim-suits and stowed them in her seemingly bottomless mum-bag. "Noah, you can carry the windbreak for Mummy, and Amy, you can take the empty cola cans and put them in your mummy's recycling bin."

The slope of the beach was long and shallow, so that once the tide turned, it came in quite quickly. All the other beachgoers were gathering up their belongings too and hurrying up the steps to the Esplanade. The amusement arcade and the ice-cream parlour would soon be doing a roaring trade, and so would Debbie's café.

"The kids are going to lose their sandcastle soon," Cassie remarked as they climbed the cliff steps.

"That's the way of sandcastles," her sister responded, laughing. "They know it always happens, but they can come back another time and build a new one. In a funny sort of way, I think it's quite good for them."

"How's that?"

"They learn to cope with disappointment, and that there's always hope for tomorrow."

Cassie laughed. "How philosophical!"

"It comes to you as you grow older."

"Ah! I remember when you dyed your hair purple. Now you're the local GP's wife and all grown up and sensible."

"For now," Lisa conceded. "But that purple dye's only on hold. It could break out again at any time."

* * *

The house was quiet when Liam and Robyn arrived home. He let Hobo off his lead and went in search of his sister-in-law. He found her in the small room which she had taken over as an office to serve all the business management for the practice.

She was sitting at her desk behind a computer and a stack of paperwork, her curly red hair caught up in a loose bunch on top of her head, her expression conveying unmistakable exasperation as he appeared in the doorway.

"There you are! Have you checked those invoices yet?"

"Auntie Julia, we been to the beach," Robyn announced before he could come up with a better excuse. "Amy was there, and Noah, and we built the biggest, bestest sandcastle *ever*!"

"Did you, Honey-bun? You look as if you've been in the sea, too."

"We did. We raced, and Amy won. And Auntie Cassie came too, and she showed me how to breathe under the water."

Julia lifted an enquiring eyebrow.

"No, sweetie," Liam corrected, trying to suppress his laughter. "How to *not* breathe under the water. Remember? You take a great big breath first, then you duck down."

"Ah." Julia nodded, smiling at the little girl. "So Auntie Cassie was there too?" The glance she slanted at Liam was full of teasing humour.

"Yes. She's ever so pretty and ever so nice, and she's got a tappoo . . . here." The child touched her shoulder to indicate the placement. "And she's going to draw one for me too."

"A tappoo?"

"A tattoo. A pretend one," Liam explained quietly.

"Ah . . ."

"Anyway . . ." He smiled down at his daughter. "I think I need to hose you down to get all that sand and gunge off you."

"The invoices?" Julia prompted. He might have known it was a vain hope that she would forget them.

"Oh . . . I'll see to them later."

"You know you won't. You've got appointments booked all afternoon, and it's darts night tonight. Do them now, while I pop this one in the shower and make us some lunch. And she can tell me all about Auntie Cassie too," she added with a mischievous wink.

Liam sighed and took the folder from her. "Okay. I need a quick shower myself first, then I'll look at them."

Upstairs in the bathroom he peeled off his clothes and stepped under the shower, letting the warm water flow down over his body. How did the sand manage to get everywhere — in his hair, in his armpits, in his groin? Once it was all washed down the drain he soaped himself all over, working up a good lather.

That wink from Julia — would everyone be speculating now that Cassie was back? In a small place like Sturcombe, anyone's business was everyone's business, and people had long memories.

Though it was ten years ago, that brief fling— barely six months, from March to September — would be fuel for the gossips now. They'd all be watching, latching onto every look, every word. It could drive you crazy — and he could well imagine that it was just the sort of thing that would drive Cassie to leave again.

Cassie . . .

He ran his hand down over his wet chest. She used to do that, when they'd been swimming — run her hand over his chest, teasing her fingers through the curly dark hair that grew there, laughing up at him.

And he'd run his hands over her body, savouring every contour — the long curve of her spine, the dip of her waist, the firm swell of her breasts . . .

Dammit! Invoices. They'd stop him letting his mind run on memories of Cassandra Channing and her soft, silky skin . . .

CHAPTER FOUR

"Hi, Mum." Cassie strolled into the kitchen and dumped the shopping bags on the counter. "Mmm, something looks good." She snaffled a pinch of the pastry her mother was kneading.

Helen pushed her hand away before she could steal any more. "What took you so long? I was about to send out a search party."

"Brenda in the shop kept me chatting." She took the frozen stuff from the bags and began to stack it into the freezer. "Then I popped round to visit Arthur Crocombe. Brenda said he'd had a nasty fall."

"He did, but he's doing okay now. His son in Canada has arranged for a full-time carer for him."

"Oh, yes. I met him. Marcus. Nice chap, ex-army medic, and Arthur seems to like him. Mmm, blackberry-and-apple pie. My favourite. How's Nanna?"

"Fine. She's been dozing most of the morning, but she ate a bit of lunch — without too much grumbling."

Cassie laughed. "Where's Dad?"

"He had to go into school. They're doing a safety inspection."

"But it's the holidays!"

"Apparently it's urgent." Helen sprinkled some flour onto the marble pastry board and began rolling out the dough. "Something to do with the roof this time."

Cassie watched her mother fondly. So many times she had sat here in the kitchen while she baked. She would be sixty next year. She had put on a little weight in the past ten years, but not much. There were threads of silver in her dark hair, and a few lines around her eyes — mostly of laughter.

Helen Channing had been the deputy head of Fowey Road Primary School — which had been a serious embarrassment for Cassie and her brother and sister when they had been pupils there themselves.

She had taken early retirement five years ago to care for her mother-in-law. Though whether coping with Edie Channing was easier or harder than coping with a hundred or so lively five- to eleven-year-olds remained a moot point.

"You're still wearing that old apron!" Cassie remarked. "It must be donkey's years old."

"It's my favourite. By the way, I was thinking. If you like, I could put you on my car insurance. That way you can borrow it whenever you need to, even if it's only for a few weeks."

"That would be good. Thank you."

A small stab of guilt pricked at her. Her mother was being matter-of-fact about it, in her usual way, but those words — "only for a few weeks"— glossed over the surface of a much deeper current.

"If the bus service is as bad as it used to be, it could come in very handy."

Helen rolled her eyes. "It's worse. Once an hour, even in high season. Off season, it's every two."

Oh yes, the buses. She remembered a long campaign by the locals to try to improve the service, but apparently it still hadn't achieved anything. With the train station demolished years ago when the rail line had been closed down, Sturcombe had dwindled into a backwater, no longer the thriving holiday destination it had once been.

Most people would stop off at the popular resorts of East Devon — Beer and Exmouth and Dawlish — or drive straight past on their way to Cornwall. Though it could still attract crowds at the height of the season, by October it would lapse almost into hibernation for the winter.

She knew that many people loved the place and never wanted to leave — her parents, her sister and her friends, even her brother. But for her, the lure of what was beyond the horizon had always tugged at her heart.

Now . . . she really didn't know. She'd had some wonderful adventures — but home was home.

Dammit, she wasn't going to think about that right now. One day at a time was enough. "Would you like a cuppa?" she asked her mum.

"Yes, please. And you could make one for Nanna while you're at it."

"Sure." She filled the kettle and got the mugs down from the cupboard. "Liam Ellis was at the beach this morning, with his little girl," she remarked, hoping her tone conveyed only casual interest. "She's such a pretty little thing. She saw my tattoo and wanted one like it. She called it a 'tappoo'."

Helen laughed as she reached for the greased pie dish and slid the rolled-out pastry onto it.

"He seems to be making a very good job of bringing her up on his own."

"He is." Helen dusted off her hands and turned to check the oven temperature. "Fortunately, he's got the family around him to help."

"Even so, it must be tough for him." Cassie fiddled unnecessarily with the mugs, lining up the handles. "Lisa said Natalie used to work for Ollie."

"Natalie? Yes, she did. He always said she was the best receptionist he'd ever had. She could even manage Edie."

Cassie's eyes danced. "That's quite an achievement."

Her mum was looking at her the same way Lisa had — questioning, slightly sceptical. As if doubting that she really

54

wasn't interested in reviving that old relationship. Which she wasn't. Too much water had flowed under the bridge, they were different people now.

There could be no going back.

The kettle had boiled, and she focused on making the tea, refusing to even notice that her hand was shaking slightly. She brought her mother's mug over to the table.

"I'll take my tea in and sit with Nanna for a while," she suggested.

"Take her a couple of chocolate biscuits too. Not too many — she'll scoff the lot, and I'm not sure they'd be good for her."

Cassie laughed. "She'd tell you that she's too old to be bothered about what's good for her."

She set Nanna's teacup down on a tray with a plate of biscuits. No mug for Nanna — it had to be a cup and saucer from her second-best bone china tea service, which had been brought down from her house when she had moved.

Careful not to let any tea spill in the saucer, Cassie carried the tray along the hall to the half-open door. "Nanna?"

The old lady was sitting in her chair, her eyes closed, her frail hands resting on the crocheted blanket covering her knees. As Cassie quietly stepped into the room, the old lady opened her eyes, glaring fiercely.

"Ah, you've brought me a cup of tea. About time, too. My mouth's as dry as the Sahara Desert." The sight of the chocolate biscuits mellowed her instantly. "Biscuits. Good girl."

Cassie set the tea tray down on the side table. "What about your teeth?"

"Ugh!" The old lady dismissed the suggestion with a snort of disgust. "Never bother with 'em. Make my mouth sore."

"They might be better if you'd let the dentist fit them properly," Cassie offered gently.

"Dentists! As bad as doctors. And they call *me* a fussy old woman! I've got nothing on them for fussy, the lot of 'em. Now, come and sit by your old Nanna and talk to me."

Cassie concealed her eye-roll as she went to fetch a chair so that she could sit close to her grandmother. "How are you feeling?" she asked.

"Pretty well, considering I'm dying. Oh, don't look so upset about it — I'm quite settled to it in my mind. It's time. Ninety-three years is more than enough for anyone." She reached over for a biscuit and dunked it in her tea. "You know, I was just fifteen when I first met your grandfather. He was a cadet at the Royal Naval College in Dartmouth." She smiled dreamily. "I thought he was the most handsome man I had ever met."

Cassie had heard the story many times, but she wasn't going to interrupt Nanna's happy reminiscences. "I've seen his photos." She glanced at the old wedding photo on the sideboard. "He certainly was handsome. He could have been a film star."

It was the right thing to say. Nanna beamed. "He could, too. When we went out together, all the girls envied me for being on his arm."

"And I bet the boys envied him just as much, for having you."

Nanna chuckled. "Well, yes — maybe they did, maybe they did." She went on nodding to herself, seeming to drift into memories.

"You didn't get married for quite a few years after you met, did you?" Cassie prompted.

"No. He had his heart set on a career at sea." Nanna sighed. "It had been his ambition since he was ten years old, to be the captain of a Royal Navy ship. I knew I couldn't ask him to give that up for me. If he had, sooner or later he would have started to feel restless, and in the end he would have resented me for holding him back." She fixed Cassie with a look full of meaning. "So, he followed his dream, and I waited. It was the right thing to do."

Cassie acknowledged the truth of that with a wry smile. "Just like it was probably right for me too, to go away. But you were lucky, you married him in the end, so you both got what you wanted."

"I did. Fifty-two years we were married." She closed her eyes again. "What's meant to be is meant to be."

She seemed to have fallen asleep again. Cassie sipped her own tea, her mind drifting back in time. Nanna had always understood her thirst to travel — she said she had inherited the wanderlust gene from her grandfather.

It was Nanna who had encouraged her to believe that she could make the dream come true. Who had nudged her into taking her PADI diving certificates, paying for the courses as a birthday present. Who had suggested that she look on the internet for information about how to get a work visa for the USA.

Then when she was seventeen, she had met Liam Ellis. Well, she had known him all her life, of course — he had been one of her brother's best friends since they were at school. But she'd just been Paul's kid sister, tagging along with the gang, probably a bit of a tomboy, determined not to be left out.

But that Easter he'd come home from university in Bristol to help out in his dad's veterinary practice. And of course he'd been invited to Lisa's twenty-first birthday party. The memories were still so vivid . . .

* * *

The house was crowded. The furniture had been moved to make space, and people were dancing in the sitting room, nattering in the kitchen, queuing for the bathroom. And probably doing other things in Lisa's and Paul's bedrooms among the coats.

The big joke was that Lisa's boyfriend Ollie and his medical student mates had brought along a stack of cardboard urinal bottles for people to drink out of instead of glasses.

Cassie had made a bit of an effort to look nice. Her mum had taken her into Exeter to get her hair trimmed, and the hairdresser had suggested she change to a centre parting. And Mum had bought her a pretty top in a soft emerald green, with a handkerchief hem. Though she'd insisted on wearing it with her usual jeans.

She'd been carting a bag of empty beer cans out to dump them in the dustbin. As she came back into the kitchen, she found Liam Ellis spreading a lump of French bread with a thick layer of butter.

"Oh!" Her heart thumped.

He turned and smiled at her, a flicker of surprise in his eyes as they skimmed over her. "Hello. I was just nicking some bread. I came straight down from Bristol and I haven't had any supper."

"Oh, that's fine." She felt as if she'd been running. "Help yourself — there's plenty. Would you like some ham or cheese with it?"

"Cheese would be good."

She turned to the fridge, hoping he wouldn't notice the blush of pink that had risen to her cheeks. "Here you are. Cheddar or Brie?"

"Cheddar will be fine."

She got the knife out of the drawer, cut him a thick wedge, and put it on his bread. He flashed her another of those smiles as he bit into it.

"Great, thanks."

"Would you like some more?"

"No. Maybe later." He smiled again as he finished the snack, and held out his hand. "Come and have a dance with me."

That smile — it made her insides melt. She put her hand into his and let him lead her into the sitting room where an old Rolling Stones album of her mother's had everyone rocking.

In spite of the press of people, he managed to make enough space for them. He didn't put his arms round her. He just laid a hand on her hip, and they moved together to the music.

It was difficult to hold a conversation, but Liam leaned down to speak close to her ear. "What have you been getting up to lately?"

"Oh, just studying for my A levels. That hasn't left me much time for anything else."

"Not even riding?"

"Sometimes. Lisa and I went up to the moor a couple of weeks ago with Tom and Ollie."

"Would you like to come out for a ride with me tomorrow? We've just taken in a youngster who wasn't making it on the racecourse. He needs a good outing, but he likes company. You could ride Missie, if you'd like."

She hesitated, longing to say yes but feeling suddenly shy. "Oh . . . Okay, yes . . ." She was struggling to project a cool demeanour while excitement was sizzling through her veins. "Um . . . I'd like that."

"Tomorrow. Say, two o'clock then?"

"That would be fine."

She wondered if he could hear her heart beating, so fast that she felt light-headed. The crowd was shoving them closer together, and she didn't notice when his arms slid round her. Was it deliberate? She let her forehead rest against his shoulder. Just dancing with him, feeling the warm strength of his body, breathing the subtle male scent of his skin . . .

It was after one o'clock in the morning when the party began to wind down. She and Liam wandered outside and across the road to lean against the wall and look across the bay, bathed in silver moonlight. So romantic. And when he tipped up her face to his, and his lips brushed over hers, warm and firm, she felt as if the whole world was slipping away.

It was a magical kiss, tender and demanding. She'd been kissed before, a couple of times, by callow boys who didn't know what to do with tongues and noses. Never like this. The taste of him, the feel of his silky hair between her fingers . . . Those things would stay with her forever.

They went riding the next day, and many days after that. They talked and laughed as if they'd been together for years. And when he went back to university, he phoned or texted her every couple of days, and came home most weekends.

And when he came home for the summer vacation, they spent time together every day. She could hardly believe that she was living her dream.

But the other dream hadn't gone away. It was still there, in internet searches for water-sports centres in Florida and around the Gulf of Mexico, and for how to get a working visa for the US. And in the PADI diving certificate and RYA power-boat handling qualification she had gained while studying for her A Levels.

She had no idea how she could reconcile the two dreams, so she just pushed the question aside, and kept them in separate boxes in her head.

It was her grandmother who had forced her to face reality. One afternoon as the date for starting university loomed, Cassie had gone up to her house with the shopping her mother had brought home, and had stayed to sit on a stool at the kitchen table, watching Nanna bake one of her fabulous coffee-and-walnut cakes.

"So then, where do you see yourself in five years' time if you stay and marry Liam?" Nanna demanded in her usual blunt fashion.

"Well, I . . . I'll be with him."

"And?"

"He'll be qualified." Why did she sound so hesitant? "Working with his dad and his brother."

"And what will you be doing?" The prodding was relentless.

"I don't know . . ."

"What about your dream of travelling the world?"

"Well, I . . ." Five years. She would be only twenty-three. "Maybe he'll come with me."

Nanna shook her head. "Do you really think he will?"

Something seemed to be constricting her throat, making it difficult to speak. "No."

Nanna put down her wooden spoon and took both her hands, forcing her to meet her gaze. "Then you have to choose which dream to follow and which to give up."

That night, gazing out of her bedroom window at the village and the long crescent of the bay, she felt as if her heart was being torn in half. She loved Sturcombe, but was it her future — all her future? If she stayed, would she begin to feel trapped? Maybe not in the next few months, but what about the next few years?

And though she didn't want to believe it would happen to her and Liam, she knew that the odds were against a youthful marriage lasting the course.

The crunch came at the end of the summer vacation. Liam had finished at Bristol and was taking up his internship at an equine medical practice near Exeter. He had been talking about them getting a flat together when she went to Exeter University.

"I'm . . . not going to Exeter University."

He frowned sharply. "But you got great A-level results," he protested. "And anyway, they've offered you an unconditional place, haven't they?"

"I know, but . . . I've got a job as diving instructor." There seemed to be a cold weight in her chest, making it difficult to speak. "In Florida."

The way he stared at her — shocked, wounded . . . She felt as if her heart was breaking.

* * *

She became aware that her grandmother had opened her eyes and was watching her shrewdly. "And you followed your dream too." She smiled, reaching out one thin hand and laying it over Cassie's. "I know it was a difficult choice for you, but I was very proud of you for having the courage to do it."

Cassie nodded. "It *was* difficult. But it would have been difficult to stay, too. Maybe not at first, but . . . You were right to make me think about five years down the line."

Nanna nodded, smug. "I'm always right."

"Everything okay?"

Cassie glanced over her shoulder, dragging her mind back from old memories as her mother poked her head round the door. "Yes, fine."

"What day is it?" her grandmother demanded.

"The twenty-third of August."

"No, no, not the date. What *day*?"

"Oh. It's Saturday."

"Right. So tomorrow will be Sunday. I'm going down to watch the cricket."

"*What*? Oh, Mama, no! Don't be silly. You can't."

"Don't call me silly," Nanna grumped impatiently. "I can and I will." Then she grinned toothlessly, her eyes sparkling with humour. "Don't fret, I'll go in my wheelchair. And if that useless son of mine won't drive me, my little Pickle can push me."

Helen threw up her hands in exasperation. "Very well, I'll see what Ollie says."

"Huh! If that nincompoop son-in-law of yours tries to say I can't go, I'll give him a piece of my mind."

CHAPTER FIVE

The Smugglers Arms was on a corner on the Esplanade, a few doors along from the fish and chip shop. Cassie had gone down with her brother and his latest girlfriend, a very attractive, long-legged blonde.

With the season at its height, the pub was crowded. As Paul pushed the door open, the cacophony of voices and laughter, and the music from the jukebox, wafted out into the street.

The place hadn't changed a bit in the past ten years. The wooden floor was worn and uneven, the bar was of the same rich dark oak. Oak beams crossed the ceiling, and one wall was rough stone, with a large inglenook fireplace. In winter they would light a log fire there. It was so cosy to sit in the circle of its warmth and listen to the waves thumping against the sea wall across the road.

But the crowd had changed. There was almost no one she recognised, apart from Alice and Wes behind the bar. Most of the people seemed to be holidaymakers — it was easy to tell from the clothes they wore, plus the peeling noses and lobster-red foreheads

She followed Paul as he eased his way to the bar. The landlord grinned at him. "Usual?" he enquired.

"Thanks. And what are you having, Cassie?"

Wes glanced at her, then looked back again sharply. "Cassie? Well I never! Alice, come and see who's here!"

The landlady finished serving a customer and came up the bar. "Who? Well, Cassie Channing, as I live and breathe!" Her broad face was wreathed in smiles and she reached both hands over the counter to take Cassie's. "Welcome home, my luvver. When did you get back?"

Cassie smiled warmly. "A couple of days ago."

"And you're staying?"

The same old question. "For a while."

"That's good. What are you drinking?"

"I'll have a white wine spritzer, please."

"Coming right up." A wide beam spread across her homely face. "This one's on the house."

At the back of the room a couple of people were playing a casual game of darts, and a few more were gathered around the pool table.

"Fancy a game?" Paul suggested to Cassie.

"If you don't mind getting beaten into the middle of next week."

He laughed, confident, and Cassie smiled to herself. He'd learn.

They took their drinks, eased through the throng, and laid their stakes on the side of the table. She watched the play with interest as they waited their turn. Tom Cullen — big, handsome Tom Cullen, one of Paul's best mates since they were at school together. He was playing against an older man whom Cassie recognised vaguely — she couldn't remember his name.

Tom straightened from the table, grinning broadly as he recognised her. "Cassie, hi." He leaned over to drop a kiss on her cheek. "I heard you were home. Lovely to see you."

"You too!" She patted his wide chest. "And I hear you're getting married in a few weeks?"

"That's right." He looked like the cat who'd got the cream. His Vicky was a lucky girl, Cassie reflected.

Tom turned back to the table, lined up his cue, and took his shot, bouncing his red off his opponent's yellow. It trickled neatly into the side pocket, leaving the yellow in an awkward position against the cushion, and the white perfectly placed for his next shot.

There was a murmur of approval around the table. "Nice shot."

He pocketed his next shot, but the ball after that teetered frustratingly at the edge of the pocket. His opponent had two balls left, which he cleared, but missed an easy shot on the black. Tom nudged his ball in, took a tricky angle on his last ball, then knocked the black perfectly into the side pocket.

"Okay, who's up next?"

Cassie sipped her drink and watched him beat his next challenger. He was good — but she could beat him.

He won the game, then Paul was up. It was a tight game and Cassie was enjoying the nip-and-tuck as they both set up tricky shots for each other, and Paul managed to force Tom into a foul.

Suddenly she felt a kind of prickling at the nape of her neck, and the group around the table shifted slightly to accommodate a newcomer. She knew it was Liam even before she caught a glimpse of him out of the corner of her eye.

He was chatting with friends — not that she was watching him. It was a few moments before he glanced in her direction. Their eyes met before she could look away, and he smiled. She acknowledged it with a cool smile of her own and turned her attention back to the pool table.

Tom won again, to a murmur of good-natured grumbles. "Liam'll get you."

"No, Cassie's up next. Come on then, girl."

Several patronising smiles confirmed that this was expected to be a bit of light relief before the return to serious bloke match-ups. She didn't react, just selected a cue from the rack and chalked the tip, calling heads as Tom tossed the coin.

She lost the toss, and Tom chose to break first. He slid her coin into the slot and released the balls, and racked them up on the table. The smile he slanted in her direction as he bent to line up his shot told her that he, at least, had guessed that she would be no walkover.

He took the break but didn't sink any balls. Cassie moved round the table, studying the angles as she considered whether to go for a quick win or to string it out a little, make it look as if she really was a klutz.

A comment of, "Beginner's luck," somewhere behind her as she sunk her first ball made the decision for her. In little more than two minutes she was on the black, while Tom stood holding his cue.

"That wasn't beginner's luck," he remarked. "Well done."

She straightened from the table, smiling. She hadn't intended to glance at Liam, but her gaze inevitably slid in his direction. He nodded, a glint of warm approval in his eyes.

"Congratulations."

"Thank you." Casual, friendly. Don't let anyone see that your heart just skipped.

* * *

Liam sipped his beer as he watched the action at the pool table. Everyone seemed to have forgotten that Cassie had been pretty good at pool before she left. They had often played, here or in the pub near his Bristol digs when she had come up to visit.

She'd clearly played a lot since then. If anyone thought that first win had been a fluke, he suspected they were soon going to find out that it wasn't.

"Okay, Terry, you're up," someone called. "Good luck."

Terry was one of the older players. It was a tighter game than Liam had expected — Cassie missed a couple of easy shots. Then he realised that she was being mindful of Terry's dignity, giving him space to pocket a few of his balls without being too obvious about it before clearing the table.

He was glad of the game as cover, enabling him to let his gaze linger without looking too obvious. She was wearing a plain white sleeveless T-shirt and well-worn jeans that clung over her trim derrière as if she'd been born in them. As she leaned over the table to line up a shot, he felt as if he'd been tasered.

But it was her smile that held his attention the most. Wide and generous, it seemed to encompass everybody while making you feel it was just for you.

It was that smile that had first caught his attention, that night at Lisa Channing's party. It was the memory of that smile that had lingered in his mind long after she had left him behind.

* * *

"Ah, that were a good game, my luvver." Terry was beaming, not minding that he'd lost. He patted her shoulder. "Well done. Where'd you learn to play like that?"

"Right here," Cassie responded, smiling. "Though I've been practising a bit since then."

He chuckled with laughter. "I bet you have, I just bet you have."

It was Liam's turn at the table next. She was aware that her smile was a little wobbly as he picked up his coin and handed it to her. "Tails."

She had a sudden moment of panic that nerves were going to get the better of her. Fumbling the coin toss would be a very bad way to start.

But hell, she'd jumped off a small metal platform and plunged almost four hundred and fifty feet attached to a bungee rope. Eight and a half seconds of free fall — pure terror, pure adrenalin. She could cope with a game of pool — even against Liam Ellis.

Smiling with a confidence she didn't feel, she tossed the coin and called, "Tails it is."

"I'll take the break." Liam's eyes glinted with amusement. "By the look of it, it could be the only time I get to the table."

"Good luck," Tom teased as Liam picked up his cue.

Lucky or not, he sank a yellow on the break, and a second on his next shot. He missed the third, but left the cue ball in a tricky place, making it difficult for Cassie to avoid a foul.

She walked round the table, carefully studying the angles. It was difficult to focus — she was all too conscious of him standing there, just a few feet away. Watching her, smiling slightly.

She needed to win the game. If she didn't, would he think she had let him beat her? Would the others remember that ten years ago they had been an item, and assume that she was still soft on him?

Dammit, that just added to the pressure. Bending over her cue, she drew in a long, deep breath and held it. *Steady, don't force it, keep it smooth . . .*

The cue kissed the white, the white bounced off the cushion and nudged one of her red balls, and she let go of the breath from her lungs as she relaxed, smiling. No foul.

Liam laughed. "Well done! You could make a fortune as a hustler."

She slanted him a challenging glance and stood back for him to take his turn.

He pocketed two more balls before failing to sink his next shot. Stepping up to the table, she studied the lay of the balls, then systematically pocketed all seven red balls in one run, finishing with an awkward long shot on the black. Liam led the congratulations, shaking her hand, and her heart skipped again.

She managed a smile. "Thank you."

"Who's next for the slaughter?" Liam asked, grinning around at his friends.

With some good-natured ribbing, another challenger stepped up, but was dispatched as effectively as the others. Finally, Cassie shook her head and put her cue back in the rack. "That's enough. I'm out."

"Well done. Very good play." Several of her rivals applauded her as she moved away from the table.

"That was a good game." Liam had moved to her side. "Loser buys the winner a drink?"

"Oh . . . Thank you." Somehow she managed a smile. "A white wine spritzer, please."

He bought her drink at the bar, but they didn't immediately move over to the table where Lisa and Ollie were sitting with Paul and his girlfriend.

"Are you coming to the cricket tomorrow?" he asked.

"Oh, yes." She conceded a faint smile. "I'll be there. And so will my grandmother."

He arched a dark eyebrow in astonishment. "Really? She's well enough to come out?"

"Not really," Cassie acknowledged wryly. "But she's made up her mind. Would you care to argue with her?"

"Not at all — she's terrifying!" He laughed. "Do you remember that time there were a bunch of yobs throwing stones at the seagulls down on the beach? She marched down there and gave them a right rollicking. Their ears must have been ringing for weeks!"

"Oh, yes. That was just like Nanna. At least she's agreed to use her wheelchair."

"Well, I suppose that's a big concession." Just then his phone buzzed, and he pulled it from his pocket, glancing at the screen. "Excuse me, I have to take this."

"Of course."

"Hello? Yes . . . Tell me . . ."

An emergency. It was too noisy in the pub for him to hear. Lifting his hand in a brief goodnight, he eased quickly through the crowd and out of the door. That was probably the last she would see of him tonight. Biting back her disappointment, she took her drink and moved over to sit down with her brother and his girlfriend. "Good game." Paul grinned. "I knew you could play, but I didn't realise you were that good."

Cassie laughed. "Ah, much you do not know there is, young Jedi."

Paul rolled his eyes. "Have you still got a crush on Han Solo?"

"Paul! I was twelve!"

He laid his hand over his heart. "Ah, first love."

She flicked a beer mat at him.

Tom Cullen came over to join them. Cassie smiled up at him. "Where's Vicky?" she asked. "I'm looking forward to meeting her."

"Working a late shift up at the hotel. But you'll meet her tomorrow if you're coming to the cricket."

He sat down, and in a few moments the conversation turned, inevitably, to football. "Who do you reckon's going to win the title this year, Paul?"

He laughed. "Oh, come on, the season's barely started. Only a fool would make a prediction after only two games."

"That new caretaker manager that's taken over from Johnson looks like he could do the business. They should keep him on. He could give them just the push they need."

"They've got some good young players coming up. There's a young striker I reckon could really go places."

"Liverpool are always going to be a good bet. Though that goalless draw at Notts Forest was a bit of a letdown."

Cassie was sitting next to Paul's girlfriend, the leggy blonde. He had always gone for the same type, even when he was in his teens. "Do you play football, Chanelle?"

The girl looked startled at the question. "Oh . . . no."

"You just like to watch?"

"Sometimes." Slightly dismissive, then she smiled brightly. "But I know loads of footballers."

"Oh?" This conversation could be hard work. "Was that how you met Paul?"

"Oh, yes. We were at a party at Ayo Chukwu's house." Happy face. "It was a great party — everyone was there."

"Ayo . . . ?"

70

Chanelle's eyes widened, evidently surprised that Cassie hadn't a clue who she was talking about. "You know. He plays for . . . some team up north." She proceeded to name drop a lot of people Cassie had never heard of but was apparently supposed to know.

Cassie sipped her drink, unable to shake the reflection that Chanelle appeared less interested in a real-life footballer than in featuring on *Footballers' Wives*. Ah well, that was Paul's business.

She took another sip of her drink, trying not to let her mind wander . . .

Liam. She had dreamed about him again last night. There had been many dreams about him over the years. Recurring dreams, that always left her waking to an aching sense of loss.

They would be strolling on a beach, or sometimes they would be riding their horses along the bridleway. He would be there, and then when she turned around he would be gone.

* * *

"Dammit. You'd have thought it might have had the decency to rain so the match would be called off," Helen Channing muttered as she gazed out at the glorious blue sky.

"No chance." Cassie laughed. "It never rains when you want it to."

Ollie had reluctantly approved Nanna's outing. "Let her have her way. It'll do her good to be out in the fresh air, and she always loved the cricket."

It was only a short drive to the cricket ground — down the hill and along the Esplanade, and up Church Road. Cassie's dad drove, and she and Ollie went in the car with Nanna while the rest of the family walked, enjoying the bright sunshine.

The ground was down a narrow lane beside the church. Richard Channing parked close to the hedge and climbed out to unload the wheelchair from the boot, then he and Ollie helped Nanna into it.

It was a bit tricky to manoeuvre the chair over the rough path. But Ollie had had plenty of practice at it and cheerfully ignored Nanna's complaints at every bump and jolt.

Inside the wooden gate, the wide green oval of the pitch was surrounded by leafy beech and ash, and one magnificent old oak tree at the far end. Beneath their shade bright wildflowers bloomed in the long grass — cornflowers and rose bay willowherb and vivid red campion. Butterflies and bumblebees hovered, and birds pecked at the ground for insects.

"Ah, there's Arthur. Do you want to sit by him?"

"Might as well," the old lady grumped. "Though he'll probably jaw my ear off all through the match, the silly old duffer."

Cassie rolled her eyes, suppressing a smile. That would make two of them. She had brought a garden chair from the car and set it up next to Arthur's deckchair, and Ollie helped Nanna into it, settling her comfortably with a blanket over her knees.

"There you go. That'll be better than sitting in that wheelchair all afternoon."

Arthur chuckled with laughter. "That's right. A bit hard on your bum, that."

"Don't you say bum to me, Arthur Crocombe," Nanna objected fiercely — not that she had ever minded raw language.

He grinned, his eyes sparkling with wicked humour. "Bum bum bum. Don't tell me you're turning prissy in your old age, Edie Channing."

"And you're turning into a rude old man. But then you always were rude."

Richard Channing smiled. "Ah, they'll be happy bickering with each other for the rest of the afternoon."

He was the umpire for the match, as he had been for years, and Cassie laughed as he pulled his wide-brimmed cotton sun hat out of his pocket. "Is that the same old hat you've always had?"

"What, this one?" He grinned, ramming it onto his head. "Of course it is."

The Sunday cricket match was always a popular event. There was a league among the local villages, with plenty of friendly rivalry. It looked as if half the population of Sturcombe had turned out to support their team today, settling themselves on picnic blankets and deckchairs beneath the trees that ringed the boundary as they waited for the game to start.

The dress code was colourful summer dresses, casual jeans, T-shirts. The same code seemed to apply to the two teams — only about half of them wore traditional cricket whites. The youngest player looked to be in his early teens, while some of the others looked old enough to be his grandfather. And there were several women on both teams.

"Nanna, would you like a cup of tea?" Cassie asked.

"Hmph! I thought you were never going to offer."

Cassie smiled to herself. "How about you, Arthur?"

He beamed up at her, showing off his dentures. "What's that, my luvver?"

"Would you like a cup of tea?"

"Oh, no, thanks all the same. My girlfriend's fetching me one."

"Your girlfriend?"

"That's right." He chuckled with mischievous laughter. "And here she is."

A tall, slender young woman with honey-blonde hair and smiling eyes approached them carrying two paper cups of tea. "Here you are, Arthur — just how you like it. Nice and sweet."

"Just like you, my luvver." He took the cup in both hands. "Thank you very much."

The young woman turned to Nanna with a warm smile. "Hello, Mrs Channing. Lovely to see you again. You're looking really well. How are you feeling?"

"Fit as a flea!" Nanna declared briskly. "Has that old goat got you waiting on him hand and foot?"

"Oh, I don't mind — he deserves it." She glanced over at Cassie, her smile open and friendly. "Hi. You must be Cassie,

Lisa's sister. I'm Vicky. It's lovely to meet you at last. I've heard a lot about you."

"Oh?" Cassie laughed, tilting her head towards her brother. "Don't believe a word he says."

"Oh no, not from him. From Lisa. She's shown me loads of the photos you've sent her. That bungee jump in New Zealand looked amazing!"

"It was." Cassie's eyes danced. "It was like flying. I went up three times. They practically had to drag me away in the end." A small brown-and-white terrier came snuffling around her feet. She tickled his ear, glancing up to smile at Tom Cullen on the other end of the lead. "Who's this?"

"Rufus. Rufty-Tufty. Rufus, sit," he commanded as the small dog tried to climb up Cassie's leg. After a brief consideration the dog decided to obey and was rewarded with a treat.

"And I see you've met Vicky." He slid his arm around the sunny blonde's waist, his eyes smiling down into hers — the kind of look that would make the heart of the Wicked Witch of the West melt into a puddle of honey.

For a fleeting moment Cassie wished that Liam might look at her like that . . .

Vicky leaned up and put a kiss on the side of her fiancé's mouth, then took the dog's lead. "Let me have Rufus. You'd better go and join your team. I'm going to sit and have a natter."

"Well, in that case, I'm definitely going to join the team," he teased, laughing. "See you later, Cassie."

"Yeah . . ." She smiled quickly. "Yes, see you later."

Hopefully, no one would have noticed her momentary distraction — she had spotted Liam out of the corner of her eye. He was with his brother and sister-in-law, little Robyn running ahead with a boy maybe a couple of years older.

Turning back to Vicky, she smiled again. "Lisa told me about Molly. I was sorry to hear she'd died. She was an amazing old woman. And she left you her cottage."

"That's right. I was thrilled. I used to love coming down to stay here in the summer holidays when I was little. I don't suppose you remember me from then."

Cassie shook her head. "No, I'm afraid I don't."

"Well, it was a long time ago — sixteen years. After my dad died, we didn't come down any more."

"That's a shame." She was trying to keep herself focused on the conversation, refusing to let herself watch Liam, who was over by the pavilion, chatting to the other players.

Vicky nodded. "It was. But I've been fascinated finding out about her, stuff I'd never have dreamed of."

"Did she really dance at the Moulin Rouge?"

"She did. I've got some photos, and some of her costumes. They were in a couple of old steamer trunks in the attic."

"Wow!" Cassie felt herself warm to the other woman. Lisa was right — she did seem really nice. And Tom certainly looked happy. "Lisa sent me a picture of that weird portrait. I remember that old drawing of my other Nanna — Nanna Marjory — that Mum had. It used to scare me a bit when I was little, but if you kept looking at it, it was sort of beautiful."

"Yes, the painting was the same. It's amazing to think it's in the Pradera in Spain. I'd have liked to have kept it, but as Debbie said, it was better for it to go to a big art gallery where lots of people could see it. We're going to visit the gallery while we're on our honeymoon."

"Oh, yes. Lisa told me you're getting married soon. Congratulations. And the wedding's going to be here in Sturcombe?"

"Of course. At All Saints." Her face was glowing with happiness. "It's in five weeks. Are you staying that long? Will you come?"

"I'd love to come." Cassie smiled warmly. "Thank you for inviting me."

"I know it might seem a bit quick — we've only known each other for a few months, but . . . Well, if you know it's right, why wait?" Her eyes danced. "My mother was just itching to tell me to be sensible. That's her favourite word."

Cassie laughed. "It's one of Nanna's, too."

Nanna must have heard that — she'd always had alarmingly sharp hearing. "There's nothing wrong with sensible. And where's my tea? Standing there nattering."

Cassie rolled her eyes. "Just going, Nanna."

"Huh!"

A long trestle table had been set up in front of the wooden pavilion, with plates of sandwiches, finger rolls and cupcakes, rows of cardboard cups, and a stainless-steel tea urn. Debbie was serving another customer, but she turned with a smile as Cassie approached.

"Hello, Cassie."

"Hi, Debs. So this is how you spend your day off?"

"I enjoy it." Debbie's beaming smile emphasised the truth of that. "It's lovely to be out in the sunshine, and I get to watch the cricket."

"Is Bill playing?"

A hint of a blush coloured Debbie's cheeks. "He's the wicket keeper. Do you want tea for your gran?"

"Yes, please. And I'll have a coffee."

"Coming up. How is she?"

"Not too bad, I think." Cassie glanced back to where the old lady was sitting, still bickering happily with Arthur. "She insisted on coming today. We were a bit worried about it, but Ollie said it was a risk worth taking. And she can be very obstinate."

"She always has been." There was a fondness in Debbie's voice. "But she's a sweetheart. Everyone loves her."

"A sweetheart?" Cassie laughed. "That could be a bit of an exaggeration. By the way, I forgot to ask the other day, how's your mum? Lisa wrote me she'd been poorly a while back."

"Yes, she was — she had a touch of pneumonia. But she's much better now, thanks." She glanced past Cassie's shoulder. "Oh, hello, Liam."

"Hi, Debs."

Cassie felt her shoulders tense. Liam, holding little Robyn's hand. As she turned, he greeted her with a smile.

"Hello. Nice to see you again."

"Hi . . . um . . . Yes. Nice to see you." *Oh, for goodness' sake, get a grip!*

The little girl was bouncing with excitement. "Daddy, Daddy, it's the tappoo lady. Ask her."

"I'm sorry." He laughed. "She's been nagging at me since Friday about having a 'tappoo'."

"You promised," the child reminded her, her huge blue eyes wide open and appealing.

Cassie laughed — could anyone resist? "So I did."

"She made me bring the pens in case you were here. Julia has them. Are you sure you don't mind?"

"Of course not. I'm not nearly as good an artist as the one who did mine, but I can probably make a decent effort. I can do it while I'm watching the cricket. They are wash-off pens?"

"Of course." His eyes glinted with amusement. "When you have kids in the house, it's wash-off pens only. Otherwise all your walls, doors and anything else they can reach would be covered in three-legged ducks and green cows."

Cassie laughed again, though she could still feel the tension in her shoulders. "Okay. Well, we're sitting over there. I just need to take my grandmother her tea."

One dark eyebrow arched in question. "So she got her way?"

"Of course — doesn't she always? You don't argue with Nanna." Her voice was laced with dry humour. "You're playing today?"

"Yes, I'm second bat, with my brother. You remember Luke?"

"Of course. Hello Luke."

She smiled up at the man standing behind him. There was a striking family likeness between the two. She knew that Luke was three years older, but Liam was slightly the taller, and a little wider in the shoulder. They both had dark curly hair — Liam wore his a little longer — but they had the same hard-boned, sculpted features and deep-set dark eyes.

"And Mrs Ellis." She recognised his mother at once. "How do you do?"

"Oh, make it Diane, please." The older woman smiled warmly . . . to Cassie's relief. If she had any lingering reservations because of Cassie's behaviour towards her son ten years ago, she had apparently set them aside. "I don't think you've met my daughter-in-law, Julia."

Ah, Luke's wife, an attractive young woman with long, curly hair the colour of autumn leaves. Her smile was as warm as her mother-in-law's. "Hello, nice to meet you."

"And this is Ben, my grandson."

"Hello, Ben." Cassie smiled at the child, dark-haired like his dad, maybe a couple of years older than Robyn.

"Can I have a tattoo too?" Ben pleaded.

Cassie flicked a questioning glance at the red-haired woman. "Well, if your mother says it's kay."

Julia laughed. "I have to say yes, or there'll be jealousy. That's if you don't mind."

"Of course not. Though I bet you don't want a flower?" she added to the little boy.

"No." He put on a fierce face. "I want a shark. With great big teeth."

"Oh . . . right . . ."

His mum shrugged her shoulders. "He can have whatever he likes. It'll wash off before he goes back to school."

"Okay. Well, let me just take Nanna's tea to her, then I can do them while I watch the match."

The game was about to start. Lisa and Ollie were setting up the scoreboard beside the pavilion, while Cassie's mum had settled on a blanket on the ground, with baby Kyra in her infant carrier. Vicky was sitting with them, along with little Amy. Noah and Ben had gone off to play with their friends in a corner of the field.

"Hi. Is there room for a couple more there?"

"Oh, hi, Julia." Cassie's mum patted the blanket beside her. "Of course, come and sit down."

Little Robyn scrambled into Cassie's lap. "Will you do my tappoo now?" she pleaded excitedly. "I want one just like yours."

Julia smiled and reached into her bag for the pens, and handed them over. "Sorry — she won't rest until she gets it done."

"That's okay. Do you want the same colours?" she asked the child.

She nodded vigorously. "Yes, please."

"Right. Sit still then. No wriggling or it'll all go wrong."

She took the blue pen and began to draw carefully on the child's shoulder. Beside her, Nanna and Arthur Crocombe were still bickering happily. A thrush was singing in a beech tree nearby, and a heavy bumblebee was lumbering lazily over the long grass.

A summer Sunday at a village cricket match. Heaven.

The home team had won the toss and had chosen to bat first. The fielders were walking out to their places, the bowlers were taking a few practise run-ups, the wicket-keepers were checking the stumps. Cassie's dad had taken up his umpire position as Liam and his brother strolled out onto the field swinging their bats.

"That's my daddy," Robyn announced with pride.

"Yes, it is. Is he going to get lots of runs?"

"I bet he'll get a *hundred*."

Cassie gave her a little hug. "Let's hope so, then we'll be bound to win."

It took a couple of deliveries for bowler and batsmen to get the measure of each other, then Luke knocked the ball towards the outfield and he and Liam began to run.

"Go, Daddy!" Robyn squealed, clapping her hands with excitement. "Go, go."

"Hold still!" Cassie protested. "I nearly made a smudge then."

The child twisted her head around to beam up at her. It wasn't clear which was more important to her — the tattoo or cheering her daddy on.

Out on the pitch, the match was beginning to warm up. Cassie watched the play. If she happened to be watching Liam more than any of the others, no one would be any the wiser.

Even hampered by the bulky shin pads, he moved with an easy athleticism as he ran between the stumps, his wide shoulders hinting at leashed power as he swung the bat.

She enjoyed these traditional village cricket matches — liked the slow, easy pace, no one needing to really raise a sweat. The essential politeness of it, even when questioning a call or bowling a viciously fast ball, and the archaic names for the fielding positions — backward square leg, fly slip, silly mid-off.

She had often watched them when she was young — she had even been drafted into the team a couple of times when they were short of players. They had always taken them seriously, although the main purpose had been fun, enjoying the game with your friends and neighbours.

And she'd watched quite a few matches at all levels in Australia, where they took the game more seriously than almost anything except beer and Aussie rules football. The staff of the water-sports resort where she had worked had even had their own team, competing in a local league.

She managed to finish Robyn's 'tappoo', being careful to lift the pen away at moments it seemed likely that the child would wriggle. The little girl's face lit up with delight as she twisted her head over her shoulder to see it.

"Oh, it's pretty. It's *exackly* the same as yours." The child flung her arms round Cassie's neck and planted a smacking kiss on her cheek. "Thank you. It's the bestest tappoo ever."

Cassie felt as if her heart was wrapping itself around this adorable little girl. "It's not quite the same — I'm afraid I'm not as good at drawing as the man who did mine."

"I'm going to show my granny and Auntie Julia." She bounced over to them and proudly showed off the colourful design. They duly admired it, and Diane Ellis smiled across at Cassie.

"Thank you. She's gone on about nothing else since she saw yours."

"I'm not very good," Cassie admitted. "The artists in New Zealand are amazing. But I hope it'll keep her happy, at least until it fades or washes off."

"Oh, she'll have forgotten all about it by then."

Luke had run up a score of fifty-six in seven overs before getting caught out at cover point. As he walked back from the crease, Tom Cullen strolled down to take his place.

"Good luck, Tom," Vicky called to him.

He smiled down at her as he passed.

Oh, wow! That man was seriously in love! What would it be like to have someone smile at her like that? She glanced out towards the crease where Liam was treading down a divot with his foot.

Something like hot lava seeped through her bones. *Oh no, don't even think it.* That time had come and gone. She couldn't imagine that he would want to revisit it.

Liam was on bat, and he walloped the ball out towards the boundary. The fielder stopped it with his foot, inches before it crossed the boundary and tossed it quickly back to the wicket keeper, but Liam just got his bat over the line before he could be stumped.

All the home supporters cheered as Ollie, who was on the scoreboard, added the three runs to their total.

"Doesn't Ollie play?" Cassie asked her mum.

"He'd like to, but he often gets called away to an emergency so that would disrupt the team." She laughed. "He's training Noah up to be his substitute."

The little boy was proudly slotting the old numbers back into their box and standing alert for the next score.

Nanna and Arthur were still cheerfully arguing. "No, you silly old duffer. Mavis Tuckett married that Ronald Witheycombe from over by Tavistock, and they went off to Australia."

"Silly old duffer yourself, Edie Channing. It were her sister Doreen married Ronald Witheycombe. Mavis never got married. She lived with her mum and worked over at the hotel as a chambermaid for years."

"Don't you call me a silly old duffer, Arthur Crocombe . . ."

Helen Channing laughed fondly. "They're happy."

CHAPTER SIX

After lunch the home team were fielding. They had run up a good score on their innings — a hundred and sixty-one for seven — so the visitors had a tough target to beat. Liam and Tom were bowling. They were a good pair — Tom the fastest, Liam with a mean leg spin. Together they made it difficult for the batsmen to settle into a regular strike.

Between his turn to bowl Liam was out on the boundary. It was pleasantly lazy out there in the sunshine. This was what he had always loved about village cricket — the chance to stand around on a sunny afternoon with not much to do but listen to the birds and the bumblebees and smell the freshly mown grass of the wicket.

Across on the other side of the field he could see his small daughter sitting on the picnic blanket with his mother and his sister-in-law.

And Cassie.

She was wearing a pair of loose navy-blue shorts which showed off her long, elegant legs, and a bright yellow cotton shirt knotted around her waist, flashing brief glimpses of her tanned, toned midriff . . .

Tom was getting ready to start his run-up, and Liam snapped his attention back to the game. Cassie Channing was a distraction he didn't need.

* * *

"Who wants an ice-cream then?" Julia opened her cool box and with a magician's flourish produced a pack of choc ices.

"Me!" The children bounced up excitedly, hands out to plead for the treat.

"And what do you say?"

"Please!"

Laughing, she passed them out, offering them to the grown-ups too. Lisa had finished feeding Kyra and laid her on the blanket. Noah was waving her yellow plastic rattle for her and she was batting at it with her tiny pink fists.

Robyn was watching, wide-eyed. "Why don't I have a baby sister?" she asked Julia.

Ooops! Awkward. The adults looked at each other. How to explain that one?

"Maybe one day," Julia managed.

"When I'm eighteen?"

"Er . . ."

"Like my tappoo!"

Phew!

"Mummies and daddies can have babies when they get married," Amy pronounced solemnly. "My mummy's going to get married to Uncle Bill, and then they can have a baby."

Cassie was struggling to keep a straight face. "Well, maybe not right away," she cautioned.

"Of course not." Young Ben was proud of his greater knowledge. "Babies take nine months to come. So do calves. Horses take a whole year, but pigs take less than four months."

Lisa was clearly having the same problem as Cassie with suppressing her laughter. "Very good," she approved. "I think I'd rather be a pig."

84

"Why?"

A silent plea for help.

"Because . . . pigs can eat lots and lots," Cassie suggested. "And they can roll around in the mud and their mummies never tell them off for getting dirty."

"Oh."

That seemed to be a sufficient answer, to everyone's relief.

* * *

Liam took the final wicket of the forty overs, leaving the visitors on one hundred and forty-three for eight. The win put the Sturcombe team at second in the league. Luke slapped him on the back as they strolled up to the pavilion.

"Not bad, little brother. You deserve a beer for that."

The two teams had gathered to toast each other with cool pints and to dissect the game.

"That was a great boundary shot in the tenth over. Poor old Colin didn't stand a chance."

"Couldn't expect him to." Neville Perkin always had to get a dig in. "Lumbering around the outfield like an old carthorse."

Colin took the teasing in good part. "I'm built for stamina, not speed," he retorted. "Anyway, you can talk, after you dropped that absolute sitter!"

"Daddy, Daddy, look!" Robyn had raced over to him and was tugging at his hand, bouncing up and down with excitement. "Auntie Cassie drew my tappoo."

Liam smiled as he picked up his little daughter and settled her on his hip. "That's a very fine tattoo," he approved. "Is that another one round your mouth?"

The child giggled. "Don't be silly, Daddy. It's chocolate ice-cream."

"Ah . . ."

"Auntie Cassie drew tappoos on Noah and Ben and Amy too. And Justin and Paige and Sophie."

"All those tattoos, eh? It sounds like you kept her busy between you all. Did she have time to watch the cricket?"

"Of course she did. And anyway, she didn't mind." Those angelic blue eyes were shining up into his. "She's really nice."

Richard Channing had strolled over to join the teams. "Hey Richard." Colin gestured with his beer glass towards the picnic blanket where the Channing and Ellis women were sitting. "Isn't that your daughter Cassie over there?"

"That's right."

"I thought I recognised her. So is she home for good now?"

Richard smiled wryly. "Ah, well, we'll have to wait and see about that."

Liam felt his shoulders stiffen. Stupid — of course she would be leaving again. He'd known that from the start. Probably sooner rather than later. She'd made a life for herself on the other side of the world — she'd only come home to see her grandmother.

Not that it mattered to him. He had a life too, and she hadn't been a part of it for ten years.

Robyn must have sensed his sudden tension. "Daddy?" Her eyes were wide.

"Sorry, sweetie. Just a bit of a twinge in my knee." It didn't matter — she could go or stay. It was no concern of his. "Come on, let's go and see if Granny and Auntie Julia are ready to go home."

* * *

Nanna and Arthur had dozed for most of the afternoon, which didn't stop them commenting loudly and critically on everyone's play. "That Neville Perkin — I don't know what he's even doing in the team. Couldn't catch a cold."

Richard Channing laughed. "Come on, Mum," he coaxed. "Time to go home."

"Huh! You're going to put me in that damned wheelchair again, ain't you?"

"Well, I'd offer to give you a piggyback but I don't think that would be very dignified for either of us. And I do have a certain position to maintain — quite a few of my pupils are here, with phones that can take photos, which would end up on Instagram."

"Huh!"

But when Ollie came over, she didn't argue, allowing him and Richard to ease her from her garden chair into the wheelchair. She leaned over to pat Arthur on the arm.

"Well, goodbye then, you old duffer."

He grinned at her. "Goodbye, my luvver. See you again soon."

"Maybe, maybe . . ."

Cassie anxiously searched her grandmother's face as they wheeled her back to the car. She looked pale and tired, but there was no doubt that she had enjoyed herself, so maybe it had done her good after all.

She seemed to doze as Richard Channing drove at a sedate pace back along the Esplanade and up Cliff Road to the house. They helped her into her wheelchair, which was then carried up the steps to the front door, and she didn't grumble at all.

"Would you like a cup of tea, Nanna?" Cassie asked as they wheeled her into her bedroom.

"Not just yet, my little Pickle." She smiled, an unusually sweet smile. "I think I'll just have a bit of a nap for now."

They settled her into her chair by the window, tucking the cushions comfortably around her and laying a blanket over her knees. Cassie made sure she had a glass of water and her bell close at hand on the table beside her. Then they all tiptoed out.

In the kitchen Richard had put the kettle on and had teas brewing by the time the rest of the family had walked back from the cricket ground.

"How is she?" Lisa asked, lifting the baby out of her carrier and settling down to breastfeed her.

Ollie smiled crookedly. "I didn't even try to take her pulse. I don't think it matters anymore."

All eyes turned to him in concern.

"You think . . . ?"

"A few days at most." His voice was heavy. "Possibly less."

"Oh . . ."

Cassie's mum wiped away a tear from the corner of her eye. "Well . . ." She sat down heavily on the wooden chair at the head of the table and picked up her teacup. "Well . . ."

No one spoke for several moments, then Richard cleared his throat. "I'd better go and mow that back lawn." Nobody bothered to mention that he had only mowed it two days ago.

"Shall I do the veg, Mum?" Cassie offered.

"Uh . . . Thank you, yes. Are you staying for dinner, Lisa?"

"Yes, if it's no trouble."

"Of course not." Helen put down her cup, the tea untouched. "Well . . . I . . . I think I'll go up and have a doze for a bit."

"Okay, Mum. I'll call you when dinner's ready."

Cassie sorted out enough potatoes for all of them and began to peel them at the sink. They were all being terribly English about it — all stiff upper lip. But if it helped them cope . . .

Noah seemed aware of the atmosphere, although uncertain of its cause, looking from one to the other of the adults for clues. "Daddy, can we watch Supertato?" he asked quietly.

"Sure." Ollie ruffled his son's curly hair. "Come on." Father and son disappeared into the sitting room.

"Well, Nanna seemed to enjoy this afternoon, anyway," Cassie remarked.

"She did." Lisa stroked baby Kyra's head with a gentle finger. "How about you?"

"It was fun." She managed a smile. "So many people I haven't seen for so long. And little Robyn's just gorgeous — like a little angel." She finished peeling a potato and dropped it into a pan of water, then picked up another one. "She doesn't take much after Liam."

"No. She's the image of her mum."

Cassie carefully dug an eye out of the potato. Natalie . . . She had kept that photo that Lisa had sent her on her phone for a long time, enlarging that small section of it and gazing at the pair of them — Liam with his arm around Natalie's waist, glancing down at her, Natalie with her head resting against his shoulder, smiling happily at the camera.

A lovely smile, not at all self-conscious, as if she really wasn't aware of how pretty she was. A heart-shaped face, bright eyes, soft blonde curls around her shoulders. Her sweet nature shone out through the photograph. Liam must have adored her.

She glanced down as Barney nudged her leg. In spite of having lost several teeth, he still loved a knob of raw potato to gnaw on. Silently thanking him for the distraction, she hunkered down and tickled his ear.

"There you are, baby. What a good boy you are."

He took his trophy, trotted happily back to his basket beside the range cooker, and settled down contentedly.

She paused for a moment to ensure that her voice conveyed no more than casual interest. "It must have been so sad for her, to have lost her mother at such a young age."

"Yes. But Liam's a great dad — you can see how much he adores her." She shifted Kyra to the other breast. "How do you feel about him now?"

"Liam? I . . ." She was going to deny everything completely, but she suspected that her sister knew her too well, even after all the years apart. "Well, he's still very attractive, of course. But I don't think it's likely that anything will happen now. It's been so long."

"Ah, well." Lisa smiled. "You never know."

Cassie dropped the potato into the pan and picked up another one. *Did* she want anything to happen with Liam? It was difficult. She couldn't deny that those old feelings were still there, but she had no idea if he felt the same. He'd given no indication that he might.

And if he did . . . That would be even more difficult. Sooner or later she would face the same dilemma as she had faced ten years ago. Whether to stay or to leave.

"No, I think I do know." She ran the peeler down the length of the potato. "He's been friendly enough but . . . there's definitely a barrier there."

"Shame."

Cassie glanced back over her shoulder, arching a quizzical eyebrow at her sister. "Because if I got together with him it might mean that I'd be staying?"

Lisa's eyes glinted with enigmatic amusement. "That too."

"Well, it's nice to know that you want me to stay. Even though I did pinch your leather jacket and ruin it by falling into the sea at Kelly-Anne Wallis's beach party."

"Ah, yes. I'd forgotten that." Lisa chuckled. "You can bugger off back to New Zealand then and never darken our door again."

They both laughed, and Cassie felt a tug around her heart. She'd missed her sister while she'd been away. They'd always been close, though they'd often fought like cat and dog when they were kids.

She'd missed the rest of her family too. And Barney, with his cute little face and fur like a coir doormat, and a tail that wagged happily all the time, in spite of his arthritis. And this house overlooking the bay.

She glanced around the cosy kitchen. So many happy memories . . . The scales which had once tipped one way were now slowly tipping the other. She'd been afraid that would happen if she came home, which was why she'd put it off for so long.

There was a tear in her eye, even though she wasn't chopping onions.

Lisa finished feeding the baby. "Time for a fresh nappy I think." She dropped a kiss on the infant's little button nose. "Come on, Munchkin."

Cassie chopped the potatoes ready to make chips, then took the chicken portions out of the freezer and defrosted them in the microwave. She was laying them in a baking tray, slathering them with butter and tarragon, when her brother strolled into the kitchen.

"Mmm, that looks good."

Cassie smiled. Though he'd lived up the road in Nanna's house since the old lady had moved into the family home, he still seemed to spend most of his time here at number nineteen.

"Make yourself useful then — lay the table."

He grinned as he opened the cutlery drawer. "When did you learn to cook?"

She flicked a tea towel at his shoulder. "Cheek! You used to gobble down my prawn curry like you hadn't eaten for a week!"

Lisa and Ollie came in from the sitting room with Noah. "The baby's asleep, so I've left her in there. I can hear her from here if she stirs."

"Dad's just putting the lawn mower away. Noah, could you run up and tell your gran that dinner's ready. I'm just going to take a little bit in to Nanna."

She had cut up a portion of chicken into small pieces, and put a few chips on the plate with a spoonful of garden peas. She picked up the plate and a knife and fork, and carried them through to the dining room.

She tapped lightly on the door. There was no reply, so she pushed it open. "Nanna? I've brought you some—" Something wasn't right. The old lady seemed to be asleep but . . . "Nanna?"

Cautiously she approached Nanna's chair and reached out to touch her thin, veined hand. The old lady didn't stir. Her eyes were closed and there was a smile curving her pale lips. But she had gone.

Very slowly Cassie put the dinner plate down on the side table and stood for a moment, feeling her heart beating against her throat. Afraid that her legs wouldn't hold her, she knelt down at her grandmother's side, holding both her hands and gazing up into that much-loved face, the mesh of fine wrinkles a map of a life well-lived.

"Thank you for waiting until I got home," she whispered. "I wish we'd had longer."

She wasn't crying — somehow she wasn't sad. That smile told her that Nanna had been happy. She would miss her. Even when she had been on the other side of the world she had felt the warmth in her heart that Nanna was here at home.

But that warmth would always be there . . .

The door behind her opened quietly and she turned her head as her mother came in.

"Cassie, your dinner's getting . . . Oh . . ."

Cassie rose to her feet. "Ollie was right, though it was sooner than he thought."

Her mother smiled and shook her head. "No, I think he knew. He was just trying to soften it a bit." She came across the room and put her arm around Cassie's shoulders, gazing down at her mother-in-law. "She looks happy."

"She does."

"She enjoyed the cricket."

"She did."

"I was worried that . . . But I don't suppose it would have made any difference. Better she went a little sooner after having a lovely day than lingering here bored and miserable."

Cassie nodded. "You're right."

"I suppose we'd better tell the others."

"Yes."

But neither of them moved. They stood there for a long time, mother and daughter, side by side, gazing down at the old lady who had filled such a giant space in their lives.

CHAPTER SEVEN

Nanna had left detailed instructions for her funeral. Well, of course she had. Cassie had laughed as she'd read the note. The writing was a little wobbly, but the voice was distinctly Nanna's.

Everyone was to wear bright colours — strictly no black. She had chosen the hymns, and had insisted that there were to be no long-winded prayers or sermons. Eva, the vicar, had laughed at that.

"Typical Edie. She'd sometimes yell at me to get on with it if she thought I was going on too long."

It had rained overnight, but it wouldn't have dared to rain on Nanna's big day. The afternoon sun was bright and the beach was full of families. It seemed a little incongruous as they piled into the funeral cars, but Cassie suspected that Nanna would have relished that.

The hearse was full of flowers, with more piled on top. As they drove along the Esplanade, people stopped respectfully to watch them pass. It was only a short distance, round past the Memorial Gardens and up Church Road.

All Saints Church had stood guard over the souls of Sturcombe since the thirteenth century. The Victorians had added a couple of bits to the original building — an imposing porch and the square bell tower, and a rather fine stained-glass window over the altar.

A low stone wall surrounded the graveyard, with a covered wooden lychgate. The hearse drew up at the kerb, the mourners' cars lining up behind it. Their driver climbed out and came round to open the rear door for them.

They stood for a moment in the sunshine, watching as the undertaker's assistants unloaded the flowers. Richard and Paul Channing would be helping them carry the coffin, along with Ollie, and Tom Cullen.

In accordance with Nanna's instructions, they were all brightly dressed. Cassie was wearing a white sundress with scarlet flowers twining up from the hem. Lisa's dress was a vivid yellow, and their mum was in mint green.

People were still filing into the church. The atmosphere was more like a summer garden party than a solemn funeral. The women had all followed Nanna's instructions too and were wearing summer dresses, and the men were mostly in colourful shirts and ties, without jackets.

As the congregation moved through the churchyard, Cassie caught a glimpse of Liam. He was wearing a pale-lemon shirt, and a virulently coloured tie patterned with cartoon fish — she strongly suspected that it had been chosen by little Robyn. For some reason that gave her heart a warm squeeze.

Beside her, Lisa laughed softly. "You know, if Nanna's looking down on us she's going to be right smug. For the final time, she's got her own way."

Cassie nodded. "There's a Maori word for it — *Mana*. It means a person has great presence, great power. It sums up Nanna perfectly."

Lisa smiled, a tear sparkling at the corner of her eye. "It does."

"Well . . ." Helen Channing let her breath go in a long sigh and linked her arms with her two daughters. "Come on, then. Here we go."

94

The three of them walked into the church. The organist was playing quietly — 'Pachelbel's Canon'. Cassie was a little surprised to see that all the pews were packed — cousins from both Nanna's side of the family and Grandpa's, as well as seemingly the whole village and many who had moved away.

They took their places in the front pew and sat for a moment, quietly listening to the organ music. The bright sunshine was streaming in through the stained-glass windows along the south side of the church, casting jewel-bright patterns across the stone floor.

The distinctive scent of old churches — dust and warm stone and beeswax polish — stirred memories for Cassie of attending Church Parades here when she was nine years old, so proud in her Brownie uniform.

The wreaths from the hearse had been set around the bier before the altar. The organist began to play the opening bars of 'Abide With Me', and everyone rose as Eva led the coffin bearers down the aisle.

The service began with a short prayer and a Bible reading, then the hymn that had been sung at Nanna's wedding so long ago — 'For Those in Peril on the Sea'.

Then Eva spoke briefly about her own memories of Nanna, stirring a few ripples of laughter. "But I only knew Edie for six years. Most of you will have known her for much longer. If any of you would like to say a few words, please do so now."

There were a few moments' hesitation, then Ollie rose to his feet. "I want to thank Nanna Edie for her kindness when I had my first experience of a patient dying on my watch. Well, as you can imagine, it was her own brand of kindness."

Laughter rippled through the congregation again.

"She sat me down and told me not to be ridiculous. People die all the time, and it mostly won't be my fault. She was right, of course — a doctor has to toughen up. But that 'mostly' also reminded me not to get too big for my boots. So, thank you, Nanna Edie. I hope I'm a better doctor for your wise words."

A few people started to applaud as he sat down again, then hesitated, wondering if that was quite appropriate. But Cassie's mum went on applauding loudly, and the vicar joined in, so the applause was taken up throughout the congregation.

Then Brenda, who ran the convenience store just a few yards up the road from the church, stood up. "I'd like to say something, if that's okay?"

"Of course. Speak up," Eva encouraged.

"Well . . . when my husband — the rat — went off, leaving me with my Bethany, just eight years old, I was at rock bottom. He'd always undermined me — I had no confidence in myself, no idea how I would cope. Edie helped me fill in all the forms and applications to take over the shop. She didn't do it for me — she showed me how to do it myself. She told me she wouldn't help me again. Instead, she gave me the belief that I really could do it myself."

There were nods and murmurs of approval. Then there was someone else with a story of Nanna giving them a small sum of money in an emergency and telling them she didn't want it back, that when they were in a position to do so, to pass on the favour.

One after another, people were standing up to tell similar stories about Nanna's no-nonsense encouragement, small acts of generosity, practical support in a crisis.

Cassie glanced at her sister, wide-eyed. "I never knew any of this," she whispered. "Did you?"

Lisa shook her head. "Not much of it."

"The Maoris have a custom like this. They call it *Tangi*. Everyone comes to the funeral and tells stories about the person who's died. They don't even have to be good stories."

"That's really nice," Lisa murmured. "Makes it a bit more interesting than a lot of English funerals."

Liam had risen to his feet. "My story's similar to Ollie's," he began. "Many of you know that my wife Natalie died three years ago." Cassie could hear the catch in his voice. "We were on holiday in Greece and . . . she was hit by a van as she was crossing the road."

He paused to drag in a long breath.

"For a long time, I blamed myself. If I had been quicker . . ." Another pause. "Anyway, Edie gave me one of her talks — as she did with many of us here. It was one sunny afternoon at the cricket, about six months after Natalie died."

The whole church was silent. The only sound was the soft trilling of birdsong drifting in on the breeze through the open doors.

"She summoned me over, the way she does . . . did. She told me that I couldn't have known what was going to happen, so there was nothing I could have done to prevent it. She told me to stop focusing on the way Nat had died, but on the happy memories of her life, our life together. For Robyn's sake. And I've tried to do that. Thank you, Edie."

The lump in Cassie's throat made it hard for her to breathe.

The last to speak was Arthur Crocombe. He rose unsteadily to his feet, helped by Vicky and his carer, Marcus.

"A lot of people have stood up to say nice things about Edie. Well, I knew her a lot longer than any of you. And I'll say this. She was a tough old bird, and had a sharp tongue that could cut you as soon as look at you. But she only used it on them as deserved it, and she never said behind your back what she wouldn't say to your face."

Marcus tried to take his arm to support him again, but he shook him off impatiently. "I can stand on my own two feet, thank you, and I ain't finished yet."

He took a moment to catch his thread again. "She was generous to a fault with her time and her money, was Edie. But she never wanted for no one to know what she did, and she didn't care about thanks. She was never bothered that someone might take advantage of her. She always said that was between them and their conscience, and she wasn't going to let someone else's behaviour change how she behaved."

He coughed and produced a large white handkerchief from his pocket to dab at his mouth.

"She came here to the church regular all through her life, but she never judged them as didn't. Nor them as got themselves into a mess through making the wrong choices. She said you only get one chance at life and you have to live it like you mean it. She was dead right about that — she was dead right about most things. But there's was one thing she was wrong about. She said I wouldn't out-live her." He finished on a note of triumph. "And I have!"

The laughter and applause rolled through the pews. Then at a signal from Eva, the organist swivelled his seat back to the keyboard and the opening notes of 'Guide Me Oh Thou Great Jehovah' swelled up to the high vaulted roof.

Cassie laughed softly. "Trust Nanna to pick this one. She always did like a good rousing hymn."

"And with the traditional words," Lisa added.

The congregation clearly liked the hymn too, belting it out with vigour, the men's voices relishing the bass pick-up at the end of each verse. Then as the last notes died away, the pall bearers stepped forward to lift the coffin from the bier and pace slowly back down the aisle.

Now Cassie found that she was crying at last, tears sliding down her cheeks. Her mum and Lisa were crying too, and the three women linked arms again as they stepped from the pew to lead the mourners out to the graveyard.

The heat and the blazing sunshine were almost dazzling after the cool of the church. Footsteps crunched on the gravel path as they followed round to the plot Nanna had planned for herself long ago, shared with her beloved husband who had gone fifteen years earlier.

"Where they can watch the cricket through that gap in the hedge," Lisa whispered with a soft laugh.

Cassie hadn't intended to look for Liam, but her gaze seemed to be drawn towards him in spite of her will. He was standing with his brother. Their mum was there, and Julia, but not their dad — he would probably be looking after the practice in case there were any emergencies.

She watched him for a moment, remembering what he had said about focusing on the happy memories of his wife. There must have been so many of them. Would he ever find someone to replace her? Would he even want to?

As if he sensed her looking at him, his dark gaze turned towards her. Her heart gave a sharp thump, and she looked away quickly, hoping the sudden heat in her cheeks wasn't a betraying blush. This was not the moment for the thoughts that were spinning in her brain.

* * *

The churchyard was a haven of peace, surrounded by trees in their full summer leaf. The grass had grown long around the gravestones, heavy bumblebees buzzed quietly among the daisies and clover and meadow crane's-bill.

Liam let his gaze drift to the left. Three years ago he had buried Natalie there, in the shade of a leafy beech tree. He brought Robyn here regularly to visit 'Mummy's garden'.

She loved to tend it, picking off any faded flowers or ragged leaves and making sure there wasn't a single weed.

His thoughts went back to that conversation with Edie Channing, that hot summer's afternoon at the cricket . . .

* * *

"Well, young man. How are you?"

"I'm fine, thank you."

"No you're not." No shilly-shallying from Edie. "I can see it in your eyes. Takes a long time to get over a loss like you've had — longer than you think."

"It's been six months." Six months already? It felt like days.

Edie waved her hand in a dismissive gesture. "Six months is nothing — part of you will grieve for her forever. And that's as it should be. But sooner or later another part of you will begin to move on, and that's as it should be too. You can't hold back life — it keeps on pushing forward."

It felt as if she was reading his mind.

"You have a little girl, and she'll be growing up. For her sake you need to focus on the happy memories. For your own sake too. You only get one life, and sometimes bad things come. But if you let yourself get stuck in that then you're wasting every other chance you might have. Don't you think Natalie would have wanted you to be happy again?"

He hesitated, struggling to admit that she was probably right. "I suppose she would."

"There's no suppose about it. She was a lovely girl, but she's gone. And you're still here, and so is your daughter. Take as much time as you need, but don't feel guilty when you find yourself beginning to enjoy life again."

* * *

He smiled to himself as he stood with the group around Edie's grave. She really had been a wise old bird. And she had been right — more and more he had found himself enjoying life.

Little things — riding along the coast path on a good horse, coming in on a cold, wet night to settle down in front of the fire with a book while his daughter slept upstairs.

At first he would catch himself with a stab of guilt — it had felt as if he was minimising everything Natalie had been to him. But as Edie had said, life keeps pushing forward.

Without any conscious intent he had let his gaze drift back to Cassie, standing with her mother and her sister. She had been crying — her eyes were still damp, her mascara smudged on her cheeks.

This must be so hard for her. She had loved her grandmother. At least she had got home in time, even if it had only been for a few days.

100

And now that Edie was gone, how long would she stay? Maybe for her old friend Debbie's wedding, and possibly for Tom's. And then . . . ? Would that deep-rooted desire for adventure lure her away again?

Yes, it probably would.

Eva spoke the last prayer, and the coffin was lowered gently into the ground. Richard and Helen Channing stepped forward to drop flowers on top, followed by their three children, then more neighbours and friends — white lilies, roses and carnations, creating a fragrant mound of white petals.

At last, with murmurs of farewell to the grand old lady who had been so much the heart of the village, everyone set off to stroll the short distance down the hill to the wake in the Carleton Hotel.

Liam fell into step with his mother and brother. Luke glanced across at him and dropped a hand on his shoulder. "You okay, Bro?"

Liam grinned back at him. "I'm getting there."

"It was a tough time for you."

"It was. But you were all there for me — I appreciate that. And Edie had it right — life keeps pushing forward."

Their mum smiled at them both but said nothing.

At the hotel a generous buffet had been set out in the function room, and the run of French windows along one wall were open to the terrace and the view of the bay.

Liam collected a small plate of food then wandered around the room, mingling. It was good to catch up with people he hadn't seen for a while — so many of them had had to leave Sturcombe because of the lack of work and affordable homes.

"I was sorry to hear about your wife."

"Thank you." The cut was still there, deep, but he had learned to acknowledge sympathy in the way it was meant.

"But you have a little girl?"

"Yes." He smiled and drew his phone from his pocket, always willing to show off photographs of Robyn.

"Oh, she's so pretty. How old is she?"

"Five."

"You must be very proud of her."

"I am."

He was focusing on the conversation, but inevitably he was aware of Cassie on the edge of his vision. She had wandered out onto the terrace. He hesitated for a moment, then followed her.

She was standing by the stone balustrade, gazing out over the bay. The sun was shining on the water, making it sparkle like sapphires and diamonds. The small town, nestling in a dip between the green hills around it, looked like a jumble of toy houses climbing the slopes.

"I'd almost forgotten the view from up here," she remarked, not turning round.

"It is pretty spectacular." He was silent for a moment. "It was a nice funeral — as funerals go."

"Yes. Trust Nanna to plan everything just the way she wanted it." She turned then, and smiled at him. "I like your tie. Did Robyn choose it?"

"I'm afraid so. It was a Christmas present."

"Ah, she's such a little darling. And so polite and well-behaved."

"Most of the time." His eyes smiled. "She's very good at winding me round her little finger to get her own way."

"She's five. Five-year-old girls are supposed to be able to wind their daddies round their little fingers. It's in the job description."

"She loved her tattoo. She was showing it off to everyone."

"Has it washed off yet?"

"Not quite. Fortunately, she seems to have been satisfied with a pretend one. I was afraid she'd keep nagging me for a real one."

"She was so sweet about it." There was a gentle warmth in her eyes. "Thank you for what you said — about Nanna. It must have been very hard for you, what happened, especially with it being so sudden like that."

"It was. It's still difficult sometimes, but you learn how to live around it." He leaned against the balustrade, watching the waves uncurl along the beach in ribbons of white lace. "It was the last day of our holiday, and we'd had a wonderful time. Someone had told Nat about a shop that sold dolls in Greek national costume, and she wanted to get one for Robyn. We'd left Robyn in the hotel's creche and gone down to the village to do some last-minute shopping for a few presents and souvenirs."

He felt as if there was a great lead weight in his chest.

"We were on our way back to the hotel when Nat spotted the shop on the other side of the road. She stepped out . . . I think in that moment she must have forgotten that they drive on the other side of the road in Greece. The poor van driver didn't stand a chance."

"Oh . . . I'm so sorry." She shook her head, her eyes dark. "That always seems such an inadequate thing to say."

"They said it was instant. She wouldn't have known a thing." And he hadn't had the chance to say goodbye.

"It's nice that you'd had a good holiday," she said softly. "Something happy to remember."

"Yes . . ." He hadn't remembered the happy times — hadn't let himself remember. But . . . yes, it had been a good holiday — lots of laughter with Robyn, a friendly crowd in the hotel, a couple of interesting sightseeing trips.

"Lisa said she was really nice. All Ollie's elderly patients loved her." She looked down at the glass of wine in her hand. "How did you meet her?"

He took a pause, letting the memories return. "It was at Widdecombe Fair. Dad was judging the livestock show and Mum, the dog show, and I'd gone along to help out." He laughed. "The first time I saw her she was eating candyfloss, and she'd got the pink all round her mouth."

Her eyes danced. "It's hard to eat that stuff without getting it round your mouth."

"Her parents' little Jack Russell was in the terrier racing — it came third. And she challenged me to enter the bale tossing. I'm afraid I didn't do very well in it."

"I'm told there's a knack to it. Some of the young farmers practice for weeks. They can get very competitive."

"They certainly can." For the first time in a long time the images shone bright in his mind — the blue sky, the colours of the fair, the music and the Morris dancing. And Natalie, the sun gleaming on her golden hair, her blue eyes laughing.

Seven years ago . . .

The sound of voices in the ballroom cut across his thoughts. He glanced back over his shoulder. "Ah — people are leaving."

"Oh, yes." Cassie smiled. "Excuse me, I'd better go and say goodbye."

"Of course." He returned the smile. "See you later."

He turned to gaze out over the bay again. The sun was warm on his face, and there was a bumblebee humming over a rosemary bush clinging to the cliff below him. There were families on the beach, building sandcastles, playing frisbee.

It was a while since he'd been here to the hotel, though it was so close. He hadn't been since Natalie was alive. They used to go for long walks along the coast path on Saturday afternoons with Bramble, his dad's springer spaniel, then come here for tea and scones.

Natalie was always full of laughter. It was the first thing he had noticed about her, that day at Widdecombe Fair — after the pink candyfloss round her mouth. He found himself smiling as the happy memories came dancing back. He'd never really talked about those good times, not to anyone.

Odd that it should be Cassie who had unlocked them.

Cassie. He was beginning to recognise the subtle changes in her that ten years had wrought. That old sparkle was still there, but now there was a warmth that spread itself generously over a motherless little girl, an eager puppy, a man who . . .

He shook his head — he hadn't worked that one out yet.

He didn't feel like going back inside and having to talk to people. A flight of stone steps at the side of the terrace led down to the beach. He took off his tie, folded it into his pocket, and unfastened his collar as he felt the red-gold sand crunch beneath his feet.

Cassie. A small smile curved his mouth. Cassie in that pretty summer dress, the hem flirting just above her knees. He had rarely seen her in a dress — even at her sister's birthday party all those years ago she had been wearing jeans.

He'd known her since she was a kid — his mate Paul's younger sister, tagging along with their gang, always game, though she had been the youngest. But that night at the party he had been startled to notice how she was growing up — no longer the tomboy, but a very attractive young woman.

It seemed so long ago now, so much had happened. He had loved her then, had assumed that they would have a future together. It had hurt badly when she'd left. It had taken him a while to acknowledge that she had probably been right to go — at eighteen, she had been too young to settle down.

And he had found happiness again with Natalie. As Edie Channing had said, life kept moving forward — no matter how hard you tried to hold it back. It was moving forward again now, letting the sunshine in as the dark clouds drifted away.

But it was unlikely to move forward with Cassie. Though the echo of that old attraction was still there, time had left all that in the past. She probably would be leaving again soon. After all, what had Sturcombe to offer to compete with the excitement of white-water rafting, bungee jumping, diving along the Great Barrier Reef.

No, there was no point even thinking about it.

CHAPTER EIGHT

"Oh, Daddy, you do look pretty."

"Pretty?" Liam suppressed a laugh.

"In your bestest clothes. Will the party be fun?"

"I hope so, sweetie." He bent over and dropped a kiss on the tip of his daughter's nose. "Remember what I told you? It's to raise money for the poor orphaned horses."

"Will you raise lots of money?"

"I hope so."

"Then they'll have plenty to eat and somewhere to keep warm," the child asserted wisely.

"That's right." He tucked the duvet up around her shoulders. "Now you be good for Granny tonight. She's going to read your bedtime story."

A wide beaming smile spread across her pretty face. "A'wight, Daddy," she promised. "Bye-bye."

"Bye-bye, sweetheart."

His mum glanced up from the sofa as he came down the stairs. "Very smart," she approved.

"Thanks. Robyn said I looked pretty."

Diane Ellis laughed. "She doesn't often see you in a dinner jacket."

"It's a rare sight. Anyway, she's tucked down and ready for her story."

"Right." She set aside her knitting and rose to her feet. "Bye then, love." She kissed his cheek. "Have a nice time."

He smiled wryly. "I'll try."

The fundraiser for the Horse Rescue Society was an annual event, held at the home of a prominent local landowner. The guests were a mix of genuine horse lovers and virtue signallers keen to be seen supporting a good cause — which was fine by him so long as they dipped deep into their pockets.

He always arrived early — as a member of the committee it was part of his duties to help welcome the guests as they arrived. There were a couple of smart cars already parked on the gravel sweep in front of the imposing porch, and he smiled to himself as he parked his work-a-day Land Rover beside them. At least he had hosed most of the mud off it this morning.

The front doors stood wide open to the gracious hall, with its Moroccan-tiled floor and sweeping staircase, and a glittering chandelier which would have looked at home in the Palace of Versailles.

Sir Malcolm's wife Caroline was descending the stairs, resplendent in a rich ruby gown, diamonds at her throat and swinging from her earlobes. "Liam, darling. Lovely to see you." She held out both hands to squeeze his and put up her cheek for a kiss. "You're looking splendid."

"My daughter said I looked pretty. But that word fits you much more appropriately. Or better still, beautiful." He smiled warmly — his hostess would probably be more at home down in the stables, mucking out, but she knew how to put on a show when the occasion demanded it.

"Lovely man!" She patted his shoulder. "Come on in. There are a few people here already — most of them you'll know. The hoards should start descending in about half an hour, but we can start on the champers now."

She linked her arm into his and led him through to the morning room, a large room at the back of the house. Most of the furniture had been removed, and the carpet rolled back to reveal the gleaming parquet floor. More Versailles-worthy chandeliers swung from the high ceiling. Oak panelling and some rather dull — but probably priceless — Victorian landscapes lined the walls.

Three blackjack tables, a roulette wheel and two hired slot-machines had been set up. Two pairs of French windows stood open onto the stone terrace, and beyond a marquee had been erected on the immaculate lawn.

"Now, as usual, we're going to have the drinks reception on the terrace, as the weather's so nice. Dinner will be served in the Tudor Barn. After that there'll be time to mingle on the terrace again and in the garden, with the fun casino in here, and then dancing back in the marquee until dawn. Well, maybe not quite dawn, but we don't expect to finish until after midnight."

"Sounds good," he approved.

"Ah, there's Malcolm. Is everything set, dear?"

"Pretty much." Malcolm rubbed his hands together. "Liam, come and have a look at the shooting range."

"We were just going to try the champagne," Caroline protested.

"Hah! No reason why we can't do both, eh?"

The shooting range was clearly Malcolm's pride and joy. It was a large interactive video game, using laser rifles, set up in a black tent in the wide hallway between the morning room and the library.

"You can set it for different levels according to someone's shooting experience, and you can choose your scenario," he explained, as excited as a twelve-year-old. "You can have a western-style shoot-out, or aliens, and even a marksman competition. Come on, have a go."

He fiddled with the console and the screen lit up.

"Ah, this is a good one. Dinosaurs. You have to hit them exactly on the red spot, and some of them move pretty damn quick, I can tell you. I only managed fifty-eight the last time I had a go. See if you can beat me."

He handed Liam a rifle, and the creatures on the screen began to move. It was great fun. All sorts of weird monsters were running towards him, quite slowly at first but getting faster and faster. Some were flying pterodactyls, swooping and soaring, others fearsome Tyrannosaurus. And to add to the challenge, the red dots were getting progressively smaller.

He could see how it could be quite addictive, but he was careful not to beat Sir Malcolm's score.

"Fifty-two! Jolly well done," the older man applauded with just a hint of smugness. "You got off to a great start there, but you weren't quite quick enough towards the end."

"Come on now, boys," Caroline chided. "Time to stop playing with your toys. People are starting to arrive."

Sir Malcolm raised his eyes heavenwards, but didn't argue. "Coming dear."

Liam put the rifle back in its cradle, and turned.

"Oh, Liam. I don't believe you've met my niece." At Caroline's side was a stunningly beautiful young woman with hair the colour of burnished copper tumbling round her shoulders. "Annabel, this is Liam Ellis — our vet. He's an absolute wonder, the way he handles the horses."

A smile curved those perfect peach-pink lips. "Hello." Her voice was soft, melodic. "Nice to meet you."

Very nice... Liam smiled back — what red-blooded man wouldn't when those sapphire-blue eyes were looking at him like that? "Good evening."

Her skin glowed like ivory, her features as flawless as a cameo. She had the body of a supermodel, tall and elegant, flattered by a long, slinky dress of midnight blue that skimmed over every slender curve.

She arched one finely drawn eyebrow. "You seem to be in need of a refill of champagne."

He glanced at his empty flute. "So I am."

He fell into step beside her as they strolled back through the French windows to the terrace. "So you're Caroline's niece. Do you live here in Devon?"

"No, I live in London now, but my family are in Bath. I came down to help Aunt Caroline with the arrangements for tonight."

"That's very kind of you."

"It's so much work for Aunt Caroline — and besides, I enjoy it."

"And what do you do when you're not arranging charity balls? Can I guess that you're a model?"

A soft, husky laugh. "Oh dear. Is it so obvious? And you're a vet. That must be very interesting."

"It is."

"You mainly work with horses?"

He nodded. "Mainly. But my family work with farm animals — cows, sheep, pigs. And my mum runs a small animal practice."

"Here in South Devon?"

"Sturcombe. It's down on the coast."

"I've never been there."

"It's just a small town, not much more than a village really. But the bay is very pretty."

It was pleasant to talk to her, and she was certainly easy on the eye. But he was conscious that he had duties to fulfil as one of the hosts, so after a little while he suggested that they should circulate.

"Of course." Again that alluring smile. "I'll see you at dinner."

He smiled back. "Of course."

The terrace was soon crowded as more people arrived. He knew quite a few of them — their horses were his patients. The Routleys, who bred very fine showjumpers, the Chubbs who had a riding school up by the moor, the Hilsons whose three teenage daughters were all horse mad.

As he moved between various groups he would occasionally glance across the room and catch that sapphire-blue gaze, that beguiling smile. And he'd smile back. He didn't have much experience of flirting, but maybe he could try it.

At last it was time to go in to dinner. The Tudor Barn was looking splendid. The vaulted ceiling was criss-crossed with heavy oak trusses, wound with twinkling white fairy lights. The walls were the original rough brick, the floor was well-trodden stone. The tall windows at the gable ends had been covered in black cloth, so that the only illumination was from the lights set in niches in the walls.

There were twenty circular tables, spread with crisp white linen and laid out with gold-edged white plates, glittering crystal wine glasses and silver cutlery. Each table had baskets of fresh bread rolls and coils of butter in glass dishes. Each had a centrepiece of three tall, slim white candles of graduated heights, wound with a trail of ivy.

Liam was checking the name cards on the tables when Annabel slipped up beside him, tucking her hands into his arm.

"I have a confession to make," she murmured, a mischievous glint dancing in her fine blue eyes. "I switched the cards around. Do you mind?"

He arched one eyebrow in amused question. "You're sitting next to me?"

"Yes."

He laughed. "I don't mind at all."

She smiled radiantly. "What do you think of the room?"

"Very nice. You've done a great job."

"Thank you."

She had knocked him slightly off balance. She was stunning, of course — the sort of woman that most men could only dream about. And she was quite definitely interested in him. Which was very flattering to his ego — not that that had ever been something he'd been bothered about.

But he didn't feel entirely comfortable about it. If she was looking for a relationship, he suspected that she would have high expectations, and he really didn't have time for that.

* * *

"Fancy coming down the pub?"

Cassie glanced up from the newspaper as her brother strolled into the sitting room. "What's up? Been stood up by . . . what was her name?"

"Chanelle." He shrugged in casual unconcern. "Oh, we're not seeing each other anymore."

Cassie laughed, shaking her head. It was hardly a surprise that that affair hadn't lasted long. "Lisa said you change your girlfriends as often as you change your socks."

Paul put on a hurt expression that would fool no one. "That's not fair. I change my socks every day."

"I'm glad to hear it," their mother remarked on a note of dry humour, turning her head briefly from the quiz show she was watching.

Cassie tossed the newspaper aside and rose to her feet. "Anyway, yes I'll come to the pub. Just give me five minutes to get changed."

"Okay." He grinned and picked up the newspaper, and flopped down in her place on the sofa. "See you in about an hour."

"Huh!" She hurried up to her room. She had showered earlier, after her swim, and had changed into clean jeans. All she had to do was brush through her hair, throw on a fresh top and slick on a little mascara and lipstick.

But . . . she wanted to look her best. Maybe her white jeans, and that pretty silky top she had bought in Wellington — white, with a pop of green flowers over one shoulder. And a touch of grey eye shadow and kohl liner to bring out the colour of her eyes . . .

Of course it had nothing to do with the possibility that Liam Ellis might be there. Of course not.

"Right, I'm ready," she announced in triumph from the doorway of the sitting room. "Seven minutes flat, and that includes running up and down three flights of stairs."

"Wow!" Paul feigned exaggerated surprise. "Must be a world record."

She picked up a cushion and threw it at his head, but he dodged neatly.

"Okay, come on then, sis." He leaned over and dropped a kiss on their mother's cheek, raised a hand to his dad, and dropped his arm around Cassie's shoulders. "See you, folks."

The sun was sinking as they strolled down the hill. A soft lilac mist lay along the horizon, the sea was silvery grey, the waves were whispering over the beach. A single sailing yacht was scudding across the bay.

If she stayed . . .

No, dammit, that question was a constant niggle in her brain, like a grain of sand stuck between her toes. There was no point thinking about it yet anyway. She would stay for Tom and Vicky's wedding, then make up her mind.

And what would be the deciding factor? that annoying little voice in her head taunted. *Are you still hoping Liam will want you after all?*

She huffed out an impatient breath. Paul slanted her a questioning glance. "What's up?"

"I . . . Uh . . . I just remembered it's the bank holiday weekend." She gestured towards the Esplanade, crowded with people milling around outside the pub and the chip shop and the amusement arcade. "We'll be lucky to get anywhere near the bar."

The glint of sardonic amusement in his eyes suggested that he didn't quite believe her, but he didn't pursue it. He just laughed. "Don't worry — leave it to me."

He was as good as his word. As soon as they entered the pub he caught Wes's eye. The landlord nodded, and by the time they got through the crowd around the bar their drinks were waiting for them. "They're on your tab," Wes said as he pulled a beer for another customer.

They took their drinks and moved back through the throng to a table near the back, close to the dartboard. Debbie was already there, with a pleasant-looking young man with russet hair that sprang from his forehead like a scrubbing brush.

She shuffled up to make room for Cassie to sit down. "Hi. Do you remember Bill?"

"Yes of course. I saw you at the cricket. And weren't you in the same class in school as my sister Lisa?"

He nodded, his smile shy. "That's right."

Yes, she remembered him. He'd always been the quiet one, overpowered by the noisy triumvirate of Paul, Liam and Tom Cullen. He was holding Debbie's hand under the table, and Cassie smiled to herself. So this was the man who had brought that spark of happiness to Debbie's soft brown eyes. Good for him.

Cassie craned her neck to look around the bar. "Where are Ian and Greg Norrish?" she asked. "And Beverley Wotton?"

Debbie smiled a little crookedly. "Moved away. Bev lives in Exeter now — she works in a bank up there. The Norrishes both went up to Manchester, I think, and the Sladers all moved to somewhere up in Nottinghamshire."

"Oh, that's sad. It won't seem the same without them here."

Debbie's wry glance reminded her that she had left too.

They sat chatting comfortably about memories of their schooldays. Cassie was trying not to watch the door to see if Liam would come in. And trying just as hard not to watch the big brass ship's clock above the bar as the time ticked by.

It was almost half past eight when the door opened and a tall man with dark hair appeared. Cassie's heart skipped . . . But as he turned, she realised that it was Luke, with Julia. The door closed behind them — no one had followed them in.

"Hi, Luke," someone called. "No Liam tonight?"

Luke shook his head, laughing. "He's at some charity thing at the Gillard's, for the Horse Rescue. I'm afraid you'll have to put up with me on the team."

"Oh, damn. Might as well throw in the towel now, boys."

There was a lot more good-natured banter as Luke and his wife moved over to the back of the room to join the darts team. Cassie refused to acknowledge the stab of disappointment. She wouldn't see Liam tonight. So what? She wasn't bothered. Not at all.

* * *

It was a more enjoyable evening than Liam had anticipated. Annabel was a lively companion, and it did his ego no harm to have such a beautiful woman at his side.

Dinner over, there were the inevitable speeches, followed by an auction run by a well-known actor who lived locally. He whipped up the audience's enthusiasm for the items to be bid for — a crate of twenty-six-year-old Irish whiskey, a helicopter ride over Land's End followed by dinner for four at one of Cornwall's swankiest restaurants, a day at the races in the donor's private box, with champagne.

There was a certain irony in that prize, Liam reflected dryly. Over the past few years the society had taken in three of the donor's racehorses that hadn't made the grade. Maybe the donation was to ease his conscience — if he had one.

"Oh, aren't those earrings pretty?" Annabel had spotted them earlier — blue enamel on gold. "I have to have them."

She was bidding excitedly, waving her hand, and she whooped with such joy when she won that she earned herself a round of applause. Impulsively, she threw her arms around Liam's neck and kissed him enthusiastically on the lips.

He laughed, though he did feel mildly uncomfortable. But it was just her lively, open personality — he really shouldn't be churlish about it.

"Aren't they gorgeous?" Her eyes were bright as she slipped the earrings she was wearing out of her ears and put the new ones in. "Here, would you look after these for me? I don't have any pockets in this dress."

He slanted her a teasing smile as he took them from her. They looked like real diamonds. "You trust me not to run off with them?"

"Of course I trust you." She laughed merrily. "I'm a great judge of character."

The actor was announcing the end of the auction. "Okay, folks, that's all for now. I think I hear the band warming up. Let's hit the dance floor."

"Come on," Annabel urged, tugging on Liam's hand. "Let's dance."

In the marquee a live band had set up on a dais at one end — a drummer and two guitarists, and a keyboard player. They were playing a good mix of pop covers and a few classic soul numbers.

He hadn't danced for a long time. Not since Natalie. But Annabel didn't seem to even notice his lack of enthusiasm. She was enjoying herself, swaying to the music, her eyes bright, her hair gleaming in the soft amber glow of the fairy lights strung beneath the roof.

Dammit. Stop being so uptight. You're dancing with a beautiful woman — just relax and enjoy it. Stop worrying about where it might lead. Stop thinking about a girl with a Maori tattoo on her shoulder.

The dance floor was getting lively, and he was just beginning to think he should suggest that they should dance with other people for a while when Malcolm breezed up.

"Ah, there you are! We're setting up the shooting range. Come and show them how it's done."

"Oh, yes!" Annabel's fine eyes shone. "I've been dying to have a go on that. Show me how to do it."

He smiled down at her. "Come on then. Have you ever done any shooting before?"

"I did some clay pigeon shooting once."

"You've got a head start then."

They both had several goes on the shooting range, teasing each other for missing, applauding good hits. Then they spent some time in the casino, Annabel cheerfully losing a hundred pounds on the roulette wheel.

"Ah, well." She shrugged as they strolled down through the gardens to the lake. "It's all in a good cause." The moonlight was glimmering silver on the water. "Oh, it's so beautiful. And look — swans."

She turned to him and wrapped her arms around his waist, lifting her face to his. She was clearly expecting him to kiss her.

So he did.

It was a perfect romantic setting, here by the moonlit lake, a soft evening breeze rustling the leaves of a weeping willow on the bank. Her perfume seemed to surround him, faintly exotic, faintly sensual, and her slender body was curved against his. It felt good, but . . . where was the spark?

The first time he had kissed Natalie, the first time he had kissed Cassie, he had felt as if a Catherine Wheel was going off in his gut. But while Annabel was undoubtedly more beautiful than either of them, something was missing.

Maybe he was expecting too much, too soon. Maybe he was making too much of his memories. Maybe he was over-thinking it. Maybe he should try to just relax and enjoy kissing a beautiful woman. Maybe the sparks would come.

She was smiling a little wistfully when he lifted his head. "I wish I didn't have to go to Milan tomorrow."

"Oh . . . That is a shame." He should feel disappointed. Give it time. "When will you be back?"

"Not for a while. I'll be going straight on to South Africa, then it's Fiji for a magazine shoot."

He smiled. "You certainly get around."

"I'll be back around the end of September." She tipped her head coquettishly on one side. "Perhaps we could meet up again then?"

"That would be good."

She glanced back over her shoulder. "It looks like the party's winding up. Maybe we should go and say goodnight."

"Okay." He kissed her again, then taking her hand, they walked back to the house.

* * *

After the fug in the pub, it was good to get out in the cool fresh air again. As they strolled up the hill, Cassie breathed in the sweet fragrance of the rosemary bushes that clung to the side of the cliff below them.

Opposite the house she paused and leaned on the cliff wall, gazing out over the bay. The moon was a thin sliver like the imprint of a thumb nail, but the stars were making up for it in brightness.

Far out towards the dark horizon pinpoints of light showed a ship sailing down towards the open ocean. Once she would have followed the path of that ship in her mind, wondering where it might be going — fabulous places, exotic places, with plants and animals she had only seen on television.

Now... A small sigh escaped her lips. "Ah . . . This really is the most beautiful place in the world."

"It is." Paul leaned on the wall beside her. "Have you decided yet what you're going to do?"

She took a pause, then shook her head. "Not yet. I'll definitely stay for Tom's wedding. After that . . ." She shrugged her slim shoulders. "Who knows?"

A soft breeze was ruffling her hair. She closed her eyes, listening to the soft swoosh of the waves unrolling themselves lazily over the sand.

"You know Nanna left her house to the three of us?"

"To us?" She opened her eyes and glanced at him, surprised. "Why us? Why not Mum and Dad?"

"They discussed it a few years ago. They felt they didn't need it, and we were all coming to the age when we might benefit more."

"Oh . . ."

"We have to decide between us what to do about it. Lisa doesn't want it."

"She and Ollie have their own house."

He nodded. "What about you?"

"Why would I want it?"

"To live in?"

She laughed. "*If* I was planning to stay. Anyway, you live in it."

He had been renting it since Nanna had moved down to live with her son's family. Lisa had told her that he had insisted on paying the proper market rent — sometimes he could be as obstinate as Nanna.

She glanced across at him, her adored big brother, five years older than her. Tall, athletic and handsome. She had been so proud of him when at seventeen he had realised his dream of becoming a professional footballer.

Starting in a lower division, he had helped his team win promotion to the Championship League and hold their place, even hopeful of moving up into the Premier League.

Then at thirty-one a bad knee injury had kept him out of the game for half a season. Even when he had recovered he had rarely made it off the substitutes' bench.

"Why did you come back here when you retired?" she asked.

He smiled, understanding why she had asked. "It was always part of my long-term plan. A striker's career rarely lasts much past the age of thirty-four, thirty-five, unless you go into coaching or management, and that wasn't my thing. Once it became clear that none of the top clubs were going to come bidding for me I knew I needed another string to my bow."

"So you chose to be an investment consultant." That had been a big surprise when Lisa had told her about it. "Why that?"

"It can be just as challenging. You play defence to avoid losing money, attack to make a profit. You get to know the players on the field, their strengths and weaknesses, when to

119

hold back and when to go for the big score. Some of my team-mates saw that I was making good money and asked me for help with their own investments, and it's just gone on from there."

"I guess they prefer to work with someone they know, someone they trust."

"That's right. Someone who understands what they need because I've been in the game too."

She slanted him a teasing smile. "I never had you down for a clever sod. I thought you were just all muscle."

He grinned, striking a Mr Universe pose. "That too. Anyway, about the house. If you don't want it, I'd like to buy out your share, and Lisa's. I suggest we each employ an estate agent to value it, then take an average of the three. And don't argue that's not necessary," he added as she started to shake her head. "I want it all done straight."

"Okay." She hugged him, laughing. "We'll do that."

CHAPTER NINE

"Okay, people, let's hit the road. Exeter here we come!" Lisa pulled out onto the roundabout at the top of Haytor Avenue and turned onto the dual carriageway. "I think the best bet would be to use the Park-and-Ride instead of trying to find a parking space in town."

Cassie was squished in the back seat of the car with Debbie and Kyra in her baby seat — Vicky was in the front. Cassie hadn't been keen to come — girlie shopping trips had never been her thing — but she needed something to wear for the two weddings, so it made sense to go along.

Debbie was going to collect her dress, Vicky for her last fitting. In spite of her initial lack of enthusiasm, Cassie found the air of anticipation and excitement was catching.

"I'm going to need shoes too," Debbie fretted.

"Don't worry, we have the whole day." Lisa changed lanes smoothly to overtake a large truck. "This is going to be fun."

The dual carriageway gave them a clear run to the outskirts of the city. The car park wasn't too crowded, and they only had to wait a few minutes for the bus. Cassie helped Lisa lift Kyra's baby buggy aboard.

"That's a good omen," Vicky declared as they settled in their seats.

The bus dropped them in the centre of town. Cassie had always liked Exeter, with its bustling modern high street and its quaint cobbled alleyways where you could discover all sorts of quirky little independent shops selling hand-made jewellery, pieces of art and vintage clothes. And lots of coffee shops to rest weary shopped-out feet and get a much-needed shot of caffeine.

Their target was just a short walk from the bus stop. The ground floor was full of fabulous evening dresses in jewel-bright colours, glamourous shoes and tempting accessories. The bridal shop was upstairs, a fairytale kingdom full of shimmering whites, ivories and creams, yards of tulle and lace, beading and sparkles.

"Oh, I love it!" Lisa spread her arms wide and spun around. "I wish I was the one getting married."

Cassie laughed. "You had your turn."

"I think I'll make Ollie do it all over again. We could renew our vows on our tenth anniversary."

The senior bridal consultant hurried out to meet them. "Ah, Miss Marston, Miss Rowley. We're ready for you. Come this way."

While Vicky and Debbie were led off to the changing rooms, Lisa browsed happily among the accessories. She picked up a long, lacy veil attached to a sparkling tiara and held it out to Cassie. "This is pretty. Here, try it on."

Cassie backed away, laughing unsteadily. "Oh . . . no . . ."

"Don't be silly. Here." She perched it on Cassie's head and fluffed out the veil. "There — it looks fabulous."

She stepped aside so that Cassie could see herself in the long mirror. It was unnervingly like something out of one of those dreams she always tried to forget — the ones where she was walking down the aisle of a church, getting married, but the aisle kept getting longer and longer, her bridegroom up ahead disappearing into a white mist.

Impatiently she pushed those thoughts aside, forcing a laugh as she tugged the tiara from her head. "I can't see me togged up like that. If I ever get married it'll be on the beach, in a bikini."

122

Lisa shook her head. "When the time comes, I'll lay money you'll go the full meringue."

"By that time I'll be walking down the aisle with a Zimmer frame."

The bridal consultant had pulled back the curtain on one of the dressing rooms. "Here you are!" she announced with a flourish.

Debbie stepped out, smiling shyly. "What do you think?"

"Oh . . . It's fabulous!"

Debbie hadn't gone the full meringue either. Her dress was a matt ivory satin in a very simple but beautifully cut style — sleeveless, a round neckline and a skirt that reached just an inch or two above her knees. Over it, she wore a bolero embroidered with silver thread and glass beads, with bracelet-length sleeves and a stand-up collar.

"It's perfect," Cassie assured her warmly. "And I love your shoes."

"Do you think they're all right?" She pointed one dainty foot in a strappy silver sandal, with a neat low heel. "They'll be comfortable enough to wear all day and I'll be able to wear them again any time."

"They're lovely. Bill's going to be over the moon when he sees you."

Debbie's eyes sparkled. "I hope so. It's all so different this time. Last time we just went to the Register Office, with Mum and Alan's brother. And then went for a drink in the pub."

"That was all?" Cassie protested, shocked.

"Uh-huh." She smiled crookedly. "I suppose it was an omen for how things turned out."

"Well, if you need an omen this time, it should be a much better one," Lisa declared.

"I don't need an omen." Debbie's soft brown eyes were warm with happiness. "This time is definitely going to be *much* better. The hotel have been wonderful." She smiled at Lisa. "Thank you so much. I never thought . . . Oh, now I'm being silly." A tear was tracking down her cheek.

Lisa darted in with a tissue before it could drop onto her dress. "It's our pleasure," she assured the happy bride. "We haven't had many weddings there these past few years, and all the staff are really looking forward to it. Anyway, what's the point of having one of your best friends as the assistant manager of a hotel if you can't have her pull out all the stops for you?"

Debbie laughed. "You've certainly done that. And you're supposed to still be on maternity leave."

Lisa waved her hand in a dismissive gesture. "Oh, Vicky doesn't mind me treading on her toes. Besides, if we left it to Mike, he'd probably faint!"

The consultant came forward again, smiling. "Are you ready for number two?"

"Oh, yes!"

She pulled open the other curtain and Vicky stepped out, spreading her arms wide. "Tah-dah!"

"Oh . . . !"

The dress was stunning — lace over layers of tulle, with an off-the-shoulder neckline edged with cut-out lace, and a full-length A-line skirt that swept back into a short train. Her veil was tulle, edged with the same lace, held in place by a coronet of white silk flowers.

"That's just beautiful," Debbie breathed.

"Isn't it?" Vicky's eyes danced with delight. "I love it."

"Oh, this is all so romantic." Lisa sighed. "I want a job here."

"Don't be daft," Cassie retorted. "That's like it being Christmas every day."

"Nothing wrong with that," Lisa insisted. "I'll work in a bridal shop all summer, and a Christmas shop all winter!"

"You're nuts!"

"Anyway, it's our turn now," Lisa declared. "Party dresses!"

A couple of hours later they were sitting in the sunshine outside a smart little restaurant beside the Cathedral Green, surrounded by shopping bags, sipping wine and eating Mexican penne with avocado.

"Oh, wow — this is delicious." Vicky's eyes were bright. "I'm having such a wonderful time. I never believed . . . !"

Lisa laughed, reaching over to gently rock Kyra's buggy. "Shopping with your besties, and the best excuse in the world. What's not to like?"

Cassie sipped her wine, gazing around at the wide grassy space, the shady trees, the golden medieval facade of the Cathedral itself. She was having a good time too.

Trying on one fabulous dress after another, picking out shoes and a pretty beaded evening bag, deciding at the last minute that she would buy that gorgeous floaty pink chiffon top with the handkerchief hem after all . . .

A girlie shopping trip — maybe the reason she had thought it wasn't her thing was because she had never really had a group of girlfriends before, at least not since she had left school. Working in water-sport centres and the safari resort and the dude ranch, she had mostly been working with men.

Which had been fine. But now, with these women, she realised what she had been missing. Something else to add to the scales when she was deciding on her future.

* * *

"Well hello, old boy. How are you doing?"

Cassie stopped dead in the doorway, startled to find Liam in the small animal surgery. He scooped Barney up and settled him on the examination table. "Oh . . . I thought . . . your mum would be here," she protested, flustered.

He smiled easily. "It's her day off." He nuzzled Barney as the little dog stretched up to sniff at his cheek. "How has he been?"

"Not too bad." She forced herself to focus, ignoring the sudden acceleration of her heartbeat. "A little stiff in the mornings, but he still enjoys his run on the beach."

"That's good. Eating well?"

"Oh, yes!" Cassie laughed. "Anything he can get hold of."

"Good." All businesslike, Liam had hooked his stethoscope into his ears and was listening to the little dog's chest. "That seems fine."

Cassie managed a smile. He was being perfectly professional — that was the problem. He was behaving as if she was just another dog owner bringing their pet in for treatment.

Which was entirely appropriate, of course. She really had no reason to object.

Barney had never appreciated the thermometer thing and tried to sit down to protect his rear end, but Liam lifted him deftly with an arm under his tummy and inserted it, laughing as the dog wriggled and tried to twist around to see what was going on back there.

"It's okay, buddy. Nearly done." He checked the thermometer and nodded. "That's fine. I just need to take a blood test to check his liver function."

"Right . . . Yes . . ."

Barney didn't object at all as Liam shaved a tiny patch of his front paw and drew a small phial of blood. He was an experienced vet — of course he had a way with animals. But Cassie couldn't help but be impressed by the gentle way he handled the little dog. Barney was a true terrier and could be quite assertive about having his own way.

"There. I'll get that tested. It won't take more than a few minutes."

"Okay. Thank you."

He disappeared into the back room, leaving Cassie to have a few moments to regain her composure. She hadn't seen him since the funeral. That conversation about Natalie had lingered in her mind. It had been clear how much he had loved her — it would have completely eclipsed that brief summer of calf-love all those years ago.

But she wasn't jealous — how could she be? She was glad for him that he had known that happiness, even though it had been so cruelly snatched away.

Now . . . Well, it probably wasn't the right moment to try to discuss their past history. He had a busy surgery to run, a

126

French Bulldog and two cats out in the waiting room requiring his attention. At least they could be friends. It would be foolish to look for anything more.

"What do you think, Barney?" she murmured in the little dog's ear, cuddling his warm body and stroking his rough fur. "Friends is good, right? Though you'll always be my bestest friend."

The door opened and Liam came back in.

"Oh . . ." She caught her breath, feeling a stupid blush rise to her cheeks — hopefully he'd just think she was embarrassed at being caught whispering sweet nothings to her pet. "That was quick."

He smiled. If he had noticed her reaction, he gave no sign of it. "Modern technology — the results will come up on the computer in a few minutes." He tickled the dog's ear, earning himself a gaze of pure adoration. "He's doing pretty well for his age. You must have missed him while you were away."

"Yes, I did," she admitted with a wry smile. "I was so happy to see him when I got back."

"I bet. So how are you all now?"

"We're fine. Trying to get used to Nanna not being there. She was such a big presence — she's left a very big hole."

"The whole town will miss her."

"She was smiling, you know — as if she was happy to go. She'd enjoyed the cricket, and bickering with Arthur."

He laughed. "Of course. She always enjoyed that . . . Ah . . ." He glanced at the computer screen beside him. "The results have come up. Everything's looking fine, within the normal range. Right, young man, just one little injection for you and you'll be running around like a puppy again. But not too much," he added quickly to Cassie. "Don't let him tire himself."

Cassie nodded, watching as Liam deftly filled a syringe and injected the contents into the loose skin at the back of Barney's neck.

"There you go — all done, mate." He rubbed the spot, and the little dog twisted his head to lick his hand.

"Thank you." She clipped on Barney's lead and lifted him down from the table. "Well . . . um . . . Goodbye."

"Will you be at Debbie and Bill's wedding?"

"Of course."

"I'll see you there then." He smiled with unexpected warmth. "Goodbye."

"Goodbye."

Cassie paid at the desk then stepped out into the bright sunshine, turning down Church Road, Barney trotting happily beside her.

She was still feeling unsettled by that unexpected encounter with Liam. Of course, it was probably inevitable that in a small town like this she would run into him from time to time, sometimes when she least expected it, wasn't ready for it. If she stayed, it would be something she would have to deal with.

If she stayed . . .

Friends. It was easy to say, not so easy to live with. She didn't want to fall in love with him again, but she wasn't sure that she could help herself.

Shaking those thoughts from her head she glanced around. There had been changes since she had been away. Brenda's shop was still there, but the hairdressers had changed hands. The pharmacy had gone and so had the off-licence and the shoe shop, which had been taken over by a second-hand furniture shop.

More of the big houses on the other side of the road had been converted to bed-and-breakfast places. She smiled to herself at the twee names: Bella Vista, Sunny Dene, Sandy Bay.

The Memorial Garden was looking very colourful, its neatly trimmed lawns and well-kept flowerbeds presided over by the old stone clock tower which had been built to commemorate the dead of the Boer War, and now carried the names of the dead in every war since.

She glanced down at the dog. "Fancy a walk on the beach?" He responded with a look that suggested he had taken it as a rhetorical question. "Okay, come on then."

They strolled down the ramp and she let him off the leash. The beach was busy again. Barney spotted an unwary seagull and set off in hot pursuit, zooming around sun loungers and deckchairs, barking excitedly.

Inevitably the seagull got away, and Barney came trotting back, his pink tongue lolling out. Cassie bent and tickled his ears. "Never mind, poppet. Come on, look who's here."

Lisa was in her usual corner with the baby in her carrier. Cassie waved as she strolled over, Barney loping along at her side. Noah and Amy were playing catch with a beach ball, but they instantly stopped their game and came to make a fuss of the little dog, who rolled over to have his tummy tickled, wriggling in ecstasy.

"Hi. How did he get on at the vet's?" Lisa asked.

"He's doing fine. He aced his blood test and had his jab. He was very good — the needles didn't bother him at all. Just the thermometer up his bum!"

Lisa laughed. "I don't blame him. You are a good boy, aren't you?" She caught the little dog and held him off as he tried to lick her cheek. Barney heaved a contented sigh and flopped down on the blanket, snuggled up against her, and promptly went to sleep.

"He's exhausted. He was chasing a seagull."

"Ah well, you're getting on a bit, aren't you, baby?" Lisa stroked a hand over the little dog's head.

Cassie sat down on the blanket. "Liam was there," she remarked lightly.

"Oh, yes. He and Luke take it in turns to cover the surgery on their mum's day off."

Cassie slanted her a wry glance but didn't answer. It would have been nice to have been forewarned.

"So how did you get on with him?" Lisa enquired with an air of innocence that Cassie didn't entirely trust.

"Liam? Fine." Her tone was dismissive.

"Only I couldn't help noticing how long you were chatting to him at Nanna's funeral."

"Oh, well, it's been a long time. We had a lot of catching up to do. But don't start getting carried away," she added warningly. "We're just friends."

"Of course." Lisa looked far from convinced, but she let the subject drop.

Little Amy came over and squeezed onto the blanket, picking up Kyra's fluffy yellow dragon and dangling it for the baby to bat at with her tiny fists.

"My mummy's getting married on Saturday," she announced proudly. "And I'm going to be a bridesmaid. My nanna's made me a dress. It's pink."

"That's lovely." Cassie smiled warmly at the child. "I bet you're looking forward to it."

"And after they're married we'll be able to have a baby of our own. And a kitten. I wanted a puppy, but Mummy said we couldn't have one because it would have to be left on its own while she's working in the café and Uncle Bill is looking after the cows and I'm at school. But kittens don't mind being left on their own so that will be better. I'm going to call her Elsa."

Lisa and Cassie shared a glance of amusement. Such a long speech — usually the child barely spoke a word, being as shy as her mother. Bill seemed to have been good for both of them.

Cassie tucked up her feet and rested her chin on her knees, watching all the activity on the beach. When she was a kid she had always felt a bit sorry for the holidaymakers from the caravan site and guest houses who could only come down here for a week or two.

Then they would have to go home again, to some dull grey town full of dull grey pavements and dull grey buildings. While she and her friends could stay here all year round, enjoying the beach, playing in the empty amusement arcade along the Esplanade or the mini golf, watching the sea in all its moods from tranquil and still to wild fury.

It had been a happy childhood, with lots of friends and plenty of grown-ups you knew well, who would sometimes treat you discreetly to an ice-cream or a packet of crisps.

Maybe she hadn't recognised at the time how special that was, dazzled as she had been by her dreams of the big wide world beyond the bay. Maybe she had had to go away and come back again in order to appreciate it.

CHAPTER TEN

"This is such a lovely idea," Cassie remarked as she and Lisa strolled down Cliff Road and along the Esplanade to the Carleton Hotel with Kyra in her buggy. "An evening wedding."

"Mmm, with the sun setting in the background. So romantic," Lisa agreed. "The photos will look fantastic."

Everyone had been anxiously checking the weather reports for days. Surely after several weeks of glorious sunshine it wouldn't choose to rain, today of all days? Of course, there was always the option of retreating to the ballroom if the weather turned, but who wouldn't want to have their wedding ceremony out on the terrace, with its sweeping view of the bay?

But it had been another beautiful day, and promised to be a beautiful evening. The sun was westering across the sky, and there wasn't a cloud in sight. The sea was sparkling like diamonds and sapphires, lazy waves rippling like white lace along the edge of the beach.

There were still lots of families enjoying the remains of the day before it was time to go home for tea. Sandcastles of various sizes bore witness to the young builders' hard labour, games of cricket and frisbee were winding down — only the dogs were still full of energy, chasing their balls and scaring up the strutting seagulls.

A sign in the window of the CupCake Café announced that it was closed for the day. Cassie laughed as they passed. "I wonder how Debbie's feeling?"

"Like she's been wired up to the mains," Lisa responded with a chuckle.

"Is that what it was like for you?"

"I could have blown up the whole National Grid!"

The hotel was at the far end of the bay, just past the Memorial Gardens, set on a low rocky cliff and surrounded by its own gardens. The original house had been built by a wealthy Victorian factory owner as a summer retreat well away from the smog and chills of the Midlands.

It had undergone many changes in its fortunes since then, with different owners, a jumble of wings and extensions added. It had seen better days, but it still maintained much of its former dignity.

Many of the guests were sentimental visitors who had been coming to Sturcombe for years, or golfers who came to play on the golf course on the rising ground behind it.

The two of them strolled across the gravelled car park and up the steps to the reception hall. Inside it was all bustle and excitement as the staff got the place ready for the wedding. A white pergola had been set up out on the terrace and Eric, the porter, was wheeling a trolley carrying a stack of folding white chairs.

In the conservatory two long trestle tables had been set up — one was displaying the wedding presents, the other would be laid out with a buffet which Chef was preparing in the kitchen. A dozen large crystal vases stood ready for the white roses, gardenias and lily of the valley that were being unloaded from the florist's van.

Vicky was coming down the stairs holding a clipboard on her arm.

"Hi," Lisa called to her. "How's it going?"

Vicky rolled her eyes. "Organised chaos. At least I hope it's organised. Your help will be much appreciated."

"Okay. What can we do?"

"Could you see to the flowers? They ought to be in water before they start wilting. If you want to drop your things off upstairs first, I've booked out Room 11 for the female guests. The men have Room 12, and the bridal party have Suite 10."

"That's great — sounds like you're really on top of it. Cassie, if you'll dump our things upstairs in the room, I'll make a start on sorting out the flowers."

"Right."

It was great fun transforming the hotel into a fabulous wedding venue for Debbie and Bill. The rather plain function room was draped in swathes of shimmering white organza hung from hooks high on the walls which had been put there for that purpose years ago. The carpet had been rolled up and the parquet dance floor beneath had had a good polish.

The flowers were arranged on small tables around the room, and the DJ had come in to set up his decks on the stage. On the terrace the pergola was festooned with garlands of white silk flowers, and the white wooden chairs were embellished with sashes of pale-pink organza. And in the conservatory, fairy lights had been twined into the potted fig trees and kentia palms.

The buffet had been brought through from the kitchen — neatly trimmed sandwiches, mini-frittatas, mozzarella sticks, both savoury and sweet kebabs, strawberry pavlova and tiramisu.

At each end of the table was a large punch bowl — one was filled with a delicious non-alcoholic cocktail of elderflower and apple juice in sparkling mineral water, spiced with a sprinkle of mint, the other a very alcoholic mix of vodka and champagne in pineapple and lime juice.

The centrepiece was Chef's masterstroke — a magnificent wedding cake. Two tiers of smooth white icing with a fall of pink and white sugar flowers cascading down one side.

"Oh, it's looking fabulous!" Vicky enthused, coming in to check on progress. She glanced at her watch. "It's probably time for us all to go up and start getting ready. Debbie will be here any minute."

"She's here now!" Cassie ran out to the door as Debbie arrived with her mum, Kate, and little Amy. "Don't peek," she insisted, putting her hand over her friend's eyes and taking her arm to lead her into the ballroom as Amy ran ahead.

"Oh, Mummy, it's so pretty!" Amy was dancing with excitement. "There are so many flowers, it's just like a garden."

"I want to see!"

"There you go."

Cassie took her hand away, and Debbie gasped in delight as she gazed around the room. "Oh, it's perfect. Thank you so much. Oh . . ." She pulled a tissue from her pocket and dabbed at her eyes.

"Mummy, why are you crying?" Amy asked anxiously.

"It's happy crying," Debbie assured her. "All this is so wonderful. I can't believe it. Thank you for everything you've done. Oh, look at the pergola. And the cake!" She hurried into the conservatory. "It's just beautiful. I have to thank your chef for that."

"He's in the kitchen," Vicky said. "Then it'll be time for you to start getting ready. You're in Suite 10. Shelley . . ." She turned to one of the housekeeping staff who had been helping with the preparations. "Could you take up a few bites and some coffee, please?"

"Of course."

"If there's anything you need," Vicky added, "just let Shelley know."

"Thank you. It's all perfect." Debbie had to dab at her eyes again.

"Is that happy crying too, Mummy?" Amy asked.

"Yes, it is. Very happy crying."

It was a lovely evening. A warm breeze was drifting in from the sea. To the east, the sky was shading from lilac to cobalt blue, and a few clouds like pink and purple powder puffs floated low over the western horizon as the sun dipped slowly down towards the sea.

Music played softly as Debbie walked out onto the terrace on Kate's arm and down the aisle between the chairs, followed by her two bridesmaids — little Amy and Bill's teenage niece Bez, in matching pink dresses, holding hands.

The silver embroidery on Debbie's bolero glinted in the low rays of the sun. Her soft brown hair had been caught up with an ivory silk flower, and she was carrying a dainty bouquet of white roses and gardenias.

And when Bill, awkward in a brand-new grey suit, turned and saw her, his homely face broke into the widest, happiest smile you ever saw, and he reached out his hand to take hers . . .

Uh-oh — tissue time.

Cassie was a little surprised at herself. She had been looking forward to the wedding, glad to see her old friend happy after the tough time she had had, but she hadn't expected to be quite so affected by it. She had never been one for all that romantic stuff — it wasn't her thing. It wasn't.

She had been trying not to let her eyes stray across the aisle to where Liam was sitting with his family. He scrubbed up well, she reflected with a flicker of amusement, in a well-cut pale-grey suit with a crisp white shirt.

As if he felt her gaze on him, he glanced across and smiled — and that warmth spread right through her veins. She couldn't stop herself returning the smile. Oh lord, all this wedding-y stuff was turning her brain to mush.

With an effort of will she focused her attention back on the couple stammering their way through their vows. Bill's ears were scarlet, and Debbie was visibly trembling.

"Ah, bless," she whispered to Lisa. "They're both so shy, it's a wonder they ever managed to get together, let alone figure out getting married."

"Vicky gave them a bit of a nudge."

"A bit of a nudge? I'd have thought they'd need a couple of super-powered electro-magnets!"

Lisa covered her giggle with a discreet cough, her eyes dancing.

The sun was slowly sinking below the horizon as the formal part of the proceedings ended, the darkening sky streaked with gold and magenta, the sea sparkling with sequins — the perfect backdrop for the wedding photos.

Then Bill tucked Debbie's hand proudly into his arm and cleared his throat. "It's . . . um . . . Well, it's . . . um . . . time for champagne, and . . . um . . ."

Debbie smiled up at him, warm and encouraging.

He laughed. "Let's hit the food."

Everyone joined in the laughter, following as he and his new bride led the way into the conservatory. The DJ was playing classic old soul songs quietly through the speakers, and hotel staff in smart white jackets were circulating with trays of champagne.

Some of the younger children, their energy pent up for too long during the ceremony, were running around and playing chase, but no one minded. Ollie was holding little Kyra on his shoulder, and she was gazing around, wide-eyed, babbling softly to herself.

Queuing for the buffet, Cassie suddenly found herself hugged by a small blonde fairy in a yellow dress, who launched herself against her, throwing her arms around her waist.

"It's the tappoo lady!"

Cassie smiled down at her, feeling a warmth in her heart. "That's right."

"Yours is still there, but mine washed off when I went in the sea."

"Ah, yes — it would do that. But like I said, when you're grown up, you can have one that stays on, like mine."

The little girl pouted. "Everything is 'when you're grown up'," she protested.

"I know. It's a pain, isn't it? But think what fun you can have when the time comes, and you can have as many tattoos as you want."

Liam had strolled over to join them. "Oh, lord. If it's going to be tattoos, I'm glad I have plenty of time to get used to the idea!"

"By then the fashion might have passed, and you won't have to worry," Cassie assured him.

"I'm keeping my fingers crossed. Robyn, sweetie, what would you like to eat?"

The child's eyes were wide as she gazed at the spread on the long table. "Can I have some of those please, Daddy?" She pointed to the frittatas. "And those. And those."

"Of course. This is a buffet, which means you can choose whatever you want. But not too much," he added quickly as she began to pile up her plate. He smiled at Cassie. "She'd eat the lot, then be sick."

Robyn turned her angel face up to his. "I won't be sick, Daddy. I promise."

He laughed. "I hope not, sweetie. Especially in that pretty dress. You wouldn't want to spoil it."

"Oh . . ." She hesitated, drawing her hand back from the savoury kebabs.

"Good one," Cassie mouthed silently over the child's head.

But then Robyn spotted the pavlova. "And can I have some of that?" she pleaded.

"Later, when you've finished what's on your plate."

Her small face crinkled into a frown. "Can't I put this back?" She picked up one of the frittatas.

"No, sweetie." He stroked his hand over her hair. "That would be rude. Come and sit down now and eat your tea."

"Can Auntie Cassie sit with us?"

Cassie managed to keep her smile in place. She really couldn't refuse, but she knew the kind of interest it would generate. The downside of living in a small place like Sturcombe was that everyone thought they were entitled to know everyone else's business.

And ten years certainly wasn't long enough for old business to be forgotten.

They found a table in the corner. Liam set a cushion on Robyn's chair to lift her closer to the table, and tucked a napkin under her chin and on her lap. "You can eat with your fingers," he told her, much to her delight.

Cassie sat down opposite him. She could feel her pulse fluttering — ten years wasn't long enough for her to forget either. She just hoped he wouldn't notice the effect he had on her — this was supposed to be just a casual friendship. Anything else . . . No, she wouldn't even think about that.

The food was delicious. The hotel may not have been the smartest in the south west, but its kitchen had a deservedly high reputation. She bit into a mini sausage roll, made with flaky pastry so light it crumbled away from her lips.

Robyn giggled. "You're making a mess, Auntie Cassie. You should have a napkin too."

She laughed, brushing the crumbs from the tablecloth onto the side of her plate. "So I should." Debbie and Bill were chatting to Bill's parents, discreetly holding tight to each other's hands. "It's lovely to see those two together," she remarked. "They should have got together years ago — they seem made for each other."

Liam nodded. "He had a thing for her even when they were at school, but he was such a noodle he couldn't work up the nerve to tell her how he felt about her."

"So she ended up with that prat Alan Gowan instead. She's much better off now. And at least it gave her Amy."

She glanced around the conservatory. It was growing dark outside, lending the place a cosy atmosphere, lit by the fairy lights in the fig trees and palms.

"We used to come here sometimes for a treat when I was little — afternoon tea on the terrace, with scones and raspberry jam."

He laughed, pausing to help Robyn cut up a wedge of pizza. "You must have seen some interesting places these past ten years."

Cassie nodded. "Oh, yes — lots."

"What was your favourite?"

"That's difficult," she mused. "There were so many. But I think I'd put New Zealand at the top of the list. Especially the South Island. It's so beautiful, unspoiled, with all those fantastic mountains and rivers, and the most spectacular waterfalls. Have you seen *Lord of the Rings*?"

"Of course."

"Well, it's just as beautiful as it looks in the films."

He seemed genuinely interested, asking questions, his eyes warm. Or was he wondering if she thought it had been worth it, to walk away from him ten years ago? At least if there had been any bitterness, it seemed that time had healed.

Time, and Natalie — and the little blonde fairy in golden yellow, tucking enthusiastically into the contents of her plate.

* * *

Liam was aware of the covert interest that was being aroused by him sitting with Cassie. The gossips would be having a fine time. Well, let them. If he and Cassie were friends now, all these years later, it was no one's business but their own.

Sitting opposite her at the small table, he could take the time to study her without appearing to stare, could see the subtle changes the years had made. Structure had emerged from the softness of her teens — strong cheekbones, a smooth oval jaw.

She wore her hair loose — it used to be long, almost to her waist, but now it just brushed her shoulders. But it still gleamed like polished mahogany. And her eyes . . . It had been her eyes that had first caught his attention all those years ago — a deep forest green, swept by long dark silky lashes.

She was wearing a very pretty dress, pale lilac, in some silky fabric, with one of those high halter-type necklines that left her shoulders bare, showing off her tattoo and a slender figure that curved in all the right places. The skirt, he had already noticed, swung to just above her knees, flashing those long, elegant legs.

He couldn't deny that the echo of that old attraction was still there. Or maybe it was a new attraction to the woman she was now. A mature woman, comfortable in her own skin. A woman who enjoyed her friends without needing to compete with them.

Who had spared the dignity of an old man at the pool table. Who loved her dog, and had shared some of that love with Hobo. Who could give a little girl so much warmth and attention . . .

She was chatting with Robyn now, telling her about whale watching on the Southern Ocean.

"*Real* whales?" The little girl's eyes were wide. "Not just in a story book?"

"Yes, real whales. Some of them would swim right up alongside us — they were bigger than our boat."

"How big?"

"Oh, enormous. Some of them were as long as the ball-room there."

"No they weren't." Robyn giggled. "They couldn't be that big."

"Oh, they could. I've got some photographs." She pulled her phone out of her bag and opened the photo gallery. "See? That's one of the other boats that was with us."

Robyn gazed at it in open-mouthed awe. "Ohhh . . . ! Look, Daddy."

The boat looked like a fifty-foot cabin cruiser, the rail lined with tourists. Alongside it, almost half as long again, was the sleek curving back of a whale.

"Do they eat people?" Robyn enquired, a little thrill of dread in her voice.

"No. This is a blue whale. They eat krill."

The little girl frowned. "What's krill?"

"They're little tiny things that look like shrimps. The whales eat tons of them every day."

"Don't they eat them all up?"

"No. There's tons and tons more of them in the sea."

Liam watched the two of them, their heads close together, dark head and fair, as Cassie showed Robyn more pictures. What would persuade her to stay? Maybe take a little time to see if they could rekindle their old relationship? Would she even want that? Would he?

But caution warned him that the chances of that working out a second time were low. Sooner or later that old wanderlust would tug at her again, and she would be off.

And this time there was another factor in the equation — a very important one. Robyn. If he let his little daughter get close to her and then she left. That would be unforgivable.

"How many whales are there?" The child's curiosity was insatiable, but Cassie's patience seemed equal to it.

"We don't really know for sure," she explained. "The oceans are very, very big and it's hard to count them."

"Because they're in the water and they keep swimming around?"

"That's right. And they can dive very, very deep. Or sometimes they jump right up out of the water. I've seen them do that, but I've never managed to photograph one."

"Do they have babies?" was the next question.

"Yes, they do. They're called calves."

Robyn giggled. "Like the calves on Uncle Tom's farm!"

"Well, a lot bigger than that. The calves take about a year to come, and when they're born they're more than twenty feet long already."

"Oh . . . !" Robyn's blue eyes widened.

"And they grow very quickly. They stay with their mummies for about six months, but when they get to about fifty feet long they swim away. But they often stay together in families, at least for some of the time."

Robyn was scrolling eagerly through more photos, and came to some of elephants and giraffes. She'd only ever seen them on television, and was thrilled that Cassie had seen them in real life.

Liam laughed. "I can see she's going to want to follow in your footsteps when she gets older."

She slanted him a look of apology. "Oh, I'm sorry. I don't mean to encourage her to leave."

He shook his head. "No, it's fine. If that's what she wants, I wouldn't try to stop her."

As I didn't try to stop you. Though it was hard to let you go.

Maybe he should have guessed what she had been thinking back then. There had been clues, if he had been perceptive enough to see them. Her love of travel programmes on television, her eagerness to chat to anyone who came from another country.

And sometimes there had been a look in her eyes when she had stood at the edge of the sea, gazing out as if she could see far over the horizon to some distant land beyond. If he had ever mentioned it to her, she would just laugh it off, say she was just thinking about her next essay or what was for dinner. So he had never pursued it.

And now? Listening to her lively stories of her travels, he had little doubt that she would leave — probably sooner rather than later. And he would have to let her go again.

* * *

It was time for the speeches. The waiters had come round again to refill everyone's champagne glasses as the guests gathered around the buffet table which had now been cleared apart from the bowls of punch and the wedding cake.

As Debbie's dad had died when she was a baby, Cassie — like everyone else — had been wondering who would take his place. Kate was surely too shy to speak in front of everyone? There was a murmur of surprise when Vicky Marston stepped forward.

"I hope you won't mind this little break with tradition," she began, smiling. "I'll keep it short. When I used to come down here to Sturcombe when I was little, to stay with my Aunt Molly, Debbie was my best friend. We used to play together on the beach and build wonderful sandcastles. When I came back, I felt so lonely at first, but Debbie remembered me and it was as if I'd never been away — though these days she makes the most delicious cupcakes instead of sandcastles."

There was a small ripple of laughter and nods of agreement.

"So I'm so delighted to see my lovely friend so happy, marrying Bill at last. I'm sure he deserves her. And if he doesn't," she added sternly, "there's me and a large herd of black-and-white cows to sort him out."

More laughter.

"So, ladies and gentlemen, thank you all for coming. I give you the toast — Debbie and Bill."

"Debbie and Bill."

Then it was Bill's turn, though he was too shy to do more than mumble his thanks to everyone and smile down at Debbie as he raised his glass, which everyone accepted as his proposal of a toast.

It was left to Tom Cullen, as Best Man, to bring the jokes, with stories about how devoted Bill was to the cows, especially when they were pregnant. "I call it OCD — obsessive calving disorder."

Most of the stories involved copious amounts of cow dung, but these were country people and were used to that kind of thing.

"So Debbie, if he starts talking in his sleep about Betty or Clarissa, you'll know you have no need to worry. He won't be talking about a mistress — he'll be talking about a half-ton black-and-white prime Friesian cow."

That produced a round of laughter. Tom proposed the final toast, then it was time to cut the cake.

"It's so beautiful," Debbie sighed. "I can't bear to cut it."

"It'll be worth it when you taste it," Vicky insisted. "I got to scrape the mixing bowl."

"Greedy," Tom teased, giving her shoulders a squeeze.

There was that look again, slanting between them. Pure love. Cassie felt her heart skip, but she refused to let herself glance at Liam who was standing across to her left, his hand resting on his small daughter's curly blonde hair.

Struggling to cut the cake with both of them holding the knife reduced Debbie to giggles. They managed to get a slice onto a plate, and fed each other a bite with small silver dessert forks.

"Mmm, you're right." Debbie's eyes were dancing. "It's absolutely delicious. Do you think he'd give us the recipe?"

"Absolutely not." Vicky laughed. "He keeps it so secret, he bakes them at midnight on a full moon, with two Rottweilers guarding the kitchen."

"I don't blame him."

* * *

One of the waiters lifted the cake carefully onto a catering trolley and wheeled it off to the kitchen to be sliced. Liam smiled down at his little daughter as his mother came over. "Well now, time for you to be off home with Granny and Gramps."

"Oh, Daddeee . . ."

"Amy and Noah are coming with you for a sleepover," his mum reminded her.

"Oh, yes!" The child bounced with excitement, all objections instantly forgotten. "Night night, Daddy." She wrapped her arms around his neck and gave him a big kiss on the cheek, then did the same to Cassie. "Night night, Auntie Cassie!"

"Night night, sweetheart."

His mum slanted Liam a questioning glance, but he just smiled vaguely as Robyn ran off to fetch her friends.

"That'll be fun," Cassie murmured with a hint of dry humour. "I hope you're going to buy your mum a big bunch of flowers for dedication beyond the call of duty."

He laughed. "Of course."

With the children gone, the adults lingered a while over their champagne before drifting back into the ballroom for the evening. The room was subtly lit by the wall sconces, and the DJ was ready to start the music as the bride and groom reluctantly moved out into the middle of the dance floor for their first dance.

He glanced around for Cassie, but she was no longer by his side. He searched the room and saw she was over by the bar, chatting to her brother.

Before he could move towards her, his sister-in-law Julia came up behind him. "Ah, this is one of my favourite songs." She swayed as the strains of a beautiful old soul ballad swelled through the room.

"It's just unfortunate that Bill dances like one of his cows," Liam responded dryly.

"Debbie doesn't seem to mind — she's dancing on air."

"And she's pretty good at keeping her toes away from his size twelves."

The song ended to a soft ripple of applause, then several more couples moved to join them on the dance floor.

"Are you going to dance?" Liam asked.

Julia smiled. "If you're asking?"

In the past he'd always enjoyed dancing with Julia. She had a good sense of rhythm and moved easily, spinning out and back as they jived to a series of lively sixties hits. When at last the music changed to a slower number, Luke appeared at his shoulder.

"Do you mind giving me my wife back?"

"No way," Liam retorted. "We're running away together."

"Oh, fine." Luke shrugged his shoulders in casual dismissal. "You're welcome."

He pretended to turn away, but Julia caught him by the collar. "Hey, you don't get away that easy!" she protested.

"You're the one who's running off with my brother."

"Maybe next week."

The two of them moved into each other's arms as naturally as breathing, still laughing and teasing. Liam felt a twinge of envy as he watched them. That was the sort of relationship he had had with Natalie — the sort of relationship he wanted again. But he was beginning to doubt if he would ever find it.

* * *

Cassie was enjoying herself. She'd dragged her brother out for a dance, she'd danced with Ollie, she'd taken a turn round the floor with Tom Cullen's dad Jack. They'd amused themselves by trying to work out exactly how they were related to each other, with her sister being married to his nephew.

She'd even braved a turn with the bridegroom, but he'd been so shy he'd barely said a word, concentrating all his attention on moving his feet while not treading on her toes.

Liam had been dancing with Julia, his sister-in-law. The tall redhead was very striking, and they danced well together. Now she was dancing with her husband, and Liam had been sitting out for a while, chatting at the bar with his father.

Would he ask her to dance? The thought of it made her heart beat a little faster. To be in his arms again, after all these years . . .

"Hi." Tom Cullen appeared at her elbow. "How are you? I haven't had a chance for a proper chat to you since you got back."

She smiled up at him. "I'm great, thanks. And you're looking very well — impending matrimony to the contrary notwithstanding."

He laughed. "Ah, well. I hit the jackpot." He glanced across at Vicky, who was dancing with Bill's dad. And there it was again, that look in his eyes. Any woman would crawl over broken glass to have her man look at her like that.

"Just a few more weeks, isn't it?"

"That's right." He held out his hand. "Would you like to dance?"

"Love to."

Tom danced well, easy on the rhythm — there was no need to be careful of her toes. They chatted as they danced and he told her the amazing story of the auction of Vicky's portrait of her Aunt Molly.

"Wow! That must have been so exciting!"

"It was. I thought Vicky was going to faint when the final number came up."

"I'm not surprised."

Over his shoulder she could see Liam dancing with Lisa. Then he danced with Debbie, then young Bez, Bill's niece, who had been Debbie's chief bridesmaid. Was he ever going to ask her to dance?

Did she want him to?

It was eleven o'clock when the evening began to wind down. Debbie and Bill were getting ready to leave for their honeymoon. All the guests had gathered in the reception hall as they came down the stairs, having changed out of their wedding outfits. The waiters had brought round trays of champagne, and everyone raised a final toast to the happy couple, then followed them out to the front of the hotel.

The car that was to take them to the airport for their flight to Paris had been festooned with ribbons and balloons, with 'Just Married' written in shaving cream on the rear window. Before they could escape, they were showered with confetti. They laughed as they ducked into the car and were driven away to cheers and applause.

As the guests all drifted back into the ballroom she felt a light touch on the small of her back. Liam. "Dance?" he suggested.

"Sure." She managed a smile, hoping for a casual air. Just friends . . .

But now she was dancing in his arms. He had taken off his jacket, and she could feel the warmth of hard male muscle moving beneath her hand, stirring up old memories — and stirring a new awareness. An awareness that made her heart beat faster.

But did he feel the same? Okay, he had sat chatting with her — old friends, and mainly at Robyn's instigation. And he had asked her to dance — finally. And now he was holding her close in his arms . . .

It would be all too easy to read too much into it — both her own feelings and his. And that would be a mistake, could risk awkwardness on both sides. Better to just keep it cool.

She drew back a little and smiled up at him — the sort of smile she might have given Luke, or Tom Cullen. "Your parents are looking well."

His smile was equally neutral. "Yes, they are."

"And Julia seems very nice."

"She's a tyrant." The glint of amusement in his eyes completely belied his words. "She makes me do invoices."

Cassie laughed. "Oh, dear. Not your favourite pastime?"

"About on a par with anything the Spanish Inquisition could have dreamed up."

"And her little boy — Ben." *Think of something else to say — keep the conversation going.* "He seems very bright."

"He's as smart as a whip. Beats us all at Cluedo."

"Is he going to be a vet when he grows up, like the rest of you?"

"It's on his list." There was pride and affection in his voice. "Along with detective, train driver and spaceman."

"Well, if he's good at Cluedo, he'd probably make a good detective, anyway."

"Actually, he cheats," Liam confided with a laugh. "But none of us let on that we know."

The music changed to an upbeat number, and they moved apart, swinging into a lively jive. Their feet seemed to remember the moves from all the times they had danced together long ago, hitting the rhythm, twirling and spinning as if all the years between were forgotten.

At last the DJ spoke into his mic. "Okay, people. It's coming on for midnight — the witching hour. So here's your last dance. Hope you've all had a great time and get home safely. Goodnight."

It was a slow, sultry song of love and longing. Liam's arms were around her — she hadn't expected him to hold her so close. Closing her eyes, she let her head rest against his wide shoulder. She could feel the smooth power in his body as they moved to the music, the warmth of his breath stirring her hair.

It was as if she had been spun back through time, to that night when she was seventeen years old, the memory as vivid as if it had been only yesterday. How was she supposed to separate the 'then' from the 'now'?

Neither of them were the people they had been back then. They'd been little more than kids, everything had been brand new, exciting. Had it been love she had felt then, or nothing more than an adolescent crush?

And now? The attraction was strong. But was it no more than the echo of those old feelings, mixed up with a dollop of homesickness for Sturcombe — with a side-dish of sexual interest? She was too confused to work it out.

She didn't notice that the music had ended until the lights came up, stark and bright. It was as if a bubble had burst. She blinked, glancing around the ballroom with its dull beige walls and scuffed wooden floor, half-empty glasses on the tables along with the debris of the buffet.

Liam was still holding her hand. She had to escape before he read in her eyes the thoughts that had been running through her head. "Well, goodnight then." She forced a brittle smile. "See you around."

"Yes."

That was all he said. Had she hoped he would say more? Try to detain her? Of course not – why would he? They were supposed to be just friends. She drew back her hand and turned away, trying not to run.

* * *

Liam watched her go, cursing himself softly. He had wanted to say something, but he didn't know what. He had wanted

150

her to stay. Holding her in his arms, feeling the supple length of her body moving against his, breathing the subtle fragrance of her skin, had brought back so many memories.

His house was just a short walk away . . .

But that was impossible. Robyn and his mum and dad were there, with the other two kids having their sleepover. He couldn't just walk in with Cassie on his arm, and climb the stairs to his bedroom as if it was the most normal thing in the world.

Besides, he'd never been one for casual sex, and he was pretty sure Cassie wasn't either. And anyway, with her it could never be casual.

Maybe he could persuade her to stay. But for how long? Would he always be wondering when she would decide to leave again? He could survive a blow like that — he was a grown man. He knew how to keep things in perspective.

But Robyn . . . She had already grown fond of Cassie. If he let her get too attached to her and then she left, it would break her little heart.

No. He could indulge in the occasional fantasy, but he knew it was never going to translate into real life. Shaking his head, he strolled over to hook up his jacket from the chair where he had left it, and with a brief goodnight to the DJ and the hotel staff who were clearing up he headed for home, and his empty bed.

CHAPTER ELEVEN

With the bank holiday week over and the tourist season winding down, the town was much quieter than it had been for the past couple of months. Soon the locals would have it to themselves again.

The Smugglers was less crowded too. Cassie had come down with her brother and his latest girlfriend — another leggy blonde, Olivia Something-Something. She seemed nice — at least she didn't seem to be auditioning for *Footballers' Wives* like the last one. But if Paul was true to form, she'd be gone in a couple of weeks.

The jukebox was playing a twenty-year-old hit, and a group of elderly men were seated around a fiercely competitive game of dominoes at a corner table. There were a few people at the pool table, including Liam and his brother.

"Ah, here's the Queen of the Pool Table!" Luke declared as Cassie walked in. "Fancy trying your luck against someone who can actually play?"

Paul laughed in lazy amusement. "Want to put your money where your mouth is, big shot?" he challenged.

"You're on. Make it a bullseye?"

"Oh, thank you," Cassie murmured on a note of dry humour. "Pressure or what?"

"What's a bullseye?" Olivia enquired, arching one finely drawn eyebrow.

"Fifty quid," Paul explained.

"Oh." She smiled at Cassie. "You can really play pool?"

Cassie laughed. "Well, I hope so, or Paul's about to lose fifty quid."

"Best of three?" Luke suggested.

Paul grinned. "Sounds good to me."

Cassie rolled her eyes. "You have a lot of faith in me."

"I've seen you play, and I've seen him play. He's good, but he can be overconfident. You can take him."

"We'll see." She moved over to the rack to choose a cue.

Liam winked at her. "Go on, Cassie. Give him a good thrashing."

She returned an amused glance as she turned back to the table. "But he's your brother."

"That's why I want to see him beat. He took the piss out of me for a week when you beat me. Now I want revenge."

Oh, that smile . . . But it wouldn't be wise to read anything into it. Though she might occasionally catch a glint of something in those dark eyes, he hadn't shown any sign of wanting to be more than friends.

"I'll do my best," she responded coolly.

Her best wasn't good enough for the first game. Luke broke, then potted three. She sank two, but then an awkward angle on the next ball left her without a clear shot. Luke potted another three with ease, but the fourth shivered on the edge of the pocket, to moans from his supporters and laughter from hers.

But she couldn't capitalise on the opening. She potted two more, but the white ball wasn't running for her and stopped obstinately short of where she needed it to be. Luke grinned as he returned to the table, dropped his seventh ball and moved smoothly onto the black.

"That's how you do it," he teased, grinning.

"Two out of three, remember?" Paul had brought her drink over and she took a sip. Yes, she could see Paul's point — Luke could be overconfident.

They had gathered quite an audience, some rooting for her, others for Luke. Side bets were being made — not just on who would win, but whether either of them could run out from the break, whether there'd be a foul or a snooker.

Cassie's luck changed for the second game. She took the break and sank five balls on her first run, then when Luke had sunk three, she returned to the table and cleared the rest. As the black rolled neatly into the pocket a cheer went up.

"Well done!" Luke gave her a high five, and glanced over at Paul. "Double or nothing?" he suggested.

Paul's grin widened. "You're on. Hope you're good for the cash."

"You're the one who needs to worry about that."

The good-natured banter continued as Cassie chalked her cue. She was trying not to glance across the table at Liam. She needed to focus on the game, not let herself be distracted by that beguiling smile.

Luke took the break and sank two balls, but as he lined up for the third Cassie could see the overconfidence. He had chosen a difficult shot over an easy one. If he sunk it and the white ball ran where he wanted it, he would have her snookered.

But it didn't — it ran into the pocket.

"Foul!"

And suddenly it was getting intense. Cassie now had two shots, and she could place the white ball wherever it gave her the best advantage. Breathing slowly to steady her aim, she chose her angle and sank her ball neatly. So she still had two shots.

She made the most of them. She only had one ball left by the time Luke got back on the table. He sank three, but the white ran back further than he wanted, so he couldn't get a good angle on the next shot and it just bounced off the cushion.

One to go, and the black. Cassie let her gaze flicker briefly towards Liam. He smiled and gave her a thumbs up. *Focus* . . . The white ran true and straight, her yellow ball obligingly dropped into the pocket, and the black was at her mercy.

Don't mess this up now.

"Go, Cassie!"

She chalked her cue again, then closed her eyes briefly, visualising the shot. Sometimes those easy ones were the ones that would catch you out. Finally, she bent over the table, lined up her cue and . . . *perfect!*

She straightened, drawing in a long slow breath of relief. Her supporters were cheering, bets were being settled, and several people were offering to buy her drinks. Now she finally permitted herself to glance towards Liam.

Oh, that smile . . .

The jukebox clicked and a new song came on. Her heartbeat skipped as the music started. It was one they had danced to last night — a soft romantic ballad that was being played on the radio all the time. Surely Liam hadn't put it on? *No . . . foolish.* Don't start thinking like that.

But the memory of dancing in his arms was so vivid that she could almost feel the warmth of his body against hers, the smooth movement of his muscles as they had moved to the music. For a moment she felt light-headed.

There was a small disturbance at the back of the crowd around the table as a tall young woman with a cascade of gleaming copper-gold hair eased through. She came up behind Liam and wrapped her arms around his waist. "Surprise!"

Cassie's breath caught in her throat. She was stunning — all flawless cheekbones and sun-tinted skin, a perfect mouth and endless legs in slim-fitting designer jeans. His girlfriend? Whom no one had bothered to mention to her.

But then why would they? She'd been very careful to show no particular interest in him.

Where had she been these past few weeks? Off on some glamorous modelling contract in Paris or Peru? Well, now she was back — and reclaiming him very publicly.

* * *

"Surprise!"

Liam felt a sharp shock. Annabel. "Hello." He managed to fix a smile in place as he turned. "What are you doing here? I thought you were in Paris."

He was aware that they had become the centre of attention, that Cassie had noticed her. Slipping an arm around her waist, he drew her discreetly away from the crowd around the pool table and over to the bar.

"Milan. I was. But the South Africa shoot was cancelled at the last minute, so I have a whole week off. Luxury!" Those sapphire-blue eyes were dancing. "So I thought I'd come down and surprise you. I've got a room in that nice hotel up the road, and your dad told me you'd be down here, so . . . here I am! Say you're pleased."

He managed another smile, hoping it was convincing. "Of course I'm pleased."

Dammit, this was uncomfortable. It was clear that Annabel had taken their brief encounter at the Gillard's rather more seriously than he had intended. In truth, he had barely thought about her over the past week.

Okay, don't make a big thing of it. She was only here for a few days. And maybe in that time he'd find that missing spark. After all, she was very beautiful, with a sweet personality. And if he didn't find the spark . . . well, he'd try to end it as gently as possible.

"What would you like to drink?"

* * *

Damn. Cassie forced herself to stop watching the couple on the other side of the room. The girl was gorgeous — she wouldn't be able to compete, even if she wanted to. How long had they been together?

No wonder he had seemed to be keeping a distance between them. She could only be thankful that she hadn't made a fool of herself by letting him know how she felt about him.

"What's up?"

"Uh?" She turned to her brother.

"You're looking like the cat pissed in your shoe."

"We don't have a cat."

"Next door's cat?"

They both laughed.

She was lucky to have such a lovely family, she reflected wistfully. She would really miss them when she left. When she left? The scale had tipped back the other way. New Zealand had its definite advantages — and one of them was that Liam Ellis wasn't there.

* * *

"Hiya." Lisa strolled into the kitchen as Cassie was finishing a late breakfast, having already been for her regular early morning swim. "Where's Mum?"

"Gone into Exeter to look for an outfit for Vicky's wedding."

"Oh. I was going to ask if she could mind Kyra for a bit. I'm just going down to the hotel to discuss the arrangements for the wedding with Vicky."

Cassie laughed, pausing to spread a layer of butter and marmalade on her toast. "I thought you were supposed to be on maternity leave?"

"I am. But I can't leave it to her to sort out her own wedding, and Mike would get in a right mither. Could you . . . ?"

"Of course. I'll come down with you, though. I don't have my full nappy-changing licence yet. Pour yourself a coffee — it's fresh in the machine. How's my little bubs?" She tickled the baby's tiny feet. "Hey, she smiled at me!"

"Wind."

"Huh!"

157

Fifteen minutes later they set off down the hill, the baby asleep in her buggy. It was a pleasant stroll in the September sunshine. It was still warm, but there weren't as many people on the beach as there had been a week ago — just a few pensioners and families with children not yet old enough to have started school.

"When are you going back to work?" Cassie asked.

"Probably in December. We get a surge in bookings around Christmas for the Tinsel and Turkey breaks."

Cassie laughed. "Tinsel and Turkey?"

"Uh-huh. We get coach parties from all over — they come down for three- or four-day breaks. Mostly older people, but they're loads of fun. And it gives the bottom line a big boost — without them we'd be pretty dead for most of the winter months. Not so many people want to go on the beach or play golf when it's freezing cold and raining."

"Will Mum look after Kyra?"

Lisa nodded. "I wondered if she'd want to go back to work herself, but she said no. It's been five years since she took early retirement to look after Nanna and Noah, and she's looking forward to having Kyra too. She's enjoying being at home with her baking and her knitting."

"I expect it'll be much easier on her without Nanna," Cassie mused.

"Much!" Lisa laughed. "She deserves the chance to take it easy. She's worked hard for years."

Cassie nodded in agreement. "She certainly has. I can think of few things I'd less rather do than wrangle a hundred or so primary school kids, all screaming and racing around like banshees."

"I'm with you there!"

They had reached the hotel and climbed the steps to the front entrance. The door hushed quietly open and they stepped into the reception hall.

Cassie hadn't paid much attention to her surroundings last weekend, but she noticed now that the place was looking rather shabbier than she remembered from ten years ago.

The wooden floor was slightly scuffed, and the carpet in the lounge area was showing signs of wear. But the view of the bay from the wide windows was stunning.

Vicky was at the reception desk, chatting to Penny, the young receptionist. "Hi." She greeted them with a happy smile. "I'll be right with you. Would you like a coffee?"

"I'll get it," Penny offered.

"Thanks."

The three women settled themselves at a table out on the terrace in the sunshine. Lisa lifted baby Kyra out of her buggy onto her lap, where she lay gurgling and kicking her chubby little legs.

"So, less than two weeks to go." Lisa smiled across the table.

"Eleven days." Excitement bubbled in Vicky's voice. "I think I'm going crazy!"

"It's a nice crazy," Lisa assured her. "The planning's all part of the fun."

"Debbie's wedding was lovely. She really deserved to have a good day."

"Have you picked up your dress?" Lisa asked.

"I picked it up yesterday. My sister's chosen hers herself. It's actually very pretty, and she went with the colour we agreed." She rolled her eyes at Cassie. "She can be a bit of a nightmare at times."

"I know how it is." Cassie sighed heavily, shaking her head. "Sisters!"

"Hey!" Lisa protested, laughing.

Penny brought their coffees with a plate of chocolate biscuits. "Lovely — thanks." Lisa reached for a biscuit. "Right, to business." She pulled a notebook out of her bag. "Let's start with flowers. Roses, lilies and baby's breath, right?"

"That's right. Lots and lots of them."

"We've got them on order from the florists. We'll need to bring up more vases from the storeroom." She noted that

159

down. "We'll put them all round the ballroom — various pedestal heights. In Reception too."

"That sounds great."

Kyra had started to grizzle. "Here." Cassie reached for her. "I'll take her for a stroll round the garden."

"Thanks."

Lisa passed the baby over and Cassie settled her into the buggy, then wheeled her across the terrace to the garden. It was a very popular feature of the hotel — a lush sub-tropical paradise wrapped around three sides of the building and overlooking the bay.

Gravel paths and shallow steps wound around beds planted with tree ferns and Chinese fan palms, fiery red ginger, fragrant gold and white frangipani.

She recognised the vibrant spiky leaves of New Zealand cordyline, the scarlet puffs of pohutukawa, the tall stems of pretty agapanthus. Butterflies flashed their bright wings over the flowers, and bumblebees hummed lazily as they searched for nectar.

Kyra liked being wheeled. She had stopped grizzling and was waving her small fists in the air, gurgling happily as she found her own toes. "What a clever girl you are," Cassie purred to her. "Lots of lovely pink toesies."

She turned a corner and stopped dead. Liam's girlfriend.

"Hello." The woman's smile was warm and friendly, her eyes the sapphire blue of the sea on a sunny day. Her hair gleamed like burnished copper, caught up in a stylish messy bun on top of her head, skinny designer jeans flattered endless legs. Her cheekbones could slice through steel.

"Oh, hi." Cassie instantly felt as if she'd been hit with the ugly stick.

"Oh, what a gorgeous baby. What's her name?"

"Kyra."

"Ah, that's a pretty name. You're a little cutie, aren't you?" She leaned over gracefully to tickle the tot's foot. "She's your daughter?"

160

"My niece."

"Ah. I saw you in the pub last night, didn't I? You were playing pool. Liam said you've beaten all the boys." She laughed, a low musical laugh. "Good for you."

Cassie managed a smile. "Thank you."

"I'm Annabel, by the way."

"Cassie."

"Yes, I know. Liam told me."

"Oh . . ."

"It's really beautiful here." She glanced out over the bay. "You're so lucky to live here."

"Yes." *Oh, come on. You can do better than that.* "Have you known Liam long?"

"Not very long. We met at a fundraiser for the Horse Rescue Society." Her eyes were bright. "I suppose you must know him quite well. He's such a lovely man — so different from most of the men I know. They're all over you like a rash, but Liam's a real gentleman, you know what I mean?"

"Yes, I know." *Oh lord, she had to escape.* "Well . . . um . . . it's nice to have met you. I'd better be getting this little one back to her mum."

"Of course. Goodbye. See you around."

"Yes . . . Goodbye."

Trying not to look as if she was running away she trundled the buggy around the corner of the path and circled back up to the terrace.

Lisa and Vicky still had their heads together over wedding plans. "Hi." Cassie parked the buggy next to the table. "She's been as good as gold. Another coffee, anyone?"

Vicky glanced up with a smile. "Yes, please."

"Right." Cassie slipped away to the bar in the lounge.

So that was Liam's girlfriend. Dammit, she seemed really nice, as well as being stunningly beautiful. It would have been so much easier if she'd been a bitch . . .

No it wouldn't. She'd hate to think of Liam being with a woman who was horrible. And it wouldn't be very nice for little Robyn, either.

Oh well, she'd known all along that there was no future for her with him anyway, so there was no point letting herself be bothered about it. Schooling herself to put on a smiling face, she set the coffee mugs down on a tray and carried it out to the terrace.

CHAPTER TWELVE

What was a black Lexus doing parked outside the house, gleaming in the early afternoon sunshine? Cassie glanced at the rental company sticker in the rear window. Of course, it might not be anyone visiting them — there were quite a few cars parked on Cliff Road.

"Hi, Mum — I'm home," she called as she opened the front door.

"Ah, here she is." Her mother appeared in the doorway of the sitting room, a big smile on her face. "You've got a visitor, love. All the way from Australia."

"What . . . ?" Startled, Cassie dumped her shopping bag in the hall and dodged past her mother as six feet five of gorgeous blond Australian surfer dude rose from the sofa and held out his arms.

"Hey, babe!"

"Dougie!" She crossed the room straight into a big Dougie bear hug. "What are you doing here?"

"I came to see you, babe."

"Oh yes?" She laughed up at him. "You flew ten thousand miles just to see me?"

"Of course. Well, no," he confessed, his sunny blue eyes smiling. "I had some business in London. Then I thought, hey, why not pop down and see Cass while I'm here?"

"*Pop* down? It's almost two hundred and fifty miles."

"Two hundred and fifty miles?" His curly blond fringe flopped as he shook his head. "That's no distance."

"Dougie, you're a walking cliché. Okay, it's nothing for you to drive two hundred and fifty miles to get a pint of milk, but people who aren't from Queensland regard it as a *long* way."

"It's a long way on your piddling little English roads, all bendy twisty," he conceded. "But it only took around four hours."

"Bendy twisty? Didn't you use the motorway?"

"Is that what you call it? Looked like a red-belly on the satnav."

Cassie rolled her eyes. "Why didn't you let me know you were coming?"

"That would have ruined the surprise."

"I might not have been here," she pointed out dryly.

"Yeah, well . . ." He shrugged those wide, handsome shoulders. "I'd just have had to hang around." He squeezed her hand. "I was sorry about your gran, by the way."

Her mouth quirked into a wry smile. "Thanks."

Her mother bustled in with a tray holding two mugs of coffee and a plate of bacon sandwiches. "Here you go." She set the tray down on the table beside Dougie. "If you've eaten nothing but aeroplane food for the past twenty-four hours, you must be starving."

"Actually, it's usually pretty good food in first class," Cassie remarked dryly.

Dougie just laughed. Back in Australia he usually flew his own plane, but when he flew commercial he always took the best option.

"Where are you staying?" she asked.

"I thought I'd get a room down at that little hotel along the beach there. Looks like a dinky little place — cosy."

"Oh, there's no need for that," Cassie's mum insisted. "You can have Paul's room."

His eyes lit up, though he had the decency to glance at Cassie to make sure she wasn't horrified by the idea. "Well, if it's no bother, Mrs Channing — that's very kind of you."

"Of course it's no bother. And call me Helen."

"Well, good on ya, Helen. Bonzer!" He threw up his hand to give her a high five.

"If he's stopping for dinner you'd better stick a whole side of beef in the oven," Cassie warned with a quirk of dry humour. "He can eat enough for three, even after a plate of bacon sandwiches."

"Well, he's a big lad."

Dougie laughed with the easy good humour of one on whom nature had showered every blessing.

Cassie sipped her coffee. "Anyway, back to why you're here. You don't seriously expect me to believe you drove two hundred and fifty miles just for the pleasure of my smile."

His gaze was wide-eyed and innocent. "Why wouldn't I? Okay, okay, there is something," he conceded with a mischievous grin that could melt a thousand female hearts — including, briefly, her own. "But it's a good something, right? I gotta go to one of these fancy black-tie shindigs you Poms are so fond of, but it's a plus-one and I don't have a plus-one."

"Dougie, you could walk down the street and have a hundred girls falling over themselves to be your plus-one in less than five minutes."

"Oh, Cass, come on," he protested. "I'm not that bad."

"No — you're that good. So what is this do?"

"It's for the kiddies hospital — Great . . . Great Ormorond Street?"

"Great Ormond Street. How come you've got an invite there?"

"One of the guys I came over to meet with is one of the sponsors, so I need to show my best face. That's why I need you. I don't know anyone else in Pommyland, and I can

165

hardly rock up at some fancy do with some Sheila I just pulled off the street, now can I?"

Cassie smiled, shaking her head. "Fair enough. Okay, I'll be your plus-one. When is it?"

"Saturday. I thought in the meantime you could show me round town a bit. You know, do the tourist thing. That is, if you haven't got other stuff to do?"

"No, I don't really." And it would be good to get away for a while, so she wouldn't have to risk seeing Liam with Annabel — at least until she had got used to the idea. "Just one thing." She held up a hand in stipulation. "Separate rooms, okay? I'm not sleeping with you."

"Cass! As if."

"Quite. Well, if we're clear on that, I'll be your tour guide. Though to be honest, I'm really not familiar with most with the touristy places in England."

"That's okay, we can explore together. Why don't we start right here? This looks like a right pretty little place."

"There's not much of it. You can see most of it from our front step."

"That's okay. Looks like a decent beach you've got — let's go for a swim."

* * *

"Come on then, kiddo. Have you had a nice time playing with Amy?"

"It was really *really* good. We watched *Frozen* and we had pink cupcakes."

Kate laughed apologetically. "They were hungry when they got in from school. I hope they don't spoil her tea."

"I doubt it." Liam smiled fondly down at his little daughter. "She seems to have a bottomless tummy. Say goodbye and thank you to Auntie Kate."

The child ran over and threw her arms round Kate's waist. "Goodbye, Auntie Kate. Thank you — *espeshly* for the cupcakes."

166

"Goodbye, cherub. Honestly, Liam, it's a delight having her. She's so polite and well-behaved — you're doing a great job with her."

"Thanks." That felt good, though if he was honest, a large part of bringing up his daughter fell to his mother and his sister-in-law. "Have you heard from Debbie?"

Kate smiled. "She rang me when they got to the hotel. She's over the moon. They have a fabulous room with a view of the Eiffel Tower. I'm so glad the money from that sketch of my mum meant I could give my girl the send-off she deserved. And I got a lovely big freezer too!"

"Good. You deserve it, both of you." He took Robyn's hand. "Come on then, let's get you home and have some tea."

"Can I have scones?"

"On top of cupcakes?"

"Just one?"

He couldn't help laughing. "That child could wheedle for England! Let's wait and see what's for tea before we settle on scones, eh? There could be apple pie."

"Oooh, yes!"

"No promises, mind. Anyway, cheerio Kate." He leaned in and kissed her cheek. "Bye-bye, Amy."

A shy little smile. "Bye-bye, Uncle Liam."

The late afternoon sun was shimmering on the sea. A couple of white-sailed yachts were skimming across the bay, and further out towards the horizon a large container ship was waiting to get into Plymouth Harbour.

"Can we walk home along the beach, Daddy?"

"If you like."

Holding his hand, Robyn skipped along at his side as they crossed the road and walked along to the steps leading down to the beach. There weren't many people about — a few packing up deckchairs and picnic blankets to go home for tea, a couple of dog walkers with boisterous mutts racing after balls and frisbees.

"There's Auntie Cassie!" Robyn bounced up and down, waving excitedly.

Yes, there was Cassie, wading up out of the sea like Venus reborn in her bright orange swimsuit. With Adonis beside her — tall, tanned, and built like some kind of Greek god. If Adonis ever wore lime-green budgie smugglers.

She saw them and waved back. Liam set his jaw and lifted his hand briefly, then tugged at a reluctant Robyn. "Come on, poppet. Grandma will have your tea ready."

Fortunately, the child didn't argue, though he realised a moment later that he was walking so fast that she was struggling to keep up with him.

* * *

"I love this pub. Look at those beams on the ceiling. I bet they're real. in most pubs these days they're just fake."

Liam managed a smile, though the minute he'd opened the door he wished he had taken Annabel for a drink in the hotel after their dinner date, instead of coming down to the Smugglers.

He should have guessed they'd be there. They were gathered round the pool table — Paul Channing with his latest girlfriend, Ollie and Lisa Cullen, and Cassie with the Greek god.

Fortunately, he wasn't in his budgie smugglers. He was wearing grey jeans and a sleeveless white T-shirt that showed off his wide shoulders, and now that his hair was dry it was a gleaming gold, flopping over his forehead.

He was laughing, showing a row of even white teeth. His laughter and his voice were loud, booming over the music from the jukebox, drawing the attention of everyone in the room, but the beaming smile on his handsome face earned him a friendly reception.

"Who's he?" Annabel asked, clearly impressed.

Liam shrugged. "I don't know. A friend of Cassie's I suppose."

Who was he? The accent — and those budgie smugglers — suggested Australian. And he'd come all this way to see her — that must mean it was pretty serious. So she'd probably be going back with him. Maybe she wouldn't even stay for Tom and Vicky's wedding.

And he'd watch her go, knowing that it had been inevitable that it would end like that.

The place wasn't so busy now that the high season was over so Liam had an unobstructed view as the guy dropped an arm casually around Cassie's shoulders.

"And she wins again! Any more of you Pommies up for a little bet on the next game?"

"If you're going to try to con us into betting against Cassie, forget it," Ollie Cullen asserted on a note of dry humour. "We've seen how lethal she can be with a pool cue."

A loud guffaw. "Too right, cobber. You don't play my girl unless you want your balls handed to you on a plate."

Liam forced his mind away from the image of Cassie and the guy on the beach, making the effort to tune in to Annabel's conversation. She was telling him a very funny story about how she had fallen into a swimming pool on a photo shoot, in full evening dress, complete with diamonds.

"The wardrobe mistress was almost in tears, but the photographer thought it was hilarious. He got a load of shots of me, soaking wet, my hair all in rat's tails. And would you believe it, that was the one the magazine published!"

He laughed. Over by the pool table, the Aussie guy was telling his own funny story.

"So I was surfing off South Straddie. You can get some real awesome breaks up there — four, five metres and more. I'm coming down the barrel when I completely mullered out. So I come up, spluttering my guts up, and I can feel something tugging at my swimmers, trying to tug them off. I thought my luck was in, but when I look round it's only a chuffing dolphin!"

"What's the biggest wave you've ever surfed?" someone asked amid the laughter.

He grinned broadly. "Eighteen metres."

"*What*? But that's . . . damned nearly sixty feet."

"Sure is. Greatest ride of my life. And it wasn't even in Oz — it was right here in Europe. Portugal — Nazaré, not too far from Lisbon. There's a kind of off-shore gorge running out to sea. When the Atlantic swell hits it, it builds up to colossal heights. In the winter you can get a surf of thirty metres."

"Surely no one's ever ridden a wave that big?"

He laughed, loud and cheerful. "Not yet, mate — the biggest one anyone's taken would be around twenty-four, twenty-five. But you can bet your bottom dollar someone will. Oh boy, what wouldn't I give to catch one like that."

He was like a giant Labrador puppy, boisterous and happy and keen that everyone else should be happy. Cassie looked happy too, her face lit up with laughter.

Liam took a long swallow of his beer. He should be happy for her. Well, at least he would try. If this was what she wanted — this rumbunctious, roistering Aussie . . .

Meanwhile, he had to decide what to do about Annabel. It had been a pleasant evening. She was easy to talk to, and certainly easy on the eye. But . . . *pleasant*? That wasn't nearly enough.

Well, she'd be leaving in a couple of days, off on another glamorous photoshoot in Fiji. Although from what she'd told him, photoshoots usually weren't all that glamorous, even in exotic locations.

Nevertheless, she'd be leaving. He'd tell her before she left, explain . . . Oh lord, not that trite 'It isn't you, it's me'. He'd have to find better words than that.

Over by the pool table Cassie was laughing, but he wouldn't let himself even glance that way. He drained his beer and smiled across the table at Annabel. "Shall we go?"

* * *

They left at eight o'clock the following morning. Dougie had always had the annoying ability to bounce out of bed like a

March hare, however much he had drunk the night before. And he had drunk twice as much beer as everyone else, while complaining cheerfully that it tasted like warm piss.

They drove up to the top of Cliff Road and round the roundabout onto Haytor Avenue, then onto the main road, leaving Sturcombe behind. Maybe it would be better if she didn't come back, Cassie reflected. She could just fly off with Dougie — back to his water-sports resort on New Zealand's stunningly beautiful South Island.

Fly back to New Zealand, and leave Liam to Annabel.

Would she make him happy? She hoped so. Though . . . somehow she couldn't see it. Annabel didn't seem the type to settle down in a sleepy South Devon seaside town.

Sooner or later she'd probably leave him — as she herself had done. She had never stopped feeling guilty about that — she'd hate to see it happen to him again.

But maybe he just wanted a casual relationship, casual sex. Though she couldn't quite imagine that of him. But then he was a man, after all — a very physical one.

She could still vividly remember the nights they had spent together in that hidden sandy cove when she was eighteen. They weren't the kind of nights you would ever forget.

Anyway, it was none of her business now. All that was long past. Sitting back in the comfortable leather seat of the Lexus, she watched the rolling green Devon countryside slide by.

Dougie had put on some Aussie hard-rock band she'd never heard of, and she tapped along with the driving rhythm on her knee, letting her mind empty of all thoughts and memories.

* * *

Liam sighed with relief as he pulled the Land Rover into the front yard. It had been a long night and a long day, with three tricky births, but now three pretty foals were beginning to find their feet and three happy mares were recovering well from their efforts.

His dad came out of the kitchen as he parked the car beside the garages. "How'd it go, son?"

"Touch and go at times, but we got there. Three safe arrivals."

"Good. You've got a visitor."

Liam's heart thumped. *Cassie?*

"Name of Annabel." His dad grinned. "Where did you find a thoroughbred like that?"

"Oh . . ." He managed a smile. "She's Caro Gillard's niece."

He'd been supposed to take her out to dinner again, but he'd had to ring her to cancel when he'd got the second emergency call to a farm up near Bodmin. By the time the third one had come in, he'd known he would be very late home.

He turned as he heard her voice at the door. "Liam! Heavens, you have had a long day, you poor thing. Your mum said you got called out at one o'clock this morning."

"That's right." He smiled wryly. "I'm sorry about dinner."

"Oh, don't worry about that." She came across the yard, wobbling slightly in her high heels on the cobbles. As she came closer she caught a whiff, and wrinkled her pretty nose. "Oh, wow. You smell awful."

"Sorry." He laughed. "I've spent most of the day up to my elbows in mares' backsides."

"Eeek!"

"It's my job. Look, I'm starving. If you don't mind waiting for about twenty minutes, I'll change out of these things and have a shower, then we could pop over to the hotel and I can get something to eat."

"Okay." A flash of that pretty smile. "I'll meet you over there."

He leaned forward carefully and brushed a kiss over her lips, then strolled round to the back door into the mud room, pausing to hose down his rubber boots at the tap.

He slid them off and carried them into the mud room to dry, then stripped off his shirt and jeans and dropped them

172

into the big white butler's sink, dousing them with cold water to wash off the worst of the muck before putting them in the washing machine.

He was cold, tired and hungry, but the hot shower went a long way to reviving him. He was used to long days, often with no more than a sandwich or a packet of crisps to eat.

It was his life, and he loved it. Especially days like today — the joy of seeing a new-born foal struggling to its feet and tottering over to take its first milk from its mother.

Stepping out of the shower he scrubbed himself briskly dry, then pulled on a fresh pair of jeans and a T-shirt from the pile beside the tumble dryer, laced up a clean pair of trainers, and stuck his head round the sitting room door to say hi to his mum.

"Did Robyn go down all right?"

"She was as good as gold. I showed her the photos of the new foals. She wants to know their names."

"I'll tell her in the morning."

She nodded. "Do you want something to eat?"

"No, thanks. I'm just going over to the hotel — I'll get something there. I . . . need to talk to Annabel."

"Okay, my luvver." His mother's voice conveyed nothing of what she was thinking, but he could guess. She was always ten jumps ahead of him. "Don't be long. You hardly had any sleep last night."

"No. We're just going to have a quick drink. See you later."

It was a pleasant evening, the warmth of the day lingering on the soft breeze blowing in from the sea. The moon was waning, a silver crescent lazing back against the inky sky amid a million stars. A perfect romantic evening.

But it wasn't romance that he had on his mind. He couldn't let this go on any longer. It wasn't fair to Annabel just to let it drift until she left for her next photoshoot.

She was leaning on the reception desk chatting to Pete, the night manager, as he walked through the front doors. She glanced up with a warm smile. "Hi. I asked the kitchen to send something through for you."

"Great — thank you. Coffee?"

"I'll have a white wine please."

As usual at this time of the evening the lounge was empty. They settled at a table in the corner and Pete brought their drinks over, and a few minutes later the young sous-chef came in with a tray. To Liam's amusement he almost fell over his own feet as he gazed in open adoration at Annabel.

She smiled up at him warmly. "Thank you."

He burbled something incoherent, blushing to the roots of his hair, and stumbled away.

"You've made a conquest," Liam remarked on a note of light humour.

She laughed, making a depreciating gesture.

He took the lid off his plate — cold beef slices, crispy golden chips, and a couple of grilled mushrooms. "Perfect." He picked up his knife and fork, and tucked in hungrily.

Annabel sipped her wine. "Your mum showed me the photos you sent. Such sweet little foals."

"They are." He grinned. "Makes it all worthwhile."

"What are their names?"

"The little roan with the white blaze will be Chester. The other two don't have names yet."

"Chester — that's a nice name."

He ate in silence for a while — you really couldn't have a serious conversation while you were eating chips. At last he set the plate aside and picked up his coffee, taking a moment to gather his thoughts.

"Annabel, look . . . I'm sorry, but . . . this just isn't working — you and me."

"I know."

He glanced across the table at her. "You know?"

She smiled a little crookedly. "I think I knew from the start that it wasn't going to go anywhere. We aren't right for each other — we have absolutely nothing in common."

Relief flooded through him — and gratitude that she was making it so easy. "I'm sorry."

She shook her head. "Don't be. It's nobody's fault. These things either work or they don't. You can't force it. It was probably silly of me to try to push it along by coming down here."

"No, it was . . . I've enjoyed your company."

"But nothing more. It's okay," she assured him. "I could see it in your eyes from the start. Or rather, I couldn't. I know how a man looks at me when he's hooked, and you've never looked at me like that."

"I should have." He smiled. "You're very beautiful."

"I know." She laughed dryly. "Good for me. I get paid a great deal of money to be beautiful."

"You're also a very nice person."

"So are you." Her eyes were warm. "You've tried very hard to pretend that you were feeling something when you weren't, just to make me feel okay. Thank you for that — even though it really wasn't necessary." She took another sip of her wine. "My agency rang this afternoon. They've lined me up a shoot in Edinburgh on Friday. I'm leaving tomorrow morning."

"Oh. I . . . don't really know what to say."

"You don't need to say anything, except goodbye." She put down her empty wine glass and rose to her feet. "I hope you'll find someone who is right for you – you really deserve to be happy." She leaned over and kissed him briefly on the lips. "Goodnight – and goodbye."

"Goodbye."

He watched her walk away, then leaned back in his chair, closing his eyes. So that was that. It had been a mistake to let himself get tangled up with her in the first place.

Finishing his coffee, he rose to his feet and strolled across the reception hall. Pete was at the desk, working through the night audit, so he stopped to say goodnight.

"So she's leaving then, your friend?" Pete was an inveterate gossip.

"That's right. She was only here for a few days. She's got a photoshoot in Edinburgh."

"Ah. Pretty girl."

"Yes." Liam smiled. "Very pretty."

"Young Cassie's left, too — with that Australian chappie. Big lad, blond hair. Name of Douglas Lee Campbell the Third. Done well for herself there. Billionaire, he is. Owns a whole string of water-sports resorts and things down Australia and New Zealand. Went off this morning, early, in that fancy car of his. Don't suppose we'll be seeing her back here now."

"No . . . I don't suppose we will. 'Night, Pete."

He thrust his hands in his pockets and strolled out into the night. So Cassie had gone — as he'd known she would. It was probably just as well that she had left — before Robyn got too close to her.

Well, at least he was sure of one thing now. He wasn't going to let himself get involved with any other women, not for a long time. From now on it would just be him and Robyn, and his family. That was enough.

He pulled his phone from his pocket and found the app for the dating site he had used, and scrubbed it. There — gone.

CHAPTER THIRTEEN

Cassie stood on the balcony of their suite, gazing out over the jumbled rooftops of London. Though it was almost one o'clock in the morning it wasn't quiet. The noise of traffic drifted up from the streets below — the heavy grind of a refuse truck clearing the black rubbish bags from the shop door-ways, occasional bursts of voices and laughter from late-night revellers.

They had reached London in record time. Cassie could only hope that if they got stopped for speeding, Dougie would be able to use his Aussie charm to wheedle his way out of a ticket.

The London traffic didn't faze him at all — he just ploughed his way through, though fortunately consenting to stop for traffic lights.

She might have guessed that he would book a suite at one of London's most exclusive hotels, all Art Deco and immac-ulate staff. She had barely had time to dump her bag when he had dragged her out to grab a bite to eat then called up an Uber to take them to the Tower of London.

He'd been fascinated by everything, listening avidly to the yeoman who conducted their tour with tales of imprisonments and executions, gawping at the Crown Jewels, admiring the sleek, glossy ravens. And, of course, his favourite was the armoury, particularly the chance to draw a real longbow.

Then they'd walked down to the riverside, and he'd been as excited as a five-year-old kid when the huge bascules that carried the road across Tower Bridge had risen to let a tall sailing barge through.

How could you not love a man like that?

They'd arrived back at the hotel with time for a quick shower and change of clothes before dinner. Fortunately Cassie had found a pair of smart black trousers among the things hanging in her old wardrobe, and a nice black-and-white silk top, so she hadn't felt too out of place in the opulent restaurant.

The dinner had lived up to the promise of their surroundings. Cassie had wild mushrooms with rosemary and pine nuts, followed by a delicious tagine of lamb cutlets with cumin and tomatoes. She had watched in amusement as Dougie had demolished a large steak. He asked for it "still on the hoof, mate," and that was what he had got.

"That looks good," she had remarked, laughing.

"It's bonzer! Yours okay?"

"Bonzer," she concurred.

Now Dougie was still down in the bar, having encountered a couple of fellow Aussies — he'd probably be there for a couple of hours yet, then still be able to wake full of energy to continue their sightseeing in the morning.

But she hadn't been able to sleep. After tossing restlessly for a while she had slipped out of bed, pulled on the hotel's plush robe, and come out onto the balcony to see if a little fresh air would help.

There was quite a view from up here. In the distance, the jagged geometric shapes of the City's business fortresses were lit up against the ink-dark sky. A little further to the right, the great circle of the London Eye glowed an eerie purple.

She'd only been to London once, on a school trip. They'd visited the British Museum and the Tate Gallery, neither of which she had found particularly interesting. They'd stayed in a Youth Hostel, sleeping in dormitories on metal bunk beds with thin, hard mattresses.

She'd known then that she could never live in a city. Millions of people, millions of buildings — though she was high above it, it gave her a kind of claustrophobia. She needed air, space, the wide never-ending sea.

Her mind went back to her conversation with Dougie over dinner.

"I'm thinking of opening a new ski resort up at Ruapehu. That's why I came over to London — to talk to a few people about marketing. Jimmy's going to manage it — and I want you to take over as manager at Te Awaiti."

"Manager?"

"Sure. You'd be great. You know the business, you're great with people. What do you say?"

"I . . . I'd have to think about it. There's my work visa . . ."

"You could apply for permanent residency. Even New Zealand citizenship."

She hesitated, moving a mushroom around her plate with her fork. "Yes, I suppose I could. I don't know . . ."

It was tempting. Dougie was an excellent boss — he paid well, and he was prone to throw parties or surprise his staff with treats. He didn't interfere or try to micromanage, but he would always back you up if you needed it.

Yes, it was tempting. Standing on the balcony with the hotel's dressing gown wrapped around her, she tried to convince herself that she would be a fool to pass up such a fantastic offer. She loved New Zealand, with its stunning scenery and its warm, friendly people.

But it wasn't home.

Sturcombe was home. Quiet, pretty Sturcombe, which she had spent the first eighteen years of her life longing to escape from. Since she had come back, it had become harder and harder to think about leaving again.

The sky was inky dark, the stars dimmed by the competing light of the street lamps. A crescent moon hung low over the roofs of the great metropolis like something out of a children's story book. She could almost imagine Mary Poppins sailing past under her umbrella.

The same moon would be hanging over Sturcombe. Would Liam be looking up at it right now? Maybe just fleetingly thinking of her? Of how they used to walk on the beach beside the tranquil water of the bay, the waves whispering over the sand, a soft warm breeze drifting in to ruffle their hair.

With a small sigh she turned and walked back into the suite. Her return ticket was dated for two weeks' time, and she still hadn't made up her mind whether she was going to use it. But whether she stayed or left, she couldn't add Liam into the equation.

* * *

"There." Liam closed the book. "Wasn't Bets clever to work out where the stolen necklace was hidden?" He smiled down at his little daughter, tucked up beneath her pink duvet. She was growing — soon she was going to need a bigger bed.

"She's the very cleverest of all of them."

"She is. And it's off to sleep for you now."

"Mmm . . ." She snuggled down under the pink duvet. "Daddy, Noah said Auntie Cassie has gone away. Why did she go away?"

He hesitated, forcing his voice past the catch in his throat. "I expect she's gone on holiday, sweetheart."

"Oh." Her little lower lip was trembling. "She didn't say bye-bye to me."

"She probably didn't have time." Oh dear. He had been afraid of this. "She would have had to pack her case and find her passport, and then it would be a long drive to the airport to catch the aeroplane."

"Will she be gone for long?"

"I don't know," he responded gently. "A while, I expect."

"Oh." The small frown furrowing the child's forehead told him that another question was coming — anything from why the sun was hot to whether dinosaurs had names. Instead: "Daddy, who was that lady who came yesterday. Was she your friend?"

"Well, sort of. She's . . . someone I met."

"She had nice hair," Robyn conceded judiciously. "But she wasn't as pretty as Auntie Julia. Or Auntie Debbie. Or Auntie Cassie."

"Probably not." Ah, the subjective assessment of a five-year-old child! "Now give Daddy a kiss and close your eyes. Time for Robyn's sleepy-byes."

The child puckered up her sweet pink mouth and planted a kiss on his cheek as he bent over her, then obediently closed her eyes. In a few moments, her deep, level breathing told him that she had fallen asleep.

He envied her the ability to do that. He usually didn't have much trouble sleeping, but last night he had lain awake for a long time, even though he had been tired after his long day — thinking about Cassie. About the gamine teenager she had been, the woman she had become.

What might have been, if he'd been able to persuade her to stay? Would she have been happy? Could they have made a future together?

But there was no point thinking about it. She'd gone, as he had assumed she would. Sooner than he had expected — clearly the lure of adventure, of Australia, of an Australian who looked like a Greek god, had been strong.

He crept quietly from the room, leaving the door slightly ajar. Outside he paused for a moment, listening to be sure that Robyn was settled. The soft sound of her breathing assured him.

He nodded and walked down the stairs. A cup of coffee and a good book — with his fingers crossed that there would be no emergency calls.

* * *

The 'shindig' was a fabulous affair. Dinner was served in the Art Deco dining room — a starter of Jerusalem artichokes with crème fraiche and bronze fennel, followed by tender breast of duck with apricot and lavender, and a stunning desert of chestnut truffle with caramelised pear and rum.

There followed a charity auction. Dougie bid enthusiastically for several items. "Why on earth do you want that?" Cassie murmured as he bid for a football signed by the Chelsea football team.

"Why not?" he countered, grinning. "It'll look great in my trophy room."

She laughed, shaking her head. He didn't win the bid, nor did he for the golf lessons he wouldn't have been able to take up. Anyway, he had never shown the slightest inclination to play golf.

He did win the right to have his name used for a character in a children's book, which he thought was hilarious, especially when he found out that the character was a cowardly dragon.

After the auction, there was dancing. She felt like a million dollars, twirling around the floor with him. He was a surprisingly good dancer for such a big man, and he looked superb in his immaculately tailored dinner jacket, his blond hair gleaming in the light from the ornate chandeliers swinging from the high ceiling.

She couldn't help but notice how much attention he was attracting from many of the women in the room. If she wasn't with him, she was quite sure that one of them would have been accompanying him up to his room later.

* * *

Two days later she saw him off from Heathrow.

"Are you sure you won't come back with me?" he asked as they strolled across the concourse to the check-in desk.

She shook her head. "I promised to stay for Tom and Vicky's wedding. Besides, I haven't got my passport with me."

Had that been a deliberate omission, to ensure that she wasn't lured into making a decision by spending five days in his charismatic company?

"Well, I'll be hoping to see you soon." He swept her into one of his giant bear hugs and kissed her cheek. Then with a wave he was off towards the fast-track security gate. He had already spotted a very attractive blonde heading the same way, and in moments he had eased up beside her.

Cassie laughed, turned away, and headed for the train station and home.

* * *

Liam liked picking Robyn up from school whenever he could. It wasn't just the joy of seeing her little face light up as she spotted him waiting at the gate, it also brought back so many happy memories from the years when he had attended Fowey Road Primary School himself.

On his first day in the pre-school class — almost thirty years ago — he had met Tom Cullen and Paul Channing, and the three of them had bonded over a wooden construction set. They'd been best mates ever since.

They'd been in their final year when Paul's mum had come back to teach there. She hadn't taught their class, but Paul had come in for a lot of ribbing about it. One or two had even tried bullying him. Paul could have dealt with that on his own, but with his two friends beside him, the bullies had never stood a chance . . .

"Yes, he's got a touch of arthritis, but he loves a little walk. And he's a very good boy, aren't you, Barney?"

Liam caught his breath sharply at the sound of that voice. *Cassie?* But . . .

If he'd had any thought of avoiding her, Hobo had other ideas, dragging him across so he could greet the little terrier in traditional canine fashion, the two of them quickly twisting their leads as they circled around, each with their nose to the other's rear end.

Cassie laughed a little unsteadily as she untangled them. "Oh . . . hello."

"Hello." His jaw felt taut. "You're back." *Oh, great. How's that for stating the bleeding obvious?*

"Looks like it." She sounded just as tense.

"I thought you were going back to Australia?"

"New Zealand. No, well not yet anyway."

Damn, what a stilted conversation! At Debbie and Bill's wedding it had seemed that they were at last beginning to be a little easier with each other. And then Annabel had shown up.

Cassie was wearing slim-fitting jeans which moulded those long, elegant legs, and a sleeveless white T-shirt. And the subjective assessment of a grown man was that she looked pretty damn good.

"You're staying for Tom's wedding?"

"Oh, yes. I wouldn't miss that for the world." Her smiled looked forced. "The chance to see Tom Cullen all done up in his best smutter? Priceless!"

He managed a laugh. "Yes, it will be." A long, awkward pause. He suspected that she was struggling as much as he was to find a topic of conversation that wouldn't poke at tender spots. "How's this lad?" he asked, hunkering down to tickle the little terrier's favourite spot behind his ears.

"He's doing well. He's just been for a walk on the beach. Even managed to chase a seagull. You'd think at his age he'd have learned that he's never going to catch one."

"Oh, they never learn that. They always keep hoping that one day it'll happen!"

She laughed at that, a little awkwardly. "How's that horse I saw you riding on the beach?"

"The Bandit? He's fine. He's gone back to his training yard."

"He was beautiful." The smile seemed more relaxed, and there was a real warmth in her voice. "The way he moved — so graceful. What was wrong with him?"

"He'd torn a tendon. We gave him a carbon fibre implant."

184

"Will he be able to race again?"

"He has a very good chance."

"That's good." Another hesitation. "Do you still have Missie?"

"Of course. Though maybe it would be more polite to call her Missus now — she's had two foals."

"Oh, that's fabulous." Her eyes glowed with warmth. "I used to love that horse."

"Why don't you come over and visit her?" He spoke before he had really considered his words. "Julia rides her sometimes, but she'd be happy for you to take her out."

"I'd love to." Her face lit up. "Are you sure?"

"Of course." Whatever impulse had prompted him to invite her, he was glad now that he had. "She can be a bit lazy, so it's good to have her ridden on a regular basis." He smiled. "Come over tomorrow. Around ten?"

"That would be great! Thank you."

"Ah." The school bell had rung. "Brace yourself."

A few moments later the doors opened and a tide of small children flooded out, chattering and squealing excitedly, some of them running around playing chase, others heading straight for the waiting cluster of parents.

"Daddy!" Robyn came hurtling across the playground, clutching a piece of drawing paper. She threw herself against him, hugging his legs. "An' Auntie Cassie." Her bottom lip came out. "You wented away," she accused.

"I did." She smiled down at the child. "But I came back."

"Where did you go?"

"To London."

"We wented to London once. We wented on a big wheel that went round and round and round and you could see for miles and miles. And Daddy got a prize."

"Oh?" She slanted him a questioning glance.

"It wasn't just for me. It was for the Horse Rescue Society."

"Oh, well done."

"Thank you."

185

"I drawed a picture of my pony," Robyn announced proudly, waving the paper in her hand. The brown splodge with four legs in a row, a head and a tail was reasonably recognisable as a pony. It stood on a swathe of green — obviously grass — with a round yellow sun beaming down.

"Ah, that's very good," Cassie approved. "What's your pony called?"

"Biscuit."

"Biscuit?" She seemed to be having difficulty suppressing a laugh. "That's a good name for a pony. Why is he called Biscuit?"

"Because he's the colour of a biscuit." The child spread her hands out, patiently stating the obvious as Cassie exchanged a glance of amusement with Liam.

"Ah, here are my two." Amy and Noah had appeared at the door, their eyes lighting up when they saw Cassie.

"Auntie Cassie!" Amy ran up, smiling shyly, and slid her small hand into hers. She held up her picture. "I drawed a picture of my mummy getting married."

"Oh, that's lovely. How about you, Noah?"

"I drawed Superman!"

Cassie laughed. "Of course you did. Come on then, let's go home for tea."

"We're just waiting for Ben," Liam explained.

"Oh . . . Right. Well . . . um . . . I'll see you tomorrow. Ten o'clock."

He nodded. "Ten o'clock."

* * *

Was this really a good idea? Cassie had her doubts. She argued with herself all the way as she walked down the hill and along the Esplanade, through the Memorial Gardens and past the hotel.

But the temptation was too great to resist. And not just the chance to ride Missie again.

Beyond the hotel was a low stone wall surrounding a paved front yard, with a wooden table and chairs and a few half-barrel tubs filled with flowers.

To one side was the house, a rambling, quirky, ivy-clad L-shaped cottage built of the local grey stone. It had once been three cottages, but they had been knocked together many years ago. The roofline was a jumble of square chimneys and dormers, every window being a different size and a different level.

To the side of the yard was a tall wooden gate that led into the stable yard at the back of the house, with a sturdy brick-built stable block around two sides.

Only a couple of the stalls were occupied. The rest of the horses were in a large paddock at the far end, and she recognised Missie at once — a beautiful bay with a white blaze down her nose and one slightly crooked ear.

Cassie called her name softly, and to her delight, the horse seemed to recognise her and trotted over.

"Well, hello there. Yes, I remembered the polo mints." She held one out on the palm of her hand, and with a little whicker, the gentle mare took it from her and looked for another one. Cassie laughed. "Still as greedy as ever."

"You got that right."

She took a moment to compose herself, stroking the horse's sleek neck, then turned with a bright smile. "Hi. Are you coming out too?"

"I need to see how Hector up at the end there is doing. He's had a bad dose of pneumonia and I had to do a thoracotomy to clear it up. Do you want a hand to saddle her up?"

"No. I can manage, thanks."

She opened the gate and Missie walked through, following her across the yard to the tack room. By the time she had her saddled up Liam was ready, mounted on a handsome bay.

"He's a fine-looking lad."

"He is." Liam patted the bay's neck. "He's coming along well. He should be able to go home in a few days."

"That's good." She led Missie over to the mounting block and swung herself up into the saddle. She immediately felt comfortable — the big mare's gait was smooth, her ears relaxed, showing that she too felt comfortable.

187

They rode out of the gate and turned along the South West Coast Path. To their right was a large field, bright with buttercups, where a dozen horses, several ponies and four donkeys were grazing peacefully.

"That big roan is Luke's," Liam pointed out. "The chestnut is my dad's. And that beautiful black mare is mine." There was a world of pride in his voice. "Gitana — Spanish for gypsy."

"It suits her."

The horse had seen him and trotted over to the fence, whickering. "Yes, okay. It'll be your turn tomorrow," he promised, stroking her nose. "It's Hector's turn today."

Cassie laughed. "She really is beautiful. And very intelligent. And I'd guess that's Robyn's Biscuit?" The shaggy-maned Shetland was happily grazing at the side of the field.

"That's right."

"I love that she called him Biscuit. I bet she's a good little rider."

"She is." The warmth in his voice conveyed his love for his small daughter.

"And those others — they're from the Rescue Society?"

"Most of them."

She could see that several of the animals looked badly out of condition, their ribs and hip bones visible, their coats dull and ragged. "It's so sad to see them like that, but good to know that they're being cared for now. How many are you looking after?"

"We've got fourteen rescues here at the moment, and a few dozen more living out in foster homes, as well as the ponies and donkeys."

"It's grown a lot since I went away."

"Unfortunately, the need's grown."

"It must cost a fortune to run."

"We get support from donors and charities, and we do some fundraising ourselves. And we have a GoFundMe site attached to the website."

"Sounds like a lot of work."

"It is." He smiled, his eyes warm as he glanced back over his shoulder at the herd contentedly cropping the lush grass. "But it's worth it."

Cassie watched him silently. This was his life's work — his whole heart was in it. He would never have left it to travel the world with her ten years ago, and he would never leave it now.

They had been trotting along the path as they talked, past the golf course. Now there was farmland rolling away to their right, while to their left the sea was glittering beneath the high blue sky.

Sturcombe nestled in the dip of the hills, the houses jumbled up the slope like children's toys. The Esplanade, with its amusement arcade and ice-cream parlour and Kate Rowley's cosy café, skirted the red-gold sweep of the beach, while across on the far side of the bay she could see the rising line of the houses on Cliff Road.

Home. New Zealand might have stunning scenery, loads of exciting things to do, but it could never truly be home.

There were several parties of walkers on the footpath that ran alongside the bridleway — serious hikers with poles and stout walking shoes, casual strollers in shorts and sandals. They greeted each other with smiles and remarks on the weather. Several dogs were running around, chasing each other or sniffing along the hedges, but neither Hector nor Missie seemed bothered by them.

"Have you had much chance to ride these past few years?" Liam asked.

She nodded, smiling. "I worked on a dude ranch in Montana for a while. That was really fun, taking care of the horses and escorting trekking parties. They all thought my English accent was 'real cute'."

"Sounds good."

"It was. I really enjoyed working at the water-sports centre in Florida, but I only had a year left on my work visa and I really wanted to see more of the country. So I lined up the job in Montana, and teamed up with another girl to hire a car and drive there, taking in a few other places on the way."

"Oh?"

"We drove up to Washington and New York. We stayed there for a couple of days. Then we headed south again to New Orleans and through Texas to visit the Mission Control Centre in Houston."

"I bet young Noah was excited to hear about that."

"He was. You can see the spacecraft and the astronauts' suits, and even touch a bit of moon rock! And you can visit the room where they controlled the moon landings, with all the old computers they used. It was incredible to think that they were able to do that, all those years ago. Then we drove on to the Grand Canyon."

"It must have been a very long drive."

"It was, but we shared the driving. And those big American cars are very comfortable. We hired a Chrysler. Once you got used to it, it was a doddle."

He nodded. "So you visited the Grand Canyon? Very Thelma and Louise."

She laughed. "Well, except for the robbery at the grocery store, and blowing up the oil tanker. And we didn't meet Brad Pitt. But it's the most amazing place — so vast, and all the rock formations and different colours. And there's a skywalk, where you can walk out literally over nothing. It's got a glass floor, and you can look down four thousand feet to the river. It's mind-boggling."

"I can imagine."

"It was only a short drive from there to Monument Valley, where they made all the cowboy films. Rhona was going on to California, so we parted company there. She caught a Greyhound bus and I took the car the rest of the way up to Montana."

* * *

Liam listened with mixed feelings to Cassie's story. It was interesting, and clear that she'd had a wonderful time, fulfilling all the things she had dreamed of.

Yes, she had been right to go. But after all her adventures it seemed very unlikely that she would be content to stay here in sleepy Sturcombe. There was Tom and Vicky's wedding, and after that she would be gone again.

"Montana is just incredible. It's called the Big Sky Country, and that's certainly true. The sky is so blue, you wouldn't believe. And the mountains, the lakes, the green valleys full of pine trees. In the winter it gets seriously cold, well below freezing, and there's deep snow right through from September to March. I learned to ski, or we'd go snow-shoe trekking. It's so peaceful with all that snow on the ground."

"And you got to ride horses?"

"Of course. In the summer we'd take parties of guests out trail riding. There wasn't so much of that in the winter, of course, but we still had guests and the horses still needed to be looked after. And we ran natural horsemanship courses, teaching people how to train their horses through gentle cooperation."

He laughed dryly. "We could do with some of that here. Maybe then we wouldn't have so many horses wind up in rescue centres. So how long did you work there?"

"About a year. Then my US work visa was due to expire, so unless I was lucky enough to get a Green Card, I was going to have to leave. The cousin of the guy who owned the ranch owned a water-sports and safari outfit in Tanzania. I really wanted to see the Victoria Falls and the Serengeti, so he put me in touch with him and he offered me a job."

"Lucky."

"It was — perfect."

* * *

Missie had taken exception to an empty crisp packet blowing along the path, prancing around like a diva, and for a moment Cassie had to give all her attention to settling her. "How's Hector doing?" she asked.

"He seems fine. Try a canter?"

She laughed merrily. "I thought you'd never ask!"

The two horses seemed very happy to pick up their pace. It was exhilarating, moving smoothly with the horse's rhythm — but more than that, it brought back so many memories of riding with Liam back in the day.

Was he remembering too? He had invited her to come riding — what was he thinking now?

They rounded the headland and rode along the clifftop for about half an hour, alternately trotting and cantering. Then Liam reined Hector in to a walk as they reached the end of the bridleway. The footpath here dropped down quite steeply to the estuary below, so steeply that in places there were steps.

"That was pretty good." He leaned forward and patted Hector's sleek neck. "Did you enjoy that, boy?" he asked the horse. The animal tossed his head as if nodding in agreement, and Cassie laughed.

"He's breathing okay?" she asked.

Liam nodded. "Absolutely fine. Shall we head back?"

"If you like."

"So go on," he urged as they turned their horses' heads back towards Sturcombe. "Tell me about Tanzania."

"Oh, that was just amazing. If Montana is Big Sky Country, the Serengeti is even more so. Miles and miles of open grassland, and huge herds of wildebeests and antelopes. And the skies are just incredible, especially in the rainy season."

"You got to see the big game?"

"Of course. Elephants and giraffes, zebras, hippos, lions and cheetahs. Sometimes you could get up quite close to them, if you were very careful. And if you were lucky, you could see a cheetah hunting a gazelle."

"Was there a problem with poachers?"

"Always." Her mouth thinned. "The rangers are really brave, the way they go after them — poachers wouldn't hesitate to kill them. And sometimes the animals come into competition with the farmers over the land. Not really surprising

— both are just trying to survive. I climbed Kilimanjaro to help raise money for a wildlife reservation."

"How did you meet your Australian friend?"

She slanted him a quick look from beneath her lashes. Was there a note of constraint in his voice? "Dougie? He was on the Kilimanjaro climb with me, and a couple of his lads from the Kalagooly resort. They were raising money for conservation work along the Great Barrier Reef. He offered me a job at one of his resorts — he owns three along the coast of Queensland, and one in New Zealand. I checked them out on the 'net and they looked amazing, so I decided to take him up on it."

"He seems like . . . quite a guy."

"He is." She didn't trouble to suppress the warmth in her voice. Let him make of it what he would. "And a great boss. Really generous, and never one to set himself apart. Unless anyone takes him for a soft touch — then they pretty soon find out their mistake."

"So you moved to Australia?"

She nodded. "It was always my dream. Diving on the Great Barrier Reef is just out of this world. There are so many types of fish and coral."

"And sharks?"

"Oh yes, some of those too." She laughed. "Though most of the ones around the reef are pretty harmless — wobbegongs and white tips."

"Wobbegongs?" Now he laughed too. "You're kidding!"

"No, really, that's what they're called. In the local Aboriginal language it means shaggy beard. They have whiskers around their mouths, which help them sense fish that come too close. They're pretty stupid looking, and they tend to just lie around on the sandy bottom. They're often called carpet sharks."

"They're not dangerous?"

"Not if you don't get too close. Anyway, most shark attacks happen further south, around New South Wales, or over on the West coast. Even then, you're more likely to get struck by lightning or be killed by fireworks."

"That's good to know," he conceded dryly.

Sturcombe had come into view again. They rode down the gentle slope and into the stable yard.

"Ah, that was good." Cassie smiled as she dismounted. "Thank you."

"I'll deal with Missie," Liam offered.

"No, it's fine. I always take care of my own mount. It's a habit."

He nodded, smiling. "A very good habit. Do you remember where everything is?"

"I think so."

She unfastened the girth and lifted off the saddle, carried it into the tack room and wiped it off. Then she removed the bridle, rinsed the bit under the yard tap and hung it up on one of the hooks along the back wall.

Then she filled a bucket and sponged Missie down lightly, checking for any rubs or chafing, and ran her hands down her legs, finally picking up each foot to check her hoofs and pick out bits of compacted mud.

When she was finished, she led the mare over to the trough and let her take a drink before letting her through the five-barred gate into the grassy paddock behind the house. The horse whickered and trotted off happily to join her friends.

* * *

Liam had watched Cassie with Missie as she had ridden beside him. He had been confident that she knew what she was doing. She'd always been a good rider — her hands relaxed, her seat easy in the saddle.

And Missie had seemed quite happy. Like many horses, she was inclined to fidget and try to assert herself if she didn't respect the person riding her.

Okay, he had just wanted to watch her. She was graceful and efficient in her movements — and that neat backside in those well-fitting jeans would make any red-blooded male's pulse rate soar.

For the past week and a half the memory of holding her in his arms as they had danced at Debbie and Bill's wedding had haunted his dreams — and had too often intruded when he was awake. That slender, supple body, the subtle fragrance she wore . . . Those memories would linger long after she was gone.

She had just let Missie through the gate into the paddock, and turned as he brought Hector up.

"Well . . . Goodbye." She smiled — he did like that smile. "Um . . . Thanks for letting me ride her again. I really enjoyed it."

"That's okay. Missie enjoyed it too." Somehow he managed to push the words past the tension in his throat. "I'll see you on Saturday then."

"Oh yes, of course. See you then. Goodbye."

"Goodbye."

CHAPTER FOURTEEN

The church was looking its very best, the pews gleaming with polish and the altar banked with white roses and gardenias, their sweet fragrance filling the air.

The bells in the tower were ringing out into the clear blue sky, the afternoon sun was beaming through the stained-glass windows casting jewel colours across the white altar cloth, and the soft music of the organ was drifting up to the vaulted ceiling.

The pews were full. Cassie had settled with Lisa near the front, Lisa with little Kyra on her lap. The tot looked as pretty as a picture in a dainty pink dress, with a pink headband that sported a pink fabric flower.

"I just hope she stays this quiet," Lisa murmured. "If she starts grizzling I'll have to take her outside."

"Vicky and Tom won't mind if she cries," Cassie assured her. "Anyway, she's been fed and nappied — she'll probably fall asleep. Has Ollie got his Best Man speech ready?"

Her sister laughed softly. "He's rewritten it about twenty times. I've never known him be so nervous — not even when we got married."

Their mother turned from the pew in front. "When you got married, he was so hungover from getting drunk with Tom and Paul the night before, he didn't know what day of

196

the week it was," she remarked dryly. "And you weren't in a much better state yourself."

"Oh dear." Lisa hunched her shoulders and slid down in the pew. "I hoped you wouldn't remember that."

"I'm your mother — I remember everything. As your two will find out as time goes on."

Cassie's eyes danced. "Didn't you say something once about being respectable?" she whispered.

"That was eight years ago."

A murmur ran around the pews as the organist began playing the familiar strains of 'Bridge Over Troubled Water', and heads turned as the bridal party appeared in the church doorway. Vicky looked as graceful and serene as a swan on her stepfather's arm as they moved slowly down the aisle.

"Ah, she looks lovely," Lisa murmured, leaning close to Cassie. "It really is a gorgeous dress."

"It is."

Tom turned, his smile lighting up his handsome face as he held out his hand to his bride. The two of them drew together, gazing into each other's eyes, seemingly oblivious of everyone and everything around them.

Eva moved in front of the altar. "Dear friends and family, we welcome you today to witness and celebrate the marriage of Victoria and Thomas."

Cassie glanced across the aisle. Liam was sitting a few rows in front of her, little Robyn tucked in close to him. His pale-grey jacket was immaculately tailored over his wide shoulders, his dark hair curled over his ears, the way it always had, always tempting her to tuck it back.

Riding with him on Thursday had brought back so many memories of riding with him ten years ago. That summer they had ridden almost every day. Had the sun really always shone? Or was it just that she had been in love?

So many memories. Her mind drifted back . . . The night of her eighteenth birthday party . . .

* * *

197

It was Saturday night. Her birthday had been on Wednesday, but you couldn't have a decent party on a Wednesday, could you?

And it was a great party. Several of Paul's football team-mates were there, much to the delight of some of her friends from school who were flirting wildly with them. Lisa and her fiancé were there, with some of his friends from the hospital where he was on his final-year placement.

She had been dancing with Liam for most of the evening, though occasionally they had both danced with other people. She was jiving — of a sort, given the crowd — with Terry, the team's tall black goalie, when someone grabbed her arm.

"Hey, Cass. Got any more cans? We're running short of beer here."

"Oh, right. There's loads in the kitchen. I'll go and get some. 'Scuse me, Tel."

She slipped away to the kitchen, blinking in the bright light after the dimmed lighting in the sitting room. There were already two black bin bags full of empty cans, but there were still more than a dozen two-four cases on the table, and she hoisted one up into her arms.

"Need a hand with that?"

She turned in surprise. She hadn't seen Bill, who worked up at the Cullen farm, sitting on the back step. "What are you doing out here by yourself?"

He grinned sheepishly. "Oh . . . I . . . It's a bit crowded. I . . ."

"Why don't you go and ask Debbie to dance?"

His ears went red. "She's dancing with Alan Gowan."

"Well go and cut in," she urged.

He shook his head. "I couldn't. I . . . If she wants to dance with him . . ."

She gave him an encouraging smile. "I think she'd rather dance with you."

He looked down at his hands — big, work-roughened hands. "I don't think so. Anyway, I can't dance. I'm too clumsy. I'd just tramp on her toes."

Cassie sighed. Poor Bill — he was cripplingly shy. It must have taken all of Tom Cullen's best efforts to drag him along to the party. He'd have been happier to stay up at the farm with his cows.

Giving up on a bad job, she left him to himself and headed back into the party.

"Ah, here's the girl with the gear." Liam's older brother Luke swooped on her and took the cans of beer. "Thank you, darling. You're a lifesaver." He dropped a kiss on her cheek and disappeared into the crowd.

Cassie glanced around the room. It was heaving with her friends. All the usual crowd. People she had known all her life, in this tiny seaside town. She loved it all, but . . . Surely there was more to find in the world than this?

"Ah, there you are." Liam dropped an arm around her shoulders and drew her close.

"I was just getting some more beer."

"Good thinking. But come and have a dance now."

She shook her head, fanning her face with her hand. "It's too hot in there."

"Come for a walk then."

"I can't do that," she protested. "It's my party."

"It's your party, so you can do whatever you like."

He took her hand and drew her out to the front door. Laughing, she let him lead her across the road and down to the beach.

It was a beautiful night. The sky was velvet black, scattered with stars like a million diamonds. The moon was almost full, shining like silver on the dark, tranquil water of the bay. Tiny waves whispered along the edge of the sand, unfurling in long strands of lacy white foam.

"I love this place," she murmured.

"Good." He glanced down at her, a question in his dark eyes. "I sometimes wonder . . ."

"What?"

He smiled, shaking his head. "Never mind."

They slipped their shoes off and strolled along the beach. Cassie felt the sand crunch beneath her feet, and the soft breeze from the sea stir her long hair.

"It's weird to think that this is my last term at school. Once my A levels are over I'll be leaving! And you'll be finishing too, and you'll be a qualified vet!" She skipped along beside him. "Freedom! Isn't it great?"

He laughed. "Then come September, we'll both be in Exeter." He caught her hands and spun her round, dancing in the sand. "It'll be so much easier to see each other than with me up in Bristol."

"Mmm."

It was ten weeks now since they had got together at Lisa's party, and they had seen each other almost every weekend, when Liam had come home to Sturcombe. It still sometimes seemed unreal that she was his girlfriend — it had been her dream since she was fourteen years old.

But there was still that other dream, of flying away, far away over the ocean, seeing all those other parts of the world that she had only seen in books or on television, or on the illuminated globe on her bedside table.

That was a scary dream, but it fizzed inside her, unsettling her every time she thought of a future here in Sturcombe, with Liam. She didn't want to leave him, and now she clung to his hand with both of hers as they scrambled over the jumble of rocks at the far end of the beach beneath the hotel.

There was a tiny patch of sand, hidden from anywhere but directly out to sea. They had often come down here to spend time alone, to swim, to enjoy a picnic, or just to laze in the sunshine and enjoy long, slow, warm kisses.

They sat down, Cassie snuggled between Liam's legs, his arms wrapped around her from behind. She tipped her head back against his shoulder. "Look at all those stars. Aren't they beautiful? There must be a million trillion of them."

Liam laughed softly and kissed her ear. "At least."

"And the sea. Isn't it amazing to think that far out there over the horizon it goes on and on, down past Africa and Australia and the Antarctic, and all the way over to America. Do you know, the Pacific is so big that there's a place on the west coast of South America where, if you could poke a stick right through the centre of the earth, it would come up on the far side still in the ocean — in the Gulf of Tonkin, near Vietnam."

"That's wild."

"And just think, these little waves here — in a few weeks they could be lapping the shores of Fiji or Patagonia." She gazed out into the far distance, as if she could see it all just by imagining it. "Let's go for a paddle." She scrambled to her feet and gathered up her long skirt. "Come on!"

"It'll be cold," he warned her, but as she ran down to the water's edge he was right beside her, his jeans rolled up. Hand in hand they splashed into the waves.

Cassie squealed. "Yikes! It's *freeeeezing*!"

"I told you so."

Hopping from one foot to the other she gasped for breath. "I can't . . . believe . . . how cold it is."

"It's almost one o'clock in the morning, and it's still May," he reminded her. "Of course it's cold."

"Okay, okay. You were right." Laughing, she ran back up the beach and threw herself down in the sand. "I think my toes have got frostbite."

Laughing with her, he knelt and picked up one foot, rubbing it to massage warmth back into it.

"Mmm." She lay back with a sigh of pure bliss. "That feels good."

He picked up her other foot, his dark eyes glinting as his hand slid along her calf. And further, up her smooth thigh. As he laid down beside her, she turned into his arms and their lips met, and lingered, long and sweet.

His skin smelled of sandalwood and the sea. She moaned softly and moved against him, his name soft on her lips. Any other dreams had been forgotten — this was the only dream she wanted.

Her pulse was racing as his hands stroked up over her waist and round to the firm swell of her breast. He was dusting tender kisses over her trembling eyelids, across her temple and over the delicate shell of her ear. She could hear the ragged drag of his breathing, feel the powerful thump of his heartbeat.

These past few weeks their kisses had been growing hotter, more urgent, but they had always stepped back from the brink. But tonight, as if through some unspoken agreement, they both knew it would be different — something had changed, clicked into place.

Maybe because she had turned eighteen, would soon be leaving school. She was no longer a child.

He undressed her slowly, his hand smooth over her skin. Overhead the stars were spinning as time drifted away like the ripples of the sea. In all her dreams she had never imagined it could be like this.

His head bent over hers as he kissed her again, his sensuous tongue swirling deep into her mouth. She curved her body close against his, wrapping her arms around him.

She hadn't even noticed that he had shed his own clothes until she felt the rasp of his hair-roughened chest against her naked breasts. She moaned softly, revelling in the movement of the hard muscles across his shoulders and down his back.

His hand slid down between her thighs, seeking the sweetest, most secret caresses. And then he moved above her, and with a hand that shook slightly he brushed her hair back from her face.

"Cassie?" His voice was a husky growl. "Is this right?"

"Yes." It was no more than a sigh. "Oh yes please."

She was vaguely aware that he had slid open a small foil pack, and then there was nothing but a golden flow of pleasure that seemed to melt her bones.

Time slipped away as their sensuous dance echoed the hushed whisper of the sea lapping against the moon-silvered sand, and she felt herself soaring, soaring, over the edge of the world, to collapse at last wrapped up in his arms . . .

* * *

A sharp nudge from her sister brought Cassie abruptly back to her surroundings. The organist was playing 'Unchained Melody' as the bride and groom walked back down the aisle, followed by their bridesmaids — Vicky's stepsister and two little cousins in pale tangerine dresses — and both sets of parents.

How had she paid so little attention to the ceremony? She must have been on autopilot, standing and sitting with the rest of the congregation, probably even singing along to the hymns. Fortunately, no one seemed to have noticed her distraction.

Her heart was still beating a little too fast as the vestiges of those memories lingered in her brain, but she managed to get to her feet. Then as she stepped out of the pew, she came face to face with Liam.

"Oh . . . Hi." Somehow she forced a smile. Past and present swirled together. She had to struggle to remind herself that it had been ten years, not just a few moments ago, that she had lain in his arms on that moonlit beach.

"Hello."

His smile was friendly, polite. She had almost been afraid that he would see in her eyes where she had been for the past three-quarters of an hour.

She hesitated, trying to think of something to say, but there was the pressure of people behind them wanting to get past and out to the front of the church, where photographs were being taken.

"Oh . . . Sorry." Liam moved out of their way, falling into step with his brother and sister-in-law, holding Robyn's hand. "See you later," he added to Cassie over his shoulder.

"Yes . . ."

Outside, the golden September sun was shining through the trees — already the leaves were starting to shade into their autumn colours. Vicky was laughing merrily as the photographer herded the wedding party into the line-up. The two young bridesmaids were dancing, swirling the skirts of their lovely dresses.

"Auntie Cassie!" Robyn came running over to her. "Wasn't that pretty?"

"Yes, it was." She smiled down at the excited child. "And you were very good. I saw you sitting with your daddy and Auntie Julia."

"I drew Auntie Vicky and Uncle Tom. And I had lots of sweeties," she added, leaning in to whisper as if it was a guilty secret.

"I just bet you did! And I expect you'll want lots of wedding cake when we get down to the hotel."

The child giggled, her eyes wide. "Lots and lots!" Then she spotted her best friend Amy and hurtled over to hug her.

After sitting still in the church for almost an hour, it wasn't surprising that the young contingent needed to let off steam, playing chase around the graveyard and kicking up the leaves that were already beginning to fall.

A few of the adults glanced anxiously at Eva to see if she would scold them, but she just laughed. "Let them play. They've been as good as gold, and I don't suppose the occupants of the graves will object."

It was a lovely setting for the wedding photographs — the ancient grey stone touched by the golden afternoon sunlight, the soft shadows of the trees. The churchyard was filled with wild flowers — Eva only had narrow paths mowed between the graves, letting nature flourish.

The photographer was very good at her job, efficiently marshalling everyone into various groups while keeping up a flow of casual chat to maintain a relaxed atmosphere. There was a good deal of laughter, especially among the men, teasing each other with cheerful insults: "Stick him at the back. That ugly mug'll crack your lens."

Cassie had posed with Vicky, Lisa, Debbie and a few other female friends, and also in the large group with all the guests together. She stood watching for a while, then slipped away to stroll over to Nanna's grave.

The headstone had been removed by the stonemason to add her name to that of her beloved husband. The coral bells and bee balm that they had planted after her funeral had begun to settle in and would thrive there for years to come.

As she stooped to pull out a stray weed a shadow fell beside her. She didn't need to look up to know who it was. Liam.

"Hi. I thought you might be over here."

"Yes." She managed an awkward smile. "It looks odd without the headstone, but they'll be putting it back in a week or so."

"It must be strange without her. She'll have left a big hole."

"Yes. We keep saying we'll make a start on sorting out her stuff, taking it up to one of the charity shops, but somehow we haven't managed to get round to it yet. I think we're all thinking that she'll come in and tell us off for messing with her things!"

He laughed. "I can imagine. She was never going to be one to go gentle into that good night."

"No." She tugged at another errant weed. "But in the end, she did. She was smiling."

"I see she's next door but one to Molly Marston. Bit risky, putting those two old birds so close together. They'll be biting chunks out of each other for the rest of eternity!"

"And enjoying every minute of it . . ." She glanced up as Vicky and Tom came over, holding hands, Vicky holding up the train of her dress out of the long grass.

"Hello." Vicky's smile was as bright as a thousand suns. "We just came over to say hello and thank you to Aunt Molly." She glanced up at her new husband, her eyes shining. "If it hadn't been for her, we'd never have met."

There it was again, that look of love that passed between them.

Vicky hunkered down beside Molly's grave, pulled a white rose out of her bouquet, and laid it beside the gravestone. "Thank you, Molly."

The four of them stood for a moment in silence, then Vicky smiled up at Tom. "We'd better be going." With a last glance at Molly's grave she turned away.

"Shall we go?" Liam suggested.

"Oh . . . Yes, of course." Something twisted in her heart. For one moment she found herself wishing that she and Liam could be like Vicky and Tom. So in love . . .

Afraid that she might blurt out something stupid, she excused herself quickly and hurried over to rejoin Lisa and the family.

Vicky and Tom had been driven off in a classic Beauford open-topped tourer, and everyone else followed them on foot down the short walk to the hotel.

The whole place had been transformed into a flower palace with tubs of white roses and blush-orange roses, canna lilies, myrtle and lily of the valley, their sweet scent filling the air.

Out on the terrace the photographer was doing her thing again, ushering all the family and friends into their places for more formal shots, while white-coated staff moved discreetly among the guests with trays of champagne flutes and canapes.

There were more photographs to be taken. Cassie found herself corralled into a large group photo. The children were ranged along the front. Robyn was with Liam and his parents, but spotting Cassie, she scampered along to stand with her, turning her angel face to beam up at her.

Cassie smiled and patted her shoulder, then slanted a rather awkward glance of apology towards Liam. He just rolled his eyes, laughing. That was a relief. She guessed that little Robyn often latched onto random adults, as many five-year-olds might do.

"Okay, everyone. That'll do." The photographer lowered her camera. "Thank you very much."

"Time to toss the bouquet, Vicky!" someone called.

"Phew!" Lisa smiled with relief. "At last we can sit down. I knew I shouldn't have worn these shoes."

Cassie turned to her, laughing. "Never mind, you can—" Something hit her in the chest. Instinctively she put up her hands, and found herself clutching the bridal bouquet.

As a cheer rose up, she felt her cheeks flame scarlet. Unfortunately, the stone terrace wasn't going to open up beneath her feet, so she could only smile as if she was sharing the joke. She knew exactly where Liam was, so she was able to avoid looking in his direction.

"Well, well!" Lisa chuckled. "That means you're the next bride."

"Huh!" She shook her head decisively. "Not gonna happen."

Lisa's eyes danced. "Never say never."

"Huh!"

* * *

With the photographs finished, there was time to mingle on the terrace. Everyone stood sipping champagne in the late afternoon sunshine. Time for games — quoits and skittles and giant Jenga for the adults, a treasure hunt in the gardens for the children.

Liam perched on the stone balustrade, watching the fun down among the flowering shrubs and the gravel paths. Robyn had dragged Cassie in to help, and was clinging to her hand or her skirt as they followed the clues.

That was a worry. The little girl was getting very fond of her — she was going to be upset when she left. But it would only be worse if he let himself be drawn into getting closer to her himself, he reminded himself brusquely. He needed to be careful.

"She's very attractive."

"Huh?"

His sister-in-law was smiling at him. "Cassie Channing. Not exactly beautiful, perhaps, but there's something about her."

"Mmm."

"Luke said you used to have a thing with her."

"A thing? Yes, well . . ." He managed to keep his voice even. "That was a long time ago. We were both young."

"Robyn seems to have taken to her."

"Unfortunately."

Julia arched a questioning eyebrow. "Why unfortunately?"

"Because she won't be staying."

"Did she tell you that?"

"She didn't need to tell me, not in so many words." It had been in her eyes, in the tone of her voice when she had been talking about her adventures. What had Sturcombe to offer in comparison to that?

"You could be wrong."

"I'm not wrong. Leave it, Julia," he added sharply as she opened her mouth to argue with him. "She won't be staying."

The children had finished their treasure hunt. Little Amy had won, and was thrilled with her prize — a big jigsaw of Frozen.

Robyn came running back to him, her rosy face full of disappointment. "I came second, Daddy."

"Well, that's pretty good. And Amy is your best friend, so you're very happy for her that she won, aren't you?"

A brief second, then the child's bright smile beamed out. "Yes I am!" She scrambled over to where Amy was showing her prize to her mother, and the two of them hugged.

Liam breathed a sigh of relief. He had sworn to himself at Natalie's funeral that he would do his very best to bring up a child she would be proud of, and sometimes he worried that, loving her so much, he risked spoiling her and bringing up a monster instead.

But then the sweetness of Natalie's nature would shine through in her, and he would have to smile.

* * *

The seating plan for the wedding breakfast had been set up on a large easel in the ballroom. Each group was represented by a flower — a white rose, a sunflower, an orange dahlia — to match the centrepiece on each allotted table.

"That's clever," Cassie murmured to Lisa as they found their places. "Who thought of it?"

"Vicky. I wish I'd thought of it for ours. We just had pictures of birds."

"Birds are nice. So long as they don't poop on the table."

Lisa laughed and punched her sister lightly on the shoulder. "You're so unromantic."

"That's me."

The children had been shepherded away to their own party table in the lounge, where they would have their own food and a hired entertainer, so they wouldn't be bored by adult conversation and speeches.

The adults found their tables and sat down. Cassie was relieved to find that Liam was three tables away. She wasn't sure that she could cope with being close to him for what was likely to be a couple of hours.

"Wow, this looks lovely," Lisa declared as she took her seat.

"It does. Your people have done a great job again."

The tables looked beautiful, with crisp white tablecloths and gold-edged white china, gleaming crystal champagne flutes and silver cutlery. Their centrepiece was a vase of blush-orange roses in sprays of asparagus fern.

"Has Kyra settled okay?" Cassie asked.

"Uh-huh. She's had her feed and nappy change, now she's asleep. Shelley's babysitting."

"That's kind of her."

Lisa nodded. "She's a good kid. Well, I say kid — she's twenty-four."

"Really?" Cassie's eyes widened in surprise. "She looks about seventeen."

"I know. There's not much of her, but she's a good worker. She's had a heck of a life." She cracked open a bread roll and began spreading it with butter. "Grew up in care — had a whole string of foster homes. And she's been homeless, actually slept on the streets for a while. Heaven only knows what she had to do to survive."

"Poor thing," Cassie murmured with sympathy. "It's good that she's been able to find herself a place here. How long has she worked here?"

"Almost three years. When she first arrived she wouldn't say boo to a goose, but she's a lot more confident now. I've been trying to persuade her to give it a go on Reception, but she's not interested. Or so she says."

Cassie slanted her a questioning glance, but at that moment their starters arrived, and she was able to focus on her plate. The food was excellent. A starter of melon with feta cheese and lemon dressing was followed by tenderloin of lamb with chargrilled vegetables.

"Oooh!" Lisa sat back with a sigh. "I don't think I can eat another thing."

Cassie laughed. "I bet you will when you see the desserts. Anyway, we've got the speeches first."

"Ah, I might be able to manage something then. If I'm still awake."

The speeches were more fun than they had feared. Vicky's stepfather spoke about how happy he had been when marrying Vicky's mother had brought a lovely new daughter into his life.

"Her mother has always advised her to be sensible — and what could be more sensible than marrying such a lovely young man as Tom?"

Vicky's mum blushed, smiling sheepishly at her new son-in-law.

Ollie's Best Man's speech raised a lot of laughter, roasting his cousin with a story about him slipping in a pile of cow manure when he was due to meet a representative of the bank to discuss a commercial loan for setting up his organic feed company.

"And of course, she arrived early, so if he had been hoping his magnetic charm would swing the deal . . ."

After the speeches it was time to cut the cake. It was a splendid creation of three tiers of smooth white icing with a cascade of white and blush-orange sugar flowers down one side. The photographer captured the moment perfectly.

Lisa found that she could somehow make room for a crème brulée with raspberry tuile. Cassie chose waffles with summer fruits and clotted cream. "Mmm." Lisa leaned back in her seat with a contented sigh. "That was good."

Cassie laughed. "I didn't think you'd be able to resist."

She had been careful during the meal to avoid glancing in Liam's direction — well, apart from the occasional glance. Certainly no more than every five minutes. Mostly.

He was sitting with Debbie and Bill, newly returned from their honeymoon and both looking radiant with happiness. Debbie, usually so shy, was chattering away, her eyes bright, while Bill gazed down at her adoringly.

Liam seemed to be enjoying himself. If she occasionally caught him glancing in her direction, she looked away quickly. The memories that had filled her mind during the wedding service had left her feeling . . . unsettled. Every time she thought the balance between staying and going was tipping firmly in one direction, something would happen to tip it back again.

CHAPTER FIFTEEN

The end of the wedding breakfast signalled the time for the younger children to be whisked away home by their families, for the adults to take some time to freshen up, and for some to change into their evening wear.

Several of the rooms on the first floor had been opened for the guests to use. Cassie and Lisa had left their bags and evening dresses in Room 11, as had Julia, Debbie and her mum, and several of the other women. It made for quite a crush, but everyone was happy to work around each other.

Lisa threw herself on the bed. "Oh boy. I'm full up to here." She indicated her forehead. "I really shouldn't have had that crème brulée."

"Which is why you all but licked the plate."

Lisa laughed. "It was pretty scrummy. Ah, here's my little Munchkin!" She bounced up as Shelley came into the room carrying Kyra. Taking the baby, she kissed the top of her head. "Thank you so much, Shelley. You're a godsend!"

"It's no trouble, honestly," the girl assured her. "She was as good as gold. She slept most of the time."

"Ah, you're a little angel, aren't you?" Lisa blew a raspberry on the baby's forehead, making her gurgle with laughter and kick her feet.

"She's a good little thing," Cassie remarked. "You're lucky she takes after you rather than me!"

"Aren't I?"

"Don't get smug," Cassie warned. "Wait till she gets big enough to argue back."

"Oh, she's so pretty," one of Vicky's cousins cooed. "She looks just like you."

"Thanks." Lisa's smile glowed with maternal pride. "I'll give her a quick feed now," she added to Shelley. "That should keep her happy for a few more hours. We won't be leaving later than ten."

"That's fine."

She settled in the armchair, Kyra snuggled contentedly in her arms. Cassie sat down at the dressing table to brush her hair and touch up her makeup ready for the evening. "Did Noah go off all right?"

"Yes. I think he was pretty tired, and his granddad has promised he can watch *Pirates* before he goes to bed."

Cassie laughed. "Dad sure knows how to deal with kids."

"Just as well, since he's been teaching them for over forty years!"

They all managed to get changed and ready, weaving around each other as if in a well-choreographed dance.

"Oh, that's beautiful!" Julia gazed in admiration as Cassie took her dress out of the garment bag she had hung up in the wardrobe. "It's really your colour."

"Thanks." She shook it out, making the long silk-chiffon skirt swirl. She'd bought it on that shopping trip to Exeter, to wear tonight, but then she'd worn it at the charity ball with Dougie.

She'd garnered a lot of compliments that night too. It was a rich emerald green, with a close-fitting bodice which left one shoulder bare. She shimmied into it, and Julia zipped it up for her.

"There. You'll knock him dead!"

"Who?" Oh lord, did she know?

Julia grinned mischievously. "Whoever you like!"

213

Cassie focused her attention on clipping a gold chain around her neck. It had been a present from Dougie for her twenty-fifth birthday — he loved giving presents. Every few links had a dainty rosette attached to it, which gleamed against her skin.

Lisa had finished feeding the baby. She sat her up and rubbed her back until she burped loudly, looking slightly astonished at her own achievement. "There's a clever girl!" She kissed her little button nose, and handed her back to Shelley. "She might need a fresh nappy in a little while," she warned.

"That's okay, I'll see to it."

"You're a gem. Okay, peeps. Let's hit the dance floor."

Downstairs in the ballroom the tables had been rear-ranged around the walls, the lights had been dimmed and a three-piece band had taken the small stage. As they started to play, the happy couple led off the dancing.

"Don't they look lovely together?" Cassie murmured to Lisa.

"And Tom won't tread on her toes. He's actually quite a decent dancer."

"Mike's dancing with Debbie's mum. They look good together too."

"He's a good dancer. He and his wife used to go ballroom dancing — they won a couple of competitions. She died a couple of years ago — she was Kate's best friend."

"Oh yes — I remember you telling me that. It was so sad."

The dance floor was filling up. "Look at Paul," Lisa remarked. "Straight in on the bridesmaid."

Cassie rolled her eyes. "Typical. How long has it been since he split with . . . What was her name?"

"I don't remember." Lisa laughed dryly. "He's had so many girlfriends I lose track. At least he's keeping her happy. When I heard Vicky had let her be her bridesmaid I was a bit worried she might make trouble."

"Oh?"

"She's a bit . . . Well, she was sleeping with Vicky's ex-fiancé — while they were still engaged."

"The bitch! It was very forgiving of Vicky to let her come."

"Family," Lisa concluded wryly. "Anyway, I think Tom tipped Paul off to take care of her. He'd have been more than happy to oblige, I'm sure — she's very pretty."

"And she'll be gone in a couple of days — perfect for him."

"So long as he doesn't fall for her. I don't think I'd fancy having her in the family."

Cassie shot her a look of surprise. "Do you think there's any danger of that?"

They shared a smile. "No chance! Let's dance."

* * *

The evening was winding down. Slices of wedding cake had been distributed, along with coffee or champagne, to taste. Liam preferred whisky. He had retreated to a corner of the bar, out of the way, where he could watch the dancing and be alone with his thoughts.

Okay — where he could watch Cassie. She was looking good, her hair gleaming like polished mahogany, that elegant green dress — the colour of her eyes — swirling around her ankles as she danced.

She'd been dancing all evening, fizzing with energy, laughing with one partner after another. At least she wasn't staying with one, and at least that Australian Adonis wasn't here.

With Tom and Vicky's wedding over, would she be going back to him? He had wanted to ask her about that when they had gone out riding, especially after the way she had spoken with such enthusiasm about her adventures. But he really hadn't wanted to hear the answer.

Or was he giving in too easily, letting the guy win without even putting up a fight? That wasn't like him — even though he would be fighting the Great Barrier Reef and surfing on Straddie Island, as well as a billionaire who owned a string of water-sports resorts and looked like a Greek god.

Dammit! At least he could dance with her. He finished his whisky in one swallow and put the glass down on the bar. But as he rose to his feet there was a commotion and a general move towards the double doors which lead out to the reception hall.

Of course — Tom and Vicky were getting ready to leave. They had changed out of their wedding finery into something more comfortable. They were going home for tonight. Tomorrow they would be off to Spain for their honeymoon, and a visit to the Pradora to see the portrait of Vicky's Aunt Molly, which had been painted by her lover, a famous Spanish artist.

As they came down the stairs, all the guests gathered to see them off. They certainly looked happy. Vicky looked as if she was dancing on air, hugging and kissing everyone, thanking them for coming as she said goodbye, and Tom was grinning like the cat who'd got the cream.

He wanted that — the connection with one woman who would always be there beside him. Like his parents, like Luke and Julia, like Cassie's parents. He had had it with Natalie — could he have it again? With Cassie? Was there a chance that she might change her mind, and stay?

The progress of the bride and groom was slow to the front step where the white Beauford was waiting, decked out with balloons and tin cans, and rude messages scrawled on the windows in shaving cream.

Tom hooted with laughter at the sight of it. "Did you do that?" he asked Liam.

"I'm saying nothing!" He slapped his friend warmly on the shoulder. "Cheerio, mate. Have a good trip."

"I will." He put his hand in his pocket. "We've cleared out the room, but I forgot to give this back. Drop it off at the desk for me, would you?"

"Sure." Liam took the key card and put it in his own pocket.

Bubbles were blown, drifting on the warm evening air, then the car drove off amid cheers and waving, and at last everyone went back inside. The music started up again, but when Liam glanced around for Cassie, she had already been claimed for a dance by a cousin of Vicky's.

"Come on, Liam." His sister-in-law caught his arm and tugged him onto the crowded floor. He conceded with an easy smile as the DJ began to play a lively song, perfect for a jive.

He liked dancing with Julia. She moved easily, following his lead and laughing as she spun out and back. But forced to pay attention to swinging her around without tipping her over, he lost sight of Cassie. When the song ended and he glanced around she was nowhere in sight.

A small stab of panic clenched in his gut. Surely she hadn't gone home already? If she was planning to go back to Australia soon, he may not even get a chance to speak to her before she left.

Dammit, he couldn't deny it any longer — he was in love with her.

* * *

It had grown dark outside. Cassie wandered over to the stone balustrade to gaze out over the bay. The moon was almost full, the stars were bright points against the velvet darkness, the sea an inky black.

The tide was high, the waves lapping with a soft hush right up to the rocks below, mingling with the sound of music from the ballroom behind her and the distant jangling of the amusement arcade down on the Esplanade. Further along, the pub windows glowed orange. When the door opened, the sounds of music and laughter spilled out, carrying on the warm evening breeze.

Across the bay, the line of Cliff Road was traced with street lights. Near the top she could see her house — there was a light on in her parent's bedroom. Beyond, a few lights up on the caravan site showed that people up there were still awake.

As she stood there, breathing in the soft, salt-tanged air, she became aware of someone behind her. She didn't need to turn to know who it was.

"Nice night," he remarked.

"It is."

"Not dancing?" He moved to stand beside her — it felt as if there was some kind of forcefield between them, like static electricity.

"Just having a break."

"You haven't danced with me."

She turned her head to glance up at him. "You haven't asked me."

"I'm asking now." He smiled down at her, that beguiling smile that she had always remembered, even when she had been on the other side of the world. "Will you dance with me?"

She didn't answer. She couldn't. She just slid into his arms, closing her eyes and letting him move her to the music. It was a classic soul number that she had always loved.

Out here with Liam, on the terrace in the moonlight, with the music spilling from the ballroom and the soft whisper of the waves at the bottom of the cliff . . . it felt as if this was where she had always belonged.

Oh lord, she was in love with him. She really was. In truth, she had been for all these years. How could she ever have denied it?

His breath was warm against her hair, then she felt his mouth brush over her temple, her trembling eyelids. Something was tightening in the pit of her stomach. He was going to kiss her . . .

His mouth met hers, his lips warm, tender, coaxing hers apart, his tongue sliding sensuously between them, seeking the sweet depths within. Time slid away as the stars turned overhead. She was curving her body against his, vividly aware of the rising need in him which matched her own.

Tenderness was forgotten. The heat in his kiss was fuelling the heat in her blood, and she could feel the ragged drag of his breathing, the rapid beat of his heart. His hands had tangled in her hair, but there was no need for him to hold her captive — she had been his captive since that summer ten long years ago.

Maybe it was moments, maybe it was hours before he lifted his head. Gazing up into his eyes she read the question there. There could be only one answer.

"Remember our secret beach?" Her voice was a husky whisper.

"I've never forgotten."

"Nor have I." She glanced down over the stone balustrade. "It's high tide." A hint of regret. "It'll be under water."

"It doesn't matter." He smiled slowly, a promise, and put his hand in his pocket. "I have a better idea." He drew out a key card.

"What . . . ?"

"It's the room Tom and Vicky were using. Tom asked me to hand it in to reception, but I hadn't got around to it yet."

"Oh . . ." Her breath jerked in her lungs. All she could think of was the way he had kissed her, and how much she wanted him. "Well, that would be . . . a lot more comfortable than the beach."

"It would."

He held out his hand to her, and she placed hers in it. Together they slipped through the doors and across reception, swift and silent, laughing as they ran up the stairs to the first floor.

Up here all was quiet — everyone was downstairs in the ballroom. Suite 10 was the first door at the top of the stairs. As Liam drew her over to it she felt the craziness spiralling through her. She hadn't intended for this to happen — it was the last thing she had expected.

But as he spun her round and crushed her against the door the excitement spiked inside her, sweeping away any uncertainty. And then he was kissing her again, his mouth hard and hungry. And she was kissing him back. This was all she wanted, all she needed.

She heard the scraping as he struggled to fit the key card into the lock, then the door opened and they fell inside, stumbling over their own feet, laughing and breathless.

The elegant sitting room with its stunning view of the bay was wasted on the pair of them. They didn't bother to notice the half-empty champagne flutes on the coffee table, the scatter of rose petals that had fallen to the floor.

Somehow they made it to the bedroom, and on to the bed. Cassie was fumbling frantically to unfasten the buttons of Liam's shirt as he dragged down the zip of her dress. As he laid hot kisses on the sensitive column of her throat she twisted herself like a pretzel to unfasten the ankle-straps of her silver sandals and kick them to the floor.

He was shaking with laughter as he drew the dress up over her head, the long flow of the chiffon skirt seeming endless. "What is this?" he protested. "A marquee?"

"Rude!" She was laughing too as she fought her way out of the fabric. "It's the most expensive dress I've ever owned."

"And a beautiful dress it is too." His dark eyes gleamed. "But nothing like as beautiful as what's underneath."

With the tip of his finger he traced the lacy edge of her bra, then reached round behind her back to unhook it, casting it aside, his hot gaze scalding her skin as he let it slide over her naked curves.

"You too." Her voice was husky and impeded, her pulse racing, her fingers fumbling as she unfastened the buttons of his shirt and dragged it back over his shoulders. She could have returned the compliment as for a long moment they just gazed at each other. Anticipation was locking her breath, clenching her stomach.

With a growl that was almost feral he bent his head and his mouth claimed hers again, deep and demanding, fierce and hot. And she responded with equal heat, her tongue sparring sinuously with his. She stroked her hands down his back, feeling the ripple of hard male muscle under her palms, and she moaned softly, her heart fluttering.

Her fingers tangled in his hair as she curved her supple body against his hard length. Soaring through the air on a bungee rope had nothing on this — wild, out of control. His hands were rough, impatient, as they slid down over her smooth skin.

His kisses were tracing a scalding path down the long column of her throat and into the hollow behind her collar bone as her hard white teeth bit into his shoulder.

She dragged in a ragged breath, all her senses focused on his touch as he caressed the firm, ripe swell of her aching breast, tormenting the tender nipple, pinching it lightly, rolling it between finger and thumb, sending a spark like static electricity sizzling along her taut-strung nerve-fibres.

And then he bent his head over her ripe breasts, his hot tongue lapping around the exquisitely sensitised peaks, his teeth nipping first at one, then the other, before his lips closed over one, drawing it deep into his mouth as ripples of pleasure flooded through her.

She closed her eyes, losing herself in the magical world he was spinning around her. This had been all her dreams for the past ten years. But this was real, and far, far beyond anything she could have dreamed.

His hand slid slowly down over her slim midriff, and her breath caught in her throat as she felt him ease her dainty lace briefs down over her slim thighs.

She barely noticed as he shed his own clothes until seconds later he was as naked as she was, his skin as hot as hers, his breathing as ragged. She was conscious only of the subtle male scent of his skin, drugging her mind.

His hand was smoothing up over her slim thighs and slipping between, his strong, sensitive fingers coaxing their way into the soft velvet folds hidden beneath the cluster of dark curls at the apex.

His touch was as light as a butterfly's wing as he found the secret core within and stroked over it. A gasp became a moan as with exquisite skill he stirred a wave of heat that surged through her veins.

At last she could stand it no longer. "Now — please."

He took a few seconds to slide a gossamer sheath onto his hard length, then as she arched beneath him, taking him into her, she wrapped her arms tightly around him, their mouths meeting — fierce, mutually demanding.

After that there was nothing but fire, fast and furious, dangerous. They moved together in a primitive rhythm — there was no slow, no steady, just a raw hunger, so intense that she felt as if it would consume her.

Molten heat was pooling low in her stomach and pulsing through her veins, dizzying her. A low, purring growl escaped her throat, and she felt her spine curl as she responded instinctively to his every movement, their bodies melding together as one.

A fever was burning through her as she spun out of control, spiralling higher and dizzyingly higher, until she heard her own voice crying out, felt him tense in her arms, and they fell together, both utterly spent.

* * *

Liam lay on his back, staring up at the ceiling as the first light of dawn crept into the sky. It wasn't his ceiling, it wasn't his bed. Beside him, Cassie lay sleeping quietly. It had been an incredible night, with an incredible woman.

He had thought he could never feel like this again. Love . . . It had seemed like an impossible dream . . .

But now the dream was slipping away, reality was seeping back — all the doubts and dilemmas. Maybe he could somehow persuade her to stay. But in a few weeks, a few months, would that restless spirit stir again, luring her away?

Maybe this time he could go with her . . . But that thought was dismissed before it was barely formed. Robyn.

He couldn't take his little daughter away from all the people she loved — her grandparents, her aunt and uncle, her cousin, her friends. The home she had known for all her five years.

And then there was Natalie's parents. Today was the day he was due to take her for her monthly visit to them. Losing Natalie had broken their hearts. He couldn't do that to them again.

And what if she stayed? Robyn had adjusted well to losing her mother. Could he really ask her to make another adjustment — a major one? It had been just the two of them for the past three years, and they had got along very well.

She liked Cassie, but that was different to having her as a stepmother. That could confuse her. What if she felt Cassie had come between them? What if she resented it? She could end up hating him, as well as Cassie.

Very carefully, so as not to disturb her sleep, he slipped out of bed and picked up her dress. Such a lovely dress. A soft waft of the perfume she had been wearing drifted around him. Shaking his head with regret, he shook it out and laid it carefully over the back of a chair.

She didn't stir as he picked up his own clothes and padded through into the lounge, closing the door silently behind him. Dressing quickly and slipping on his shoes, he strolled over to the French window, opening it to step out onto the small balcony.

The stars were gone. In the west the sky was still a deep indigo, but in the east it was shading to a pale silvery blue, washed with misty gold, the sea shimmering like mother-of-pearl. The air was cool. He breathed in slowly, struggling to clear his head.

Ten years ago he had been shocked, angry, hurt when she had walked away. Then slowly he had come to realise that it had been the right thing for her to do. He had been assuming that she wanted the same things he did, that she would be content to spend her life in this small, tucked-away seaside village. He should have known that she could never be content with that.

And though he had never quite stopped loving her, he had been able to lock that love away in some deep, secret vault in his heart, never to be opened.

Then he had met Natalie. She had been the complete opposite to Cassie — angelically blonde and dainty, with lovely blue eyes and the sweetest smile, and a quiet, gentle nature. Who wouldn't love her? And he had, truly and sincerely, thanking whatever stars guided his fate that he had found her. Losing her had torn him apart.

And now . . . Could he risk his heart again? For himself, maybe. But for Robyn, a little girl who had lost her mother — no. And she had to be his priority. Nothing else mattered.

A soft sound — the bedroom door opening. He turned his head. Cassie was standing in the doorway, wrapped in the hotel's bathrobe, her hands deep in the pockets. She didn't speak.

He wanted to tell her that he loved her. But how could he say that when there was no future in it? He felt as if his tongue had turned into a lump of cold concrete, refusing to form any words.

For a long moment she just stared at him, no expression in her eyes. Then she slowly nodded her head and turned and walked back into the bedroom, closing the door behind her with a firm click.

He dragged in the breath he had forgotten to take. That was it. His bridges were burning. There was nothing left for him to do. Shaking his head, he moved swiftly across the room and out of the door.

The hotel was silent. No one was awake yet, not even the domestic staff. He crossed reception in a few strides, picked up his jacket from where he had left it in the ballroom, and hurried out into the cool morning air.

CHAPTER SIXTEEN

It was a little over half-an-hour's drive to the pretty village on the edge of Dartmoor where Natalie's parents lived. Liam had slid an audio CD of one of Robyn's favourite stories into the CD player to keep her entertained as they drove along the narrow country roads with their high Devonian hedges.

The Brayley's home was a pretty whitewashed cottage surrounded by a low stone wall. The lush garden was full of buddleia and roses and hollyhocks and chrysanthemums, with spikes of delicate pink veronica and bright cosmos.

Liam pulled onto a patch of rough ground on the opposite side of the lane. "Here we are!" he announced brightly. He could do this. Those lingering memories of last night were safely tucked away in the back of his brain.

He unfastened the seatbelt on Robyn's child seat, and took her hand as she scrambled out of the car. She skipped along beside him as they crossed the road and opened the garden gate.

"Granma!" She broke from him as the front door opened, and raced up the path to be caught in a smothering embrace.

Sylvia Brayley was in her early sixties, with soft grey-blonde curls and her daughter's soft blue eyes. "Ah, my little cherub. How lovely to see you."

"Granma, we brought you flowers."

"Though it's a bit like bringing coals to Newcastle." Liam laughed, glancing around the colourful garden.

"Oh, never mind that. They're lovely." She took the bouquet and put up her cheek for a kiss. "Come on inside. Martin," she called back over her shoulder. "They're here."

"Can I go find Grampy?" Robyn pleaded.

"Of course, darling. He's in the garden."

Liam followed Sylvia into the sitting room. It was a cosy room, old-fashioned, with flower-patterned wallpaper, a comfortable three-piece suite in front of the fireplace, lots of flourishing pot-plants on the sideboard and several small occasional tables.

And photographs, of Natalie and her two older sisters — as toddlers on a beach somewhere, smart in their school uniforms in school photos, as bridesmaids at each other's weddings. And then grandchildren.

A happy family.

And there was the one he had given them, in pride of place. A copy of the one on Robyn's bedside table — of Natalie and Robyn on the sun lounger by the pool of their hotel in Greece. He felt that familiar twinge of guilt. If he had been quicker . . . And the guilt that he was still living, while Natalie was gone.

He knew that Natalie wouldn't have wanted him to feel that. That Sylvia didn't. But it never quite went away. He could only imagine how it must be for Sylvia, to have lost her youngest daughter. He knew how he would feel if anything happened to Robyn.

"Go and sit down while I put these in a vase," Sylvia urged. "Then I'll fetch in the tea."

The sun was streaming in through the window, and he could hear Robyn's voice out in the garden, chattering away to her grandfather, nineteen to the dozen. He smiled to himself. It was important to keep up these regular visits. It always would be.

Though he suspected that in ten years or so a teenage Robyn would grumble and pull a face: *Must we?* Then a few years after that, driving her own car, she would happily drive over herself to see her beloved grandparents. Heavens, he was pushing the time away . . . !

"There." Sylvia came in with a pretty flower-painted tea tray. On it was a teapot and milk jug, three dainty teacups, and a plate of chocolate biscuits. She set it down on the low coffee table. "I brought orange juice for the baby."

"That's good. Thanks." *Just don't let her hear you call her a baby.*

"So how have you been?" She smiled at him as she poured the tea.

"Well enough, thank you." He always tried to calibrate it carefully between assuring her that Robyn was happy while not appearing to have forgotten their loss. "She's started in the reception class now. She loves it."

"Goodness, how the time rushes on! Is she still with her little friends?"

"Amy and Noah — yes. They're all in the same class."

Robyn came running in, dragging her grandfather by the hand. "Granma, I saw a butterfly! A really pretty one."

"Did you, sweetheart?"

"It was this big." She held her thumb and forefinger a couple of inches apart. "It was blue."

"That's lovely. Come and sit down now and have your orange juice."

The child bounced up onto the sofa beside Liam and took the glass he handed to her, her little face creasing into a frown. "Don't I have cola please?" she asked.

"Not right now, sweetie." Liam flicked a glance towards Sylvia, registering the hurt on her face. "You like orange juice."

"But I like cola better."

"Oh, sweetheart." Sylvia looked genuinely distressed. "I don't have any cola. I forgot to get it."

"That's fine," Liam insisted firmly. "You can have cola another time, but drink up your orange juice now, and say thank you to Granma."

To his relief, the sweet side of the child's nature came to the fore, and her beaming smile appeared like the sunshine. "Thank you, Granma." She drank the juice, leaving an orange moustache on her top lip.

He laughed, pulling a tissue from his pocket to wipe it clean. "There you go." He bent to drop a kiss on the top of her head. "Good girl."

Tea and biscuits finished, they all strolled out to look round the garden, admiring Martin Brayley's immaculate flowerbeds. Then they walked down to the small park beside the river to feed the ducks and for Robyn to play on the slide and the swings.

"Ah, bless her." Sylvia smiled fondly as she watched the little girl swoop backwards and forwards, squealing with excitement, begging her grandfather to push her higher. "Thank you for bringing her over. It means so much to her granddad to see her."

Liam smiled to himself. What she really meant was that it meant so much to her, too.

"Sometimes it seems like it was only yesterday that Natalie was here, playing on those swings with her daddy." Fumbling in her pocket for a tissue, she dabbed at her eyes. "I'm sorry. I'm being stupid. I don't mean to cry."

"No, no. It isn't stupid at all," Liam assured her gently. "It isn't something you ever really get over. I still cry myself sometimes."

She dabbed at her eyes again, watching as Robyn jumped from the swing and ran over to the slide.

"Look at me, Granma." The child waved, full of excitement. "I'm going down the slide!"

"She's growing so fast," Sylvia sighed. "And she's adjusted so well. You've been such a good daddy to her. But I suppose . . . No, no." She shook her head. "It's none of my business."

"What is it?" he asked, smiling down at her.

"It's just . . . I suppose one day . . . You're still a young man. I suppose one day you're likely to think about getting married again."

Oh lord. His breath seemed to have locked in his chest. "I don't think so," he managed.

She glanced up at him, her mouth a little crooked. "You don't have to say that just so as not to upset me. I'd understand. It's just . . . You would still bring her to visit us, wouldn't you?"

"Of course."

Robyn was zooming down the slide and Martin caught her at the bottom, swung her up in the air then set her on her feet to race round for another go. Liam felt a knife twisting in his gut. Any lingering thoughts he might have had of flying off to Australia with Cassie really were out of the question.

"Oh, take no notice of me." Sylvia smiled resolutely and tucked the tissue back in her pocket. "I'm just being a silly old thing. I know you'll always do what's right for her."

They strolled back from the park, Robyn between her two grandparents, holding both their hands. After lunch they had a very noisy game of Snap and then settled down to watch CBeebies, Robyn snuggled on the sofa between them.

They stayed to tea, then drove home. It had started to rain quite heavily, and Robyn dozed off when they were half-way home. She woke as he parked the car beside the garages, and they laughed as they splashed together across the yard and into the kitchen. His mother glanced round with a smile as they came into the house.

"Hi. Did you have a nice time?" she asked Robyn.

The child nodded vigorously. "I went on the swings and the slide. Can I have cola please?"

"Of course, sweetie." She opened the fridge and pulled out a can. "Here. What do you say?"

"Thank you, Nanma. Can I watch KrazyKat?"

"Yes, sweetie. Ask Gramps to put the DVD on for you." As the child scampered away she arched an eyebrow at Liam.

"How was it?" The note of restrained sympathy in her voice reminded him that she knew it was likely to have been difficult.

He shrugged and went over to the coffee maker in the corner, and poured himself a mug. "Much as always. They're a really nice couple. It must be so hard for them." He sipped the coffee. "She was talking about . . . would I still take Robyn to visit if I ever got married again."

"Oh?" An arch of an enquiring eyebrow. "Is that on the cards?"

He shook his head decisively. "No. Not for the foreseeable future. Maybe never. "

"And Cassie?"

There was a teaspoon on the counter beside him. He picked it up and absently stirred his coffee with it. "What about her?"

"Julia said you were dancing with her out on the terrace last night. And you didn't come home until this morning."

"I'm an adult, Mum. I can stay out all night if I want to."

"Who said you couldn't? But you had a thing with that girl . . ."

"Ten years ago."

"Ten years ago. And since she came back . . . I'm your mother, Liam. I can read you like a book."

"Okay. Well, yes, since she came back it's stirred up some of the old memories. But I'm not going there, Mum. Once was enough." He put the teaspoon down. "I think I'll go and watch KrazyKat. That's about as much as my brain can cope with at the moment."

* * *

It had been raining since Sunday afternoon. Cassie sat on the window seat in her bedroom, Barney snuggled up beside her. Outside, the view of the bay was obscured by the darkness and the thick raindrops trickling down the glass, distorting the glow of the coloured lights along the Esplanade.

It perfectly matched her mood. So much hope, so quickly destroyed.

For a moment she closed her eyes, then opened them again to look down at the piece of paper in her hand. Her airline ticket, her return ticket to New Zealand. Dated the day after tomorrow.

She had kept it tucked in her poetry book for the past six weeks, with that strip of old photographs. She had known it was there, but she had chosen not to think about it, not to mention it. But now . . .

"Hello, dear." Her mother appeared in the doorway. "I've brought you a cup of coffee and these last few bits from the wash."

She smiled thinly. "Thanks, Mum."

"You haven't finished packing yet?"

"Not quite."

Helen came over and sat down beside her on the window seat. "You're really going?"

"Yes, Mum."

"It's just . . . I wondered . . . with Liam . . ."

"Nothing with Liam." It was a struggle to keep the bitterness from her voice.

"It's just . . . You were with him on Saturday — at the wedding. And?"

Cassie laughed without humour. "Nothing gets past you, does it, Mum?"

She got one of those patented 'mother' looks. "I'm your mum."

Cassie was silent for a long moment. "Yes, we stayed the night. At the hotel. And in the morning when I woke up, he was dressed and ready to leave. He didn't say a word. So . . ." She shrugged in careless dismissal.

"You're not going to give him a chance to explain?"

"What's to explain? It's been three days. Three whole days. More than enough time, however busy he might be, if

231

he wanted to speak to me. Clearly he doesn't." Her mouth quirked into a crooked smile. "I chose to walk away ten years ago. I could hardly expect to come back and pick up where we left off. So, message received and understood."

Her mother nodded slowly. "Please don't stay away for ten years again."

Cassie reached over and took both her hands, squeezing them tightly. "I won't, Mum. I promise."

* * *

"Okay, that ought to do it." Liam carefully withdrew the naso-gastric tube and dropped it into the disposal bag. After endless weeks of sunshine, the weather was catching up with itself. It had rained continuously for three days, and was still pounding heavily on the corrugated roof of the stable.

He stood for a few moments watching the pretty roan. She had got to her feet, and already she seemed a little more settled, her breathing beginning to slow to a steadier pace. He tucked the earpieces of his stethoscope into his ears and put the diaphragm against the horse's heart. The rhythm was almost back to normal.

"Are they going to be all right?" Penny asked anxiously.

"They should both be fine in a few days. Give them warm, clean water, with the electrolyte. If they won't drink it, make up a dilute bran mash and try them with that, two or three times a day. Put a few bits of apple or carrot in it, if you like."

The girl nodded solemnly, taking in everything he was saying, though he had a print-out to leave with her. He sym-pathised. Colic was a nasty condition for horses. It must have been horrible for her to see her beloved horses rolling on the ground, sweating and clearly in pain.

"No grain feed for a few days. Watch their droppings. Feed them about a quarter of their normal amount of hay, walk them for about fifteen minutes several times a day, and turn them out to the paddock for an hour or so, building up to a couple of hours. Any concerns, ring me at once."

"I will." She brushed a tear from her eye. "Thank you. Thank you so much."

"No trouble."

The roan whickered and nuzzled against her cheek, and she stroked her hand down her neck. "Oh, Elsa. I'm so sorry I let you get ill."

"It wasn't your fault," Liam assured her gently. "I know your horses are very well cared for. It's likely it was the change of feed that caused it."

"We had to change it. The place we were getting it from has closed down."

Liam nodded. "The thing is, if you have to change their forage, it's best to do it gradually. Mix some of the new in with the old so their stomachs can get used to it. If you'd like to try them with organic feed, I'd recommend Cullens."

"Cullens? Oh, yes. Dad uses them for the pigs. I didn't know they did horse feed too."

"They do the whole range. Anyway, I'll come back on Friday." He pulled out his phone and checked his appointments. "Two o'clock, if I can make it." He folded up his ultrasound scanner and ran through the rain to stow it in the boot of his SUV, coming back for his equipment case and the disposal bag. "Goodbye then."

"Goodbye."

She stood waving to him as he drove away. The clock on the dashboard told him it was almost ten o'clock. It had been a long day, starting early with a call to another colic case, followed by a crashed horsebox on the main road. Fortunately, there had been no more damage than a bruised fetlock and a bit of a fright.

At least keeping busy had left him no time to think about Cassie. What could he have said? What *should* he have said? An apology, at least? Or would she have taken that as an insult?

He had never intended it to be a one-night stand. He hadn't really intended anything. He hadn't been thinking at all. He had just let himself be swept away by his own need.

He had hurt her, and he regretted that, but perhaps it was a good thing after all. It had put an end, once and for all, to any forlorn hope that might be lingering that there could be some kind of relationship between them.

And now she'd soon be gone, back to the New Zealand sunshine, and he could try to find a way to go on with his life. He'd done it before — twice. He could do it again.

He shook his head, accelerating as he turned onto the main road, his headlights stabbing through the darkness, the windscreen wipers splishing and splashing against the rain. The only important female in his life was Robyn.

That thought was still uppermost in his mind as he turned into the front yard and parked the car, and splashed around to the back of the house. In the mud room, he kicked off his boots and hung up his dripping jacket, and changed his work clothes for something to relax in, then strolled into the kitchen to pour himself a coffee.

His mum and dad were watching television in the sitting room.

"Hi, Mum." He dropped a kiss on the top of her head.

She glanced up. "Ah, hello, love. You've had a long day."

"Tell me about it."

"If you want some dinner, there's some lasagne in the freezer. You just need to pop it in the microwave."

"Great, thanks. I'll just nip up and look in on Robyn first. Did she go down okay?"

"No trouble."

"Thanks."

He climbed the stairs and walked quietly down the corridor. Robyn's door was slightly ajar, the pink glow of the night-light spilling out, and to his surprise he heard her voice. He paused, listening — he could just see her without pushing the door further open.

She was kneeling up on her bed, talking earnestly to Hobo. The dog was sitting in front of her, very still, his whiskery grey head on one side, listening intently.

"...I could be a bridesmaid like Amy. And Amy says that when people get married they can have a baby, so if Daddy got married, I could have a baby sister too, like Noah."

He reached out to open the door, but then drew his hand back.

"And if Daddy got married I could have a proper mummy like Amy's mummy and Noah's mummy. I know I have Mummy Natalie, and she'll always love me, but she isn't here — she's in heaven. And if he married Auntie Cassie, she'd be the best mummy ever, and she'd play with me and help me build sandcastles and read me stories and tuck me up in bed."

He drew in a slow, silent breath. This was something he hadn't anticipated. He pushed open the door.

"Oh!" Robyn dived under the duvet. "I was just going to sleep, Daddy. Truly."

"That's all right, sweetie." He sat down on the edge of the bed, easing Hobo aside. "I'm sorry I wasn't here to read your bedtime story."

"Nanna read it to me."

"That's good." He paused, thinking what to say. "Robyn, do you want me to get married?"

"Yes. Yes, please." Those angelic blue eyes were wide, gazing up into his. "If you married Auntie Cassie, she'd be my mummy and she'd really love me and I'd love her."

Oh...The urgent pleading in his daughter's voice struck right into his heart. And with it came a sudden thought. He'd assumed that Cassie would be leaving, but he hadn't actually asked her to stay. And didn't he know her well enough to trust that if she said she would stay, she would keep her word?

Edie Channing had said it — you only get one life. Don't waste whatever chances you might have. It was a risk. If he asked her to stay, she might just throw it back in his face. But if he didn't take this last chance, Edie would have called him a fool.

He smiled down at Robyn. "Well . . . we'll see. You go to sleep now, eh? Do you want Hobo to stay here?"

"Yes please."

"Okay." He bent and kissed her rosy cheek, then tucked the duvet around her shoulders. "Night night then."

"Night night, Daddy."

Outside on the landing he stood for a moment, feeling the beat of his heart. Cassie . . . He loved her. He would be crazy to let her slip away without a word.

Huffing out a breath he hurried back down the landing and down the stairs. His mother looked up, startled, as he strode across the room. "You're going out again? Another emergency?"

"Yes. An emergency." Somehow he knew that it was urgent that he see her. "I'll see you . . . later."

"Hope it goes okay . . ."

It was still pouring with rain, but he hadn't stopped to pick up his jacket. He ran down the lane, past the hotel and the Memorial Gardens, and along the Esplanade, the buffeting wind almost strong enough to knock him off his feet.

The sea was rough, white-capped waves rushing in from far out in the bay to thump against the sea wall and throw up fountains of spray. There was no one else around. Who would be daft enough to be out in this weather?

He raced up Cliff Road. There were lights on in the sitting room of number nineteen, and a light up in the dormer window that he knew was Cassie's room.

His jumper was soaked, rain was dripping from his hair and trickling down his neck as he waited on the doorstep for someone to answer his urgent ring, but he didn't care. Footsteps. Her mother opened the door.

"Ah. Hello, Liam." If she was surprised to see him, she didn't show it. She stood aside. "You know where to find her."

"Thank you, Helen."

He took the stairs two at a time, breathless as he reached the top. The door to Cassie's room was slightly ajar, and he pushed it open. There was a backpack on the bed, half full, and she was folding a sweater ready to go in it.

She turned sharply, her green eyes wide and shocked when she saw him standing in the doorway. "What the fuck are you doing here?" she demanded through clenched teeth.

"I . . . You're packing."

"Yes."

"You're going back to Australia."

"New Zealand."

"Don't go."

* * *

Cassie stared at him. "You're wet." Stupid, but it was the only thing she could think of to say.

"It's raining." He ran a hand back over his hair, sprinkling raindrops everywhere. "Don't go."

Her laughter was bitter, humourless. "You've left it a bit late. Couldn't you have said this on Saturday night? Or even yesterday?"

"I should. I can't give you any excuse. I was stupid." He took three paces across the room towards her, but seemed to sense the invisible 'don't touch me' forcefield she had spun around herself. "Ever since you came back . . . I've been an idiot. I was so sure you'd leave again that I was afraid to take the risk of asking you to stay. But I'm asking you now. Please don't go. I know I'm not offering you anything more than I did before, and it wasn't what you wanted then. But . . . Maybe . . . Might you change your mind?"

She sat down heavily on the bed. Even if she could have thought of something to say, she doubted it would get past the tension in her throat.

He knelt and took both her hands in his. "I loved you before, but we were not much more than kids then. I was hurt when you left, but I recovered. Now . . . I love you as a man loves a woman — truly and for ever. So I'm asking you to stay — I'm asking you to marry me. That's all I have."

237

Cassie didn't realise that there were tears streaming down her face until they splashed on her hands. Her globe of the Earth was there on the table beside her, lighting up all those places she had dreamed of going, all those adventures. But she had done that now. It was time for a new adventure.

"Yes." The word had slipped out before she had consciously realised she was going to say it. "Yes, I will."

* * *

Cassie had had a dream, many times, that she was walking down the aisle of a church to her wedding, but the aisle kept getting longer and fading into a distant mist.

It wasn't like that today. Cassie glanced up at her dad with a crooked smile. He returned the smile, his eyes warm, and patted her hand where it rested on his arm.

"Ready?"

She drew in a long, deep breath. "As I'll ever be."

She really was walking down the aisle. In a long white satin dress with a boat-shaped neckline and bracelet-length sleeves, and a skirt that flowed out into a short train, her hair coiled up on her head and laced with small white silk flowers.

The church was gaily decked out for Christmas, with the nativity scene she remembered from her childhood in its usual place on one side of the altar, a large Christmas tree on the other. The end of each pew was trimmed with a garland of holly, shiny scarlet baubles and a bow of scarlet ribbon.

The pews were fuller than she had anticipated, with family and friends of both her and Liam. They hadn't wanted to separate them into his and hers, so everyone was jumbled together. Natalie's mum and dad were there too, smiling bravely and dabbing away a tear.

And there at the front was Liam, turning to look back at her and holding out his hand. She put hers in it, feeling the reassuring squeeze of his fingers. As she drew level with him she managed a flicker of a smile.

"I can't believe we're going through this pantomime just to get married."

He laughed softly. "I know. You'd have preferred to slip away to the Register Office and get married in jeans, wouldn't you?"

"So would you."

"Right."

"Remind me again why we're doing this?"

His eyes lit with amusement as he nodded his head slightly down towards the small blonde angel standing behind them in a pretty pink dress of crinkle chiffon, with a puffed-out skirt and a satin sash at her waist, and an expression of pure rapturous delight on her sweet face.

"Oh, yes."

He lifted Cassie's hand to his lips and placed a light kiss on her fingers. "Let's do this."

Eva stepped into her place in front of the altar. "Dear friends and family, we welcome you today to witness and celebrate the marriage of Cassandra and Liam."

Yes, she really was doing this. Never mind all the fuss about flowers and dresses and getting her hair done — that was all just froth. She was marrying Liam Ellis, the love of her life — for better or worse, richer or poorer.

And as he slipped the slim gold ring on her finger, and she slipped a matching one on his — to rest beside the one Natalie had put there seven years ago — she felt as though they were exchanging pieces of their hearts.

The formal ceremony seemed to be over very quickly. Eva was pronouncing them husband and wife, and Liam was kissing her, and she felt as if she was dancing on air as they walked hand in hand back down the aisle and out to the churchyard, blinking in the cool December sunshine.

Then it was all laughter and kisses and photographs and people blowing bubbles that glittered and shone like miniature rainbows in the crisp December air. Cassie posed with Liam, with Liam and Robyn, with Liam and Robyn and both their set of parents, then both their families.

Then everyone crowded together for a large group photo, slapping their hands together and hunching their shoulders, and smiling against the cold.

* * *

At last there was a moment of peace as the photographer lined up various groups of guests which didn't need to include the bride and groom. Liam glanced down at Cassie, laughing.

"Phew. Maybe we should have opted for the Register Office and jeans after all."

Her eyes danced. "Never mind, this bit's nearly over now. Then it'll be cake and champagne."

"I could go for that!"

"Daddy." Robyn was tugging at his jacket. "Can I put my flowers on Mummy Natalie's garden?"

He felt a pang as he smiled down at her. "Of course, sweetheart. That would be lovely."

He glanced across at Cassie, but she was smiling too. How lucky was he to have found two such loves, and the second had accepted without doubt or question that the first would always have a space in their lives.

He took her hand, and they followed the child over to the grave. It was in a sheltered corner beneath a tall beech tree, holding up its bare branches like a net of lace against the pale-blue sky.

Natalie's parents were there. Sylvia was quietly dabbing at her eyes with a tissue. As they approached, she glanced up with a slightly watery smile.

"Oh . . . It was a lovely wedding." She reached out and took Cassie's hand. "I . . . I hope you'll be very happy." She glanced down at the grave. "Natalie would want you to be."

He could see that Cassie was struggling. "Thank you."

"I can see how Robyn's so fond of you. Take good care of them both, won't you?"

"I will."

"Come on then, dear." Martin Brayley patted his wife's shoulder. "Let's go home."

"You're not staying for the reception?"

"No, dear. It . . . would be too much."

Liam nodded and shook his hand, watching as they walked away.

* * *

Robyn crouched down beside the headstone and carefully laid her small posy of white roses and mauve gerberas on the ground. "Here you are, Mummy Natalie. These are for you. They're my bridesmaid flowers, but I want you to have them."

Oh lord, she was going to cry. Cassie was struggling to breathe, watching the child at her mother's grave.

But then with the joyful resilience of childhood, she jumped up, having spotted little Amy, and hurtled off to join her friend.

"She's having a lovely day," Liam remarked.

Cassie smiled. "She is. It wouldn't be the same in jeans. "

"Daddy," the child called to him. "Come and have your picture taken with me and Amy."

"Another one?" he murmured dryly, but obeyed the instruction.

Cassie lingered a moment longer, looking down at the grave. "I will take good care of them both," she whispered. "I promise."

She scooped up the long skirt of her dress, tossing it over her arm, and walked back to where everyone was still milling around the church porch. On the steps, she had paused to chat to Julia, her new sister-in-law, when Robyn came hurtling down the aisle of the empty church.

"Mummy, Mummy, come and see the navity scene."

Mummy . . . She felt her heart flip over. It was the first time she had called her that. She glanced uncertainly at Julia, who smiled and nodded.

"Go on, *Mummy*," she urged softly.

Robyn had taken Cassie's hand. "It's got sheep and a donkey, and the baby Jesus. We're going to have our picture taken beside it."

Cassie allowed herself to be towed down the aisle to the pretty arrangement next to the altar — the stable, the animals, the crib and the little figures, with a slightly chipped angel presiding over the whole.

The photographer was laughing, shaking her head. "She insisted."

"She can be very insistent."

Cassie hunkered down beside the small wooden stable, and Robyn came to pose beside her. She put her arm around Robyn's waist, and the little girl laid her own arm around her neck. And as the camera clicked, she turned her head and put a kiss on Cassie's cheek.

"Mummy, why are you crying?" she asked anxiously.

"Oh . . ." She brushed one tear away with her finger. "They're happy tears, sweetheart."

"Like Auntie Debbie cried at her wedding, and Auntie Vicky cried at hers?"

"That's right."

"Do ladies have to cry when they get married?"

Cassie laughed. "I guess they do." She glanced up as Liam came to join them.

"Daddy, come and have your picture taken with me and Mummy by the navity," the child pleaded.

"Okay." He knelt on one knee beside Cassie. "I'll be next to Mummy, shall I?" His eyes held amusement, and something deeper — love for his small family that was binding together in so much warmth.

"So, are you looking forward to Christmas, Robyn?" the photographer asked.

The little girl beamed. "We're going on our honeymoon."

"What, all together?"

A vigorous nod. "We're going to the North Pole to see Santa."

"Oh . . . that'll be nice."

"Lapland," Cassie explained quietly.

"Ah. And what do you want Santa to bring you for Christmas?"

"A baby sister!" Robyn declared without hesitation.

Beside her, Liam spluttered as he tried to suppress his laughter. "Maybe we'd better get a move on with that — she'll give us no peace," he murmured, his breath soft against Cassie's ear.

"It . . . um . . . might be a baby brother," Cassie cautioned, her own laughter bubbling up.

The child thought about that for a moment, her head on one side. Then she shrugged her small shoulders, spreading her hands. "Whatever."

THE END

ACKNOWLEDGEMENTS

My thanks to Becky, Kate, Elizabeth, Julie and all the lovely people at Choc Lit and Joffe Books, who have helped pull this book into shape.

Also to Geoff for keeping me supplied with cups of tea, and Pippa for always reminding me of the importance of walks on the beach and chasing balls — even though she doesn't fetch them back.

THE CHOC LIT STORY

Established in 2009, Choc Lit is an independent, award-winning publisher dedicated to creating a delicious selection of quality women's fiction.

We have won 18 awards, including Publisher of the Year and the Romantic Novel of the Year, and have been shortlisted for countless others. In 2023, we were shortlisted for Publisher of the Year by the Romantic Novelists' Association.

All our novels are selected by genuine readers. We are proud to publish talented first-time authors, as well as established writers whose books we love introducing to a new generation of readers.

In 2023, we became a Joffe Books company. Best known for publishing a wide range of commercial fiction, Joffe Books has its roots in women's fiction. Today it is one of the largest independent publishers in the UK.

We love to hear from you, so please email us about absolutely anything bookish at choc-lit@joffebooks.com.

If you want to receive free books every Friday and hear about all our new releases, join our mailing list here: www.joffe-books.com/freebooks.